Quietly Dead

Laura Belgrave

An Imprint of The Overmountain Press
JOHNSON CITY, TENNESSEE

This book is a work of fiction. All names, characters, places, and events are either the product of the author's imagination or are used fictitiously. Any resemblance to actual events or persons, living or dead, is entirely coincidental and beyond the intent of either the author or the publisher.

Hardcover ISBN 1-57072-172-6
Trade Paper ISBN 1-57072-173-4
Copyright © 2001 by Laura Belgrave
Printed in the United States of America
All Rights Reserved

1 2 3 4 5 6 7 8 9 0

*For my husband, John C. Caramanica, Jr.,
a man astonishingly undaunted by dreamers,*

*and in memory of my mother, Mary L. Belgrave,
who seeded my passion for all things written, so many years ago.*

ACKNOWLEDGMENTS

For the encouragement, enthusiasm, insistence, insight, and brainstorming that were essential—and at times critical—in making this book happen, I can only offer a huge and heartfelt "thank you" to the people most persistently fundamental to my creative orbit: my sisters, Linda Liska Belgrave (a tireless draft reader) and Leslie Curtis (a tired reader who found the time, anyway); my friends Marlene Passell, Pat Marcus, and Judie O'Connor; and finally, another newbie who bonded with me in the terror of authordom, Mary Saums.

For helping me sort out technical or procedural matters, I'd also like to thank Boynton Beach police officers John Huntington and Lou Zeitinger; Boynton Beach Police Department fingerprint examiner Brenda Anderson; and, for forensics details, Douglas P. Lyle, M.D. They were generous in sharing expertise and offering suggestions. Any errors or oversights are mine, not theirs.

Last, but certainly not least, thanks also to all of the good folks at Silver Dagger Mysteries—fearless champions of terrific storytelling. They made it happen.

CHAPTER 1

HE WOULD TAKE SOME GETTING USED TO. First, there was that hair—a red so vivid it looked painted on. Then there was his walk, a bouncing gait that seemed to propel the top half of his body faster than the rest of him. Of course, it could've been that he was simply wobbling out of balance because of the heavy backpack anchored to his shoulder. From a distance, Claudia couldn't tell, and she tried to push aside the uncharitable thoughts that were already forming as he angled toward her through the Indian Run police station.

"Lieutenant Hershey! Greetings! Hi! I'm Booey Suggs, or just plain 'Boo.' My uncle told you about me, right? I can't believe I'm actually meeting you! You're even taller than you looked on TV. This is superlative. I've never been up close to anyone famous before."

"And you're not up close to anyone famous now," Claudia said. Shaking the knobby hand Booey thrust at her, she made herself smile. If he were a puppy, his tail would be wagging so hard his body would spin. "Nice to meet you," she added.

"Oh, me too, me too! That homicide you worked last fall? Brilliant! It's what made me think about maybe becoming a police officer, a detective. My uncle told me—"

"What he told me is that you're keen on being a documentary filmmaker," Claudia said swiftly. "He said you're talented with a camera."

"He told you I'm talented?" Booey said, pleased.

She nodded. The filmmaker part was true. She steered the boy toward her office, ignoring the amused expression on the dispatcher's face.

"Well, I *am* considering filmmaking too," Booey said. "When I'm done with my internship with you—"

"It's not exactly an internship," Claudia said. "It's unofficial and it's only two weeks. Just to give you a feel for detective work, which you'll find is about as exciting as reading a phone book."

Booey shrugged, bounced along beside her. "Well, anyway, when I'm done here, then I've got something lined up with a film company that mostly does Southern documentaries. Over in Orlando."

"Good for you," Claudia murmured. They'd reached her office, which had been converted from a utility closet a few weeks earlier. As closets went, it was plenty big. As an office . . . well, except when people used the stained sink in the corner to get water for the coffeepot, it made up in privacy what it lacked in size. "Sit." Claudia pointed at a metal chair beside her desk, then shuffled through a few incident reports. Lunch had come and gone. She had an afternoon to fill and no earthly idea what to do with him—and this was only Monday.

"Just let him hang out with you, Hershey," Chief Suggs had said when he sprang the Booey thing on her a few hours earlier. "He's my brother's youngest boy. Just graduated from high school and he thinks he wants to be a cop—that or a documentary movie mogul of some kind. He's got his own car—one of them little VW bugs—so you don't need to pick him up or drop him off. Just take him on calls. Let him listen in on interviews. Give him some forms to fill out."

"If he wants to be a cop, he should do two weeks on patrol," Claudia said. She resisted asking about the kid's silly-ass name, which she already knew would never flow easily off her tongue. "He'd probably love riding around in a police car."

"Nah. He wants to be a detective. He clipped every story that was written about your psychic murders last fall."

"They weren't *my* murders, and they weren't psychics," she said flatly. "They were mediums."

"Whatever. The kid thinks you're some kind of mental giant. 'Course, that's what he *said*. Could be he's just got the hots for you. And anyhow, it's of no matter. He specifically asked if he could be assigned to you."

"Oh, come on. Can't you just tell him that it's not possible? Tell him anything you want. You're the chief of police."

"My brother doesn't give a rat's ass that I'm the honcho, Hershey. He only cares that I owe him five hundred bucks, which I don't happen to have right now. I'm buyin' down my debt by lettin' Boo ride with you. Out here, barter is still part of the free-enterprise system. You're comin' up on two years here. I'm surprised you don't know that by now."

Actually, it was a year and a half. Claudia supposed Suggs was close enough, though. And yeah, she knew about barter in Indian Run. She knew a lot about the small Florida town by now. She knew that living in the dead center of the state meant you'd never catch a breeze in the summer. She knew that cows took forever to cross a road and were impervious to car horns. She knew that half the streets weren't marked, that fishing tournaments were enough to close stores on a Sunday, and that no one would smile at you if you didn't smile first. She also knew that Indian Run wasn't immune to murder.

What she didn't know—not when she moved down from Cleveland and, really, not even now—was why she stayed. Her daughter, Robin, said it was just part of Claudia's miserable stubbornness. Maybe.

"Look, Chief—and this is nothing against your nephew; I haven't even met him yet—if I have someone with me everywhere I go, it's just going to slow me down," Claudia argued. "I'll have to explain everything. Whatever I do will take twice as long as it should."

"Hershey, Hershey . . . that's pretty lame, even for you. It's summer. What're you working? A shoplifting or two? A vandalism? Stolen wallet? What's so hot that Boo's gonna get in your way?"

He had a point.

"Besides, Hershey, Boo's a good kid. Granted, he could stand a little toughening up, sure, but that's just the physical side. Bookwise, the kid's wicked smart. He can probably recite every word in the dictionary backwards, and damned if he doesn't know every one of the begats in the Bible. He's affectionate, too. He'll grow on you faster than kudzu on a telephone pole."

And that had been that. Booey was on a metal chair, beaming at Claudia, waiting. His knees were crossed and one foot was jetting up and down.

She sighed and plucked a stolen-vehicle report from the stack. "My original idea was to show you some of the administrative part of police work," she said, "but I don't know . . . maybe I'll save that for later." In close proximity, his jiggling would make her nuts in five minutes. "There's this local businessman, the guy who owns a used car lot on the edge of town. He called in this morning. Looks like an old Eldorado got boosted from his place. I guess we could head on over there, talk to the man, and—"

She didn't bother finishing. Booey was already shooting out of his chair. It scraped against the concrete floor like fingernails on a blackboard. Claudia shuddered and made a mental note to remind Suggs that he'd promised to order cheap carpeting for the closet. The *office*.

"Auto theft! That's got the potential to be big, right? I read somewhere that stealing cars isn't just about joyriding. The article said a lot of car thieves are actually part of sophisticated rings. They even have lists of exactly what kind of cars to steal. The cars get stripped, the parts get sold." Booey hefted his backpack to his shoulder. "You think that's what's going on here, Lieutenant? I remember this one movie where—"

"Tell you what . . . Booey." Claudia still had trouble with the name. "Let's just hold off on speculating until we've talked to the victim." She glanced at the report. "Mike Gorman. Gorman's Autos. We'll ride on over and see if he's got anything illuminating to add to the officer's initial report."

Two weeks, Claudia reminded herself. She only had to put up with him for two weeks. She tucked her .38 Colt revolver into her trouser holster, shrugged into her jacket, grabbed a portable radio, and headed for the parking lot, trying to ignore the kid's eyes following her every move.

Claudia's police-issue car, an old Cavalier that no longer evidenced style or substance, sat just beyond the reach of shade from a small knot of trees outside the police station. Heated by a late-June sun, the steering wheel would be almost too hot to touch. That was just one more little detail Claudia hadn't considered when she settled on Florida.

She yanked the driver's door open and peered over the hood at Booey, struggling with his own door. "You have to lift up on the handle a little," she said. "The passenger side didn't work at all before, but it got fixed a few months ago—more or less, anyway. Now it just takes muscle. You'll get used to it." She waited for him to get in and settled with his backpack before she started up the engine, wishing the car thief had scrounged the Cavalier instead of the Eldorado. She pulled onto the street and headed north, toward the outskirts of the town's small commercial district.

"So what exactly are you toting around with you, Booey? That bag looks heavy enough to be holding a set of encyclopedias."

He leaned enthusiastically toward Claudia. "Actually, this is better than encyclopedias. I've got all kinds of stuff—a laptop, a cell phone, a digital camera, a PalmPilot . . . you know, electronic equipment, so I can have quick access to anything I might need."

"What? No fax machine?"

Booey looked at her, puzzled.

"Never mind," Claudia said. She was about to ask why he thought he'd need electronics with him, when her portable crackled and the dispatcher's voice came on. "Lieutenant Hershey? You got that radio of yours turned on for a change? I got one for you."

Claudia fiddled with the squelch button and gritted her teeth. She couldn't get Sally to talk in code no matter how hard she tried. "Yeah, Sally. I'm on. What's up?"

"Animal control called right after you left. They got a call out to old Wanda Farr's trailer. Two guys went out. They want an officer to meet them."

"Farr? You talking about the old cat lady?"

"That's a 10-4, Lieutenant."

"They don't need a detective to help them pick up cats, Sally. By the way, nice code."

"Thanks. This isn't just about cats, if you get my drift."

"What? Neighbor problems again?"

"No. Shoot . . . hang on a sec. Let me look this one up."

Claudia vaguely heard Sally shuffling through papers.

"Okay, I got it. My drift is that they think they might have a Signal 7 out there because, quote-unquote, 'Something smells funny here.' That's what the animal control guy said. He said they haven't gone in yet, but that there's—"

"All right, all right, Sally. I got it now. I'll head on over."

"You know the location?"

"Ten-four." Everyone in town knew the location. Farr's trailer was one of a handful near the railroad tracks which bisected Indian Run, separating the oldest communities from the newest. Complaints about the woman periodically came from both.

Claudia clicked off and swore softly.

"What was she talking about?" Booey asked. "What's a Signal 7?"

"It means there's a dead body."

"A murder?" Booey's foot started tapping. "Shouldn't we go faster? Don't you have a siren or something you can put on your roof?"

"Don't get excited, Booey. A 5 is a homicide. A 7 is just a dead body, usually from natural causes or maybe an accident. The woman Sally mentioned is about a hundred years old. From what I hear, for the last ten years people've been taking bets on when she'd die. Sounds like maybe she just did. Anyway, we'll make a welfare check and see what's what."

"Why did you call her the cat lady? Is she into exotic cats? Or show cats?"

"My guess is, you'll be able to answer your own question when we get there."

Wanda Farr was an institution in Indian Run. Stories about who she was and what she was and why she did the things she did may have been founded in fact once, but over time the truth had become more elaborately embroidered than the lines on her face—and no one disputed how deep and intricate those were. If any of her contemporaries were still alive, maybe one or two might be willing to say whether it was accurate that Wanda Farr had actually been pretty once, and normal once, or perhaps even just average on both counts. But the Farr woman had apparently outlived them all, and no one now could remember her as anything except an ill-tempered old lady who shared her days and nights with too many cats and too much bad wine.

As Claudia got out of the car and made her way toward Farr's trailer, Booey so close behind her that he clipped her heels once, she called to mind an image of the cat lady. She'd spotted her on the streets a few times, slightly bent but with purpose in her step. Claudia tried to recall what else she knew about the woman. It wasn't much.

Once, years earlier, a reporter from the twice-weekly *Indian Run Gazette* had tried to interview Farr for a human-interest feature, but the woman was uncooperative, and the reporter wound up writing a column loosely based on comments and details supplied by everyone but the cat lady. Claudia had still lived in Cleveland when the column was written, but Suggs showed her a faded copy shortly after she'd arrived and first noticed the old woman beside a Dumpster, muttering to herself and tossing scraps to at least a dozen squalling cats. The reporter must have been miffed that Farr wouldn't talk to him. He painted her in an unflattering light, making more of the complaints she'd generated over the years than the compassion she'd shown to the stray felines that prowled the town's shadows. Claudia hadn't given the story or the woman much further thought. Every municipality seemed to have a cat lady. Indian Run's was eccentric, crabby, and old.

A cat abruptly streaked past Claudia and Booey, the feline hell-bent, from beneath a gnarled bougainvillea bush to a recess under the trailer. Claudia jumped, swore. She could hear others from inside the trailer, Wanda Farr's cats. She could smell them, too—that, and something else.

The animal control officers fidgeted outside the door and gave her a quick rundown: They'd received a call, they'd come out, no one responded to their knocks. Claudia nodded and tugged latex gloves onto her hands. She handed a pair to Booey, then rapped hard once and again, and called out Farr's name. Nothing. She took a deep breath and tried the door. It was unlocked. Shadow and stench leached out of the trailer when she opened it.

She turned to Booey. "You don't have to come in, you know."

He swallowed and waved a hand. "No, no . . . this is all part of police work, right?"

Claudia looked at him. "All right. Don't touch anything. Don't step anywhere I don't step first."

Booey nodded. He was about to say something else, but a sudden sneeze cut him off. He covered his nose with a hand and followed her in.

Of course, Claudia didn't think Wanda Farr was literally one hundred, but that she was way up there in age seemed a certainty. Whether she was as cranky as everyone said—right now, that seemed a likely possibility, too. Even in death, bottomed-out naked in her bathtub as she was, The Cat Lady of Indian Run appeared to be glowering. Then again, maybe it was just an illusion. In life, Farr's left eye had a tendency to drift off-center—no doubt one of the reasons kids called her a witch—and that same eye now stared blankly toward the side of the tub, while her right eye seemed anchored directly on Claudia. Disconcerting.

Booey took one look at the corpse and fled, sneezing in violent bursts, both hands at his face. Claudia could hardly hold it against him. If she'd had a choice, she would've raced him for the door. The smell of death, combined with the pungent odor of cat urine, made her eyes water and her stomach lurch. Almost as bad was the racket. Cats howled and wailed from every corner of the stuffy trailer, their collective voice a shriek that raised goose bumps on Claudia's arms. She batted aside a half-grown cat that had leaped onto the edge of the tub, then peered uneasily behind her. There had to be twenty or twenty-five felines in every shape and color and size. They weren't the cute cuddlies that played with balls of yarn in cat food commercials on TV. Wanda Farr's cats were hungry and testy, and Claudia wanted to get the hell out of the trailer—now.

She looked back at the dead woman. Farr lay flat on her back in the tub, her head below the faucet and her knees slightly raised to accommodate the short length of the tub. Now and then, Claudia heard a pipe gurgle. Though she couldn't see the drain stopper under the woman's head, she assumed that bath water was slowly trickling past it. Enough had already seeped out so that, by now, it fell just below Farr's nose, but a high-mark ring of dirt around the tub suggested the water had originally been plenty deep enough for the old woman to drown in. She hadn't drowned without a little help. A glass with an inch or so of amber liquid sat on the side of the tub against the wall.

Claudia carefully leaned across the tub and sniffed at the glass. Liquor of some sort. She straightened, then stood and shook her head. Too many old people died alone and lonely. All the cats in the world couldn't change that.

She moved outside of the bathroom. The trailer was little more than a boxcar with electricity and plumbing. Besides the bathroom, it contained nothing more than a kitchenette and a long, narrow living room. She took her glasses off and wiped a smudge from the lens. Even through blurred vision, the trailer looked shabby and as dirty as the air smelled. Partly it was the cats. Claudia knew they were fastidious creatures by nature, but the litter boxes clustered in a corner were heaped with their waste, and their fur clung to every surface.

She made a face and put her glasses back on. Everywhere she looked, she saw piles of . . . stuff. Clothes were heaped in random piles. Bags filled with more bags nested two and three deep against one wall. Uneven stacks of faded newspapers, some of which had clearly become handy latrines for the cats, sprawled beside a tattered sofa. There was no bed in the room, but oily contours in the cushions of the sofa suggested that Farr used it as one. Claudia couldn't imagine shutting out the din of the cats enough to actually sleep. Then again, she didn't know much about cats. Maybe they drifted off when their owners did.

The temperature in the trailer must've been in the 90s. Claudia shrugged off her jacket, this one beige and one of many such jackets she special-ordered for their sturdy practicality. She liked the mid-thigh length. She liked the bellows pockets even more.

Robin, who had just turned fourteen and liked to tell her mother how to dress—liked to give her advice on just about everything—told her she was nuts to wear them in the summer. "News flash, Mom," she'd said a week earlier. "Half the cops in Florida wear shorts in the summer. You have to get with it. I mean, like, no offense or anything, but you look like you just got off the boat."

Claudia didn't bother pointing out that only uniformed cops had the privilege of shorts, and even then, not all of them. Robin wore her fourteen-year-old's convictions like a second skin.

Something tugged at her slacks. She looked down at a calico kitten, its tiny nails stuck in the fabric. It hissed when she bent down to free it, batted once at her hand, then dashed beneath the sofa. Tough guy, she mused. Cute, sort of. She wondered how long it had been stuck in the trailer with the dead woman.

On her way out, Claudia paused by the kitchenette, a square room separated from the living area by a faded picnic table that Farr must've dragged in—probably a trophy from someone's trash. A huge bag of dry cat food, the bag shredded almost to the point of being indistinguishable, lay on the floor beside it. The cats had spared Wanda Farr. They'd made do with what they could find.

She shuddered and examined the table. It was burdened with

crusted plates, empty cat food cans, a few drained wine bottles, and a crumpled sandwich wrapping. Claudia read the print on the wrapper: roast beef with provolone from the gourmet grocer in Indian Run's ritzy Feather Ridge community. The expiration date had come and gone two weeks earlier. Farr had probably crossed the tracks and scavenged it from a Dumpster outside the store. For the grocer, a discard. For The Cat Lady of Indian Run, a feast.

Claudia stepped outside and inhaled fresh air, one deep breath after the other. She would be at the trailer for a few more hours, trying to find neighbors and documenting the minutiae of Wanda Farr's life. Unless the old woman had been under the care of a doctor—Claudia thought not—then, in police parlance, Farr was officially an "unattended death." An autopsy would be required. Paperwork would mount. First, though, the cats needed to go. Booey, too, it looked like.

The chief's nephew was hunched beneath a scraggly pine tree, his head between his bony knees. "Booey? You all right?" Claudia asked.

"Yeah . . . I'm, uh . . . fine." He sneezed loudly—once, twice, a third time. "Really."

"There's no reason you have to stay here."

"No, no . . . I'm good. It's just, I'm . . . the cats . . . allergies."

"Your stomach all right?"

"Fine. I—" Abruptly, he swiveled away and vomited into the grass.

Claudia winced. She tossed her jacket in the backseat of the Cavalier, lit one of the cigarettes she had vowed to quit, then raised Sally on the radio and told her what she needed. She glanced at Booey again and asked the dispatcher to send a patrol officer over, too. The chief's nephew needed a ride home.

CHAPTER 2

EMORY CARELLA WAS IN HIS ELEMENT. The computers had landed and he stood knee-deep in cartons, whistling while he wrested a monitor from its Styrofoam packing. Claudia had forgotten.

She eyed the boxes and pushed her hair off her collar for a second, letting the station's air-conditioned air whisper against her neck. On a good day, her hair fell to her shoulders in gentle mahogany curls that tempered the sharp angles of her face. Just now, though, still damp from the humidity of Wanda Farr's trailer, bits of her hair jutted out in spikes that matched her disposition.

Claudia hoped Carella's good humor would jar her into a better mood. She had less confidence in the long-awaited computers. "You know what you're doing, Emory?"

Carella set the monitor on a desk and turned around. He grinned. "Child's play, Lieutenant, child's play."

"Could've used you on the road earlier. Where the hell is everyone today, anyway?"

He leaned against the desk. "Well, let's see. The chief went home with a bellyache. The sarge is still on vacation. Moody caught a missing persons call out at Feather Ridge—this Becker character again. Third time this month. His wife phoned it in a couple hours ago."

She nodded. "The name rings a bell. What's the story on him?"

"I don't know, but he's a wanderer of some sort. Old guy. He usually finds his own way home before we're done with the paperwork. But since we're talking Feather Ridge, Moody snagged two officers to scout the area with him—you know, give the wife the illusion that we're dropping everything else, yada, yada, yada. Anyway, let's see . . . we got one or two other guys cruising for speeders, aiming to make the chief's quota for the month. And one more who's chasing off some bonehead trying to make a buck with an illegal fireworks stand. Fourth of July is coming up fast."

Claudia briefly wondered if she should pick up some sparklers. Would Robin consider herself too old for that?

"So, Lieutenant, there you have it, except for me and these babies." Carella gestured at the computer boxes. "The chief made me the department's technology guru, which is fine by me. Keeps me off the street and out of the heat—at least for a day or two. Saved the budget a buck or two by picking them myself. I'll be surprised if the chief doesn't promote me all the way from officer to captain."

"Carella, you're a shameless suck-up." Claudia lobbed a pink message pad at him. He fielded it in midair.

"It's worse than you think. Guess whose desk got the first computer?"

Roselli in records had a computer, a tired thing that took five minutes to boot and froze on a regular basis. Chief Suggs had one, too, though his was acquired only after the town council boosted the department's budget and told him to upgrade its technology—which meant *get* some technology, as far as Claudia was concerned. Suggs demanded a machine that would be faster than anything the rival sheriff's office had. Once he had it, he lost interest. He turned the thing on every morning, then bitched about how much space it took up on his desk the rest of the day.

"Emory," Claudia said, "please don't tell me that a computer is parked on my desk if you're not going to tell me that it's already hooked up and ready to go, too."

Carella shrugged. "Sorry. I got as far as 'parked.' Look for 'hooked' tomorrow. Right now, I just have to get these sweethearts out of their boxes. You know how the chief hates clutter. Of course, I would've stored them in the utility closet if we had one. Come to think of it, we used to. It seems to have gone missing."

They grinned at each other. Claudia gave Carella a half salute and made her way to her office. There it was, on her desk, all right. It swallowed half the room.

"Hey, Lieutenant." Carella bounded into view. "In all the excitement of high technology, I forgot to tell you that before Moody fielded the Becker thing, he followed up on the Eldorado. He knew you were out on the Farr call, figured he'd just take the car gig before you told him to."

Claudia was the department's only bona fide police detective, but Suggs had reluctantly given her the green light to draft Moody for minor investigations if time permitted. It almost always did.

"Apparently there wasn't much to it," Carella said. "Vehicle was there one day. Gone the next. Gorman doesn't exactly have a secured lot. Anyway, Moody told him to alert his insurer, and he put a BOLO out on the car."

"Busy day for Mitch," Claudia said. "Tell him I said thanks."

She spotted Booey's flame-topped head a fraction of a second before he squeezed past Carella into her office and parked himself on the metal chair. Great. She'd hoped for a reprieve, at least until the next day.

"BOLO," Booey said, "that's 'be on the lookout,' right?"

Carella clapped him on the back. "You got it, sport." He mouthed "and you got him" to Claudia, then slipped away. She glared at his retreating back, then looked at Booey, trying to decide what to do with him next. His face had color again, but he'd been pretty sick at Farr's trailer. "You know, Booey, you didn't need to come back today. It's already—"

"Ailuromania."

"Pardon me?"

"Ailuromania. I looked it up."

The boy was speaking in tongues. "Give it to me in English, Booey."

"That cat lady—the way she is? I mean, was? It's called 'ailuromania.' That's the psychological term for someone who's got an unhealthy enthusiasm for cats. I thought you might want to include it in your report."

"Ah. Something to consider."

"I don't mean ailuromania killed her, of course. She drowned, right?"

"Probably."

"Probably? Wait—you mean that's *not* how she died?"

"I just mean 'probably,' Booey. Don't get excited. I have a few things to check. Routine things. And we'll know more when the medical examiner does an autopsy." Claudia swiftly deflected additional questions by asking Booey if he knew enough about computers to get the monster on her desk hooked up.

He did, and would—with enthusiasm. Claudia smiled. Good. Carella could baby-sit him for a while. It was four-thirty. Maybe she'd still have time to play detective. Because "probably" wasn't good enough.

Back in Cleveland, Claudia had grown close to a patrol officer whose career on the road abruptly ended the night a drunk driver slammed into him while he was helping a motorist change a tire. He'd lost a leg in the accident, but months later he told Claudia that half the time it still felt like it was there and that in his dreams, it always did. He called it his "phantom limb" and said that most amputees experienced the same phenomenon.

As Claudia steered the Cavalier toward home, it occurred to her that the smell of death was a little like that. It lingered, ghost-like, long after contact with it, a grim plea that the life it represented not be forgotten. Her stomach rolled, and she cranked the window all the way down. The fresh air helped, but there was more going on here than the odor of decay. She sniffed, picked the smell apart, and cursed. Cat urine. Of course. She'd spent a few hours walking around in it. The shoes would have to go.

By the time she reached that conclusion, she was pulling into the driveway, her headlights sweeping across the thirty-year-old house at the end. On most nights, the image was enough to induce a twinge of guilt over how much work the house still needed. Not tonight. A black BMW was parked in her spot. She didn't recognize the car, but she recognized the vanity plates instantly. Everything else dropped from sight.

Brian.

She turned off the car and listened to the tick of the engine until it spun down into silence. She hadn't seen him for a long time; didn't want to see him now. Of course, he wasn't here for her. He was here for Robin. Maybe he was between gigs. Or maybe he was just out of work altogether. That would hardly be surprising.

With a dread that made her feel a decade older than her thirty-six years, Claudia stepped out of the car. She'd have to stow her feelings because, whatever animosity she felt toward her ex, he was still Robin's father. It was really that simple.

She leaned into the backseat and fumbled for her jacket. Her hand touched something wet, and at the same time that she recognized what it was—what it only *could* be—she felt something sharp scissor her wrist.

"Ouch, damn it!" She jerked back and banged her head on the door frame. "Shit!" She rubbed her wrist and cautiously peered into the gloom of the interior. Yellow eyes glared back.

Lovely. One of Wanda Farr's cats, no doubt host to a lively community of fleas, had obviously managed to escape the sweep by animal control hours earlier. Now, here it was. Not Wanda Farr's problem. Not animal control's problem. *Her* problem. Brian in the house. A feral cat in the car. Perfect.

For a moment, Claudia merely stared at the yellow eyes, and they stared at her. The cat had moved to the other end of the backseat, as far from her as it could get. For all the movement it made, it might as well have been a stone, though she knew it could deploy itself fast enough to take out her eyes if she grabbed at it. But the stare-off had to end, so in a voice she hoped sounded soothing, she murmured nonsense at it, trying to coax it closer. To her surprise it eventually slinked nearer, and she was shocked to see that the cat was not a cat at all. It was the calico kitten that had latched itself to her trousers earlier. She let it sniff at her hand for a long time—it appeared pleased to discover its own *eau de pee* on her—and when she gently rubbed its chin with a finger, it purred lightly.

"Some tough guy you turned out to be," Claudia murmured. She sighed. "If I point you at Brian and say 'kill,' will you?"

She could take it to the pound in the morning. What she couldn't do was leave it in the car overnight. She also couldn't delay the inevitable any longer. Gently, Claudia scooped the kitten up and nestled it against her shirt. She half hoped it would leap from her hands and sprint into the trees around the house. It didn't, though, and when she felt its head quivering against her throat, she held it just a little more firmly on her march to the house.

Brian had come bearing gifts. A compact stereo in ruby casing rested on an end table by the couch. Colorful lights pulsed from a panel on the front. It was the same system she had intended to buy Robin for Christmas. Music swept through the room, some kind of throbbing rock that her daughter favored. Claudia inhaled slowly, steeling herself. They hadn't seen her yet, hadn't heard her come in. Both were hunched by the table, fooling with the stereo controls. At that moment, Claudia knew the kitten wasn't going anywhere.

"Hello, Brian. What a surprise," she said.

He turned slowly, a casual grin spreading over his face, a beguiling smile so familiar, so intimate, that for a nanosecond she felt her heart bang out of sync. *Bastard.*

"You look good, Claudia," he said, rising from his knees. Without taking his eyes from her, he reached down and lowered the volume on the stereo. "Did you—"

Whatever he was about to say was lost in Robin's screech. She'd spotted the kitten and was across the room in a moment, eclipsing the tension with an exuberance that made Claudia laugh out loud. God love this kid, this half-girl, half-woman who had made an otherwise disastrous union entirely worthwhile.

"Easy, easy, kiddo. You don't want to scare it," she said. "He's been through a lot today." She pried the kitten's nails from her shirt and gently handed it over.

Robin pressed the kitten to her face "He's for me? *You* bought *me* a kitten? I thought you said no animals. 'Not now, not ever, never. They're dirty and expensive and need too much attention.' Hello. Wasn't that you?"

Claudia shrugged. "I caved. The little guy was on his way to the pound. I looked at it and said 'no way.' This one's got Robin written all over him." She glanced over her daughter's head at Brian. *Hah. Top that, you son of a bitch.*

Robin held the kitten out, examining it. "You just need a little love, don't you," she cooed. The kitten mewed plaintively, and Robin's eyes pivoted to Claudia. "*Please* tell me you didn't forget to pick up cat food and a litter box."

Claudia held up a hand. "Give me some credit, Robin," she said smoothly. "I didn't buy anything yet because I figured you'd want to pick things out for him yourself." Oh, this was fun.

Robin nodded. "Good idea. Not to be rude, but you probably don't have a clue what a kitty needs."

Claudia happily conceded the truth in that and told Robin to go find her shoes so they could get to the store before it closed. She set off without protest, the kitten still clutched to her chest, the stereo forgotten.

"What're you doing here, Brian?" Claudia said swiftly.

"How about 'nice to see you, Brian'?" he said.

"It's not. What do you want?"

"I missed her birthday. I'm here catching up."

"The story of your life."

"I take it you're going to be sour on me to the day you draw your last breath."

"What I think or feel doesn't matter. But you can't keep bouncing in and out of Robin's life on a whim. What's the matter with you that you don't get that?"

He sighed. "Here we go, the world according to Detective Lieutenant Claudia Hershey."

She shook her head. "Leave it alone, Brian. You don't like my lifestyle. I don't like yours." She felt her hands shaking and pressed them against her legs. "Look, you brought her a present. Good for you. Now, when are you leaving?"

They both stood six feet tall. On the job, Claudia's height was an advantage. With Brian, it never had been. Almost nothing had been. She didn't look away, though.

"I want her for the summer, Claudia."

CHAPTER 3

ANYONE WHO LIVED IN FLORIDA quickly learned that come summertime, it was best not to leave the house without an umbrella. Summer storms blew in almost daily—and with a ferocity made all the more dramatic by extravagant displays of lightning. That lightning—it was nothing to fool with. It cuffed Florida around more than any other state in the union, and those who thought it was more show than sizzle claimed morgue space with sad regularity.

That was just one reason why Claudia didn't want to get out of her car when she saw a pickup truck on the side of the road and a man crouched beside it, examining a tire. The other reason was the man—Chief Suggs. What miserable luck. The stomach upset which had sent him home the day before was apparently gone now. She wouldn't be able to put off telling him about the Farr case; he wouldn't like what she was doing with it. It didn't help that she was running late this morning, either.

She eased the car behind the truck and slid out, struggling with her umbrella. Suggs had thrown a rain slicker over his clothes, but even with the hood pulled over his head, she could see the set of his jaw.

"Looks like you could use a lift," she called out, pitching her voice above the drum of the rain. "What happened?"

"You're late, Hershey," Suggs said. "You shoulda been at your desk twenty minutes ago." He kicked the tire with a boot. "I got a reason. You don't."

Well, yes, she did, actually. But Claudia wasn't about to share her personal life with Suggs. "Couldn't be helped," she said. She was spared further response when lightning flared in the west, startling them both. A second later, a thunderclap followed with force enough she could feel in her feet. "Why don't I give you a ride in? You can send someone out later to change the tire and bring the truck back."

"I don't need to rouse the troops for a foolish tire, Hershey." He cracked his knuckles and smirked. "I'm here. You're here. We're both able-bodied. And anyway, it hardly appears you're in that much of a rush today."

They locked eyes. "Fine," Claudia said. "Let's do it, then." She retrieved a hooded poncho from the trunk of the Cavalier and set a reflective cone behind her car. Traffic was light, but trucks favored the four-lane road, and she wasn't of a mind to challenge their visual acuity in a storm. By the time she was ready to test her muscles, Suggs had hauled out the spare, a lug wrench, and the jack.

Rain beat at them from an angle. Claudia's glasses quickly became extraneous and she stuffed them in a pocket. She braced her feet against the slick pavement and pried the hubcap from the flat tire while the chief angled the jack into place.

"So tell me, Hershey—and I hope this is good—what's with the melodrama I'm hearing about the Farr case? You needed *crime scene* to hold your hand at the trailer? 'Cause that's what I hear, that you brought a unit in, then sealed the trailer off when they were done. Hand me that lug wrench."

So he already knew.

"My intent was to fill you in this morning," Claudia said. She shoved the hubcap to the side with her foot, then passed the tire iron to Suggs. He eased himself to a knee and began loosening the nuts. "I brought crime scene in as a precaution," she told him. "There were a couple of incongruities in Farr's home." She winced when Suggs's grip on the wrench slipped, bruising his knuckles.

He swore and glared up at her. "'Incongruities.' Well, gee, that explains just about everything, Hershey." He shifted from one knee to the other. "Now, can the fifty-cent words and tell me why in hell you think an old lady with a liquor habit couldn't just drop dead in her tub. Matter of fact, it looks to me like she died pretty easy for an old woman who lived life so hard. Why does everything with you have to be a . . . a quest."

Quest. Good one, thought Claudia. *Must have picked that one up from Booey.* But it was as if the chief were reading her mind, because before she could respond, he said, "And this business of you sticking Boo with computer scut work . . . I won't tolerate it."

"He got pretty sick out at—"

"Horseshit, Hershey. I know exactly what you were doing. Don't do it again. Hear me?"

"I hear you."

Suggs carried about twenty pounds more than he needed to. He grunted with the effort of standing and straightening. Rain cascaded from the hood of his slicker. "Those nuts are about as loose as they're going to get." He exhaled. "Crank that jack up while I go raise Sally. I don't want her sendin' out a posse for us."

It wasn't the first flat Claudia had ever changed. It wouldn't be the last. She bent to the task and wrestled the tire off before the chief was finished on the radio. She was just pushing the spare on when he returned.

"Rain's startin' to slow a bit," he said. He leaned over to watch Claudia tighten the lug nuts. "Thing is, Hershey, you know good and well I'm not keen on havin' Flagg County lookin' up our skirts—your 'incongruities' aside."

He was referring to the Flagg County Sheriff's Office, which provided crime-scene support to Indian Run on the rare occasion when it was needed. The police department wasn't big enough to have its own. Suggs worried endlessly that one day Flagg would absorb the IRPD altogether.

"Look, Chief, it couldn't be helped." Claudia struggled for a word that wouldn't set him off again. "It might be that Wanda Farr's death was accidental. *Probably* was. But—"

"Yeah, yeah. That's what Booey *said* you said: 'probably.' And if—"

Claudia stood so abruptly that she jarred them both against the truck. "Damn it all! How about you let me finish what I'm trying to say? How about we leave Booey out of it, and we leave Flagg out of it—at least long enough for me to tell you what I need to? Because there *were* incongruities, all right?"

The rain had slowed to a drizzle, and the sun was beginning to reassert itself in the east. In another half hour it would look like it never had rained at all.

"Settle down, Hershey. This ain't the OK Corral."

Claudia leaned against the pickup and waited for a semi to hurtle past them. "Number one, Farr wasn't exactly known for her personal hygiene. You have to ask yourself why she was taking a bath in the first place—why now, why on the day she dies. Now maybe that's just one of life's tragic ironies, until you get to Number two. She socked away a lot of wine. No secret. But a glass on the edge of her tub held some kind of hard liquor. I saw wine bottles in the trailer, but no booze bottles, and I find that more than just a little out of whack. Number three, her door was unlocked. And Number four, she was on her back in the tub, with her head below the faucet. Come on; people put their *feet* under the faucet, not their heads." Claudia rooted in her pocket for her glasses and put them on, ignoring the smudges. "Oh, and one more thing, Chief. The original call to animal control came in anonymous. I don't like it."

Suggs shrugged out of his rain slicker. "Last year, you were dead-on with that psychic case. I didn't think you were, but you proved me wrong. I'm man enough to admit it. But you have a habit of lookin' for monsters under every bed and . . . stop shakin' your head, Hershey."

Claudia folded her arms across her chest.

"This Farr thing," Suggs continued. "I gotta tell you, I'm not even close to bein' persuaded. Everything you just said—it can all be explained."

"That's right. And that's what I'm trying to do."

"Uh-huh." He sighed. "So what's your next move?"

"I have people to talk to."

Wordlessly, Suggs reached down and grabbed the flat tire. He pitched it into the back of the pickup with a grunt. "Give me the wrench. I can finish up on my own." He took it from Claudia and looked at her for a long time. "Anywhere you go? You take Boo with you. I want that boy to learn a thing or two about police work—even if it turns out to be the wrong thing."

Claudia thought she heard him mutter "probably will be" while he was turning back to the tire. But maybe that was just a deceit of the road, the sound of traffic over a rain-washed highway playing tricks on her ears. She took her poncho off and shook it out. Then she picked up the safety cone and tossed it with the poncho into the Cavalier's trunk. She was thinking about the dead cat lady and didn't notice the rainbow forming in the east when she drove off.

Booey was at Claudia's desk when she got in, pecking away at the keyboard, his attention so absorbed that he didn't notice her until she stood just inside the doorway to her office. He scrambled to his feet when she greeted him, chirped a hello, and gestured at the computer.

"I almost couldn't wait for you to get in because you are going to be so blown away, Lieutenant! Officer Carella and I got you totally, totally networked. Without even leaving your desk, you can access just about everything you could ever need. You can blaze right into NCIC, FCIC, motor vehicles—you name it. Your setup is the police equivalent of the *Starship Enterprise!*"

Claudia mustered a smile, but the boy's energy exhausted her. She did *not* know how she'd go the full two weeks with him.

"I'm still tinkering with a few preferences to make accessing files easy for you, but it's basically ready to go now," he said. "You want to give it a test drive?"

"I do, Booey, but it has to wait." She plucked a sheaf of phone messages from her desk, avoiding his crestfallen expression. And then it occurred to her that with a minor infraction of the rules, she could turn his disappointment into brownie points with the chief. "Look, forget whatever tinkering you're doing. I got as far as getting Wanda Farr's Social Security number from the power company yesterday. That's not much, but it's the gold card for getting some real information, which may or may not come in handy. Hang on a second." She scrounged in her notepad, found the cat lady's Social Security number, and jotted it down for him. "Since you already know how to access data, see what you can dig up on her. See if she's got any priors. See if you can track down any next of kin. Find out who holds title on her trailer. Might've been her. Might not've."

Booey scribbled furiously on a scratch pad. Claudia waited for him to catch up, then said, "If you've got time, check into whether she ever held any sort of professional license, filed suit, got sued. See if she was a registered voter. See if she checked books out of the library." Long shots, and not all of it would come from a computer records check, but it would keep him busy and . . . you never knew. "I'm going to catch up on some phone calls and check into a few other things. Holler if you need me. When we're done we'll hit the road and talk to some people. Got all that?"

He brightened. "Absolutely! I was hoping we'd get back into the cat lady's death. Matter of fact, I told my uncle about her last night after dinner. He hadn't been feeling very well, but he sat right up when I laid it out for him. I think he's impressed with how thorough you are."

"You're staying at your uncle's house?"

"Sure. Did you think I lived here?"

Claudia nodded. "I guess I assumed you did."

"Nope. My family's in West Palm Beach. My daddy's the one who suggested I do my internship here. Uncle Mac thought it was a terrific idea, too. He's my godfather—did you know that? I think he's actually very pleased that I have such an interest in police work."

Doomed. She was doomed. The kid would be a constant pipeline to Suggs.

She left Booey tapping away on the keyboard and slid into a chair at a vacant desk in the multipurpose room. She nodded to an officer laboring over a report, then turned her back to him and leafed through the messages. Routine, routine, routine . . . she stopped at the fourth. *Dennis Heath.*

Claudia leaned back in the chair. Was it possible that she hadn't talked to him in a week? Hadn't returned the last several calls? Was she nuts? She didn't have to look far into her history to know that

Dennis was the most genuinely decent man she'd ever met. She liked that he could nudge a laugh from her, even on her worst days. She liked that he knew how to make a decent omelet, that he remembered to put the toilet seat down, that he earned a living as an artist. And in bed? No question—he had most of the right moves. Even Robin had warmed to him. But . . . *what?*

With a pang of guilt, Claudia stuffed the message into her pocket. Later. She'd call him later. *Would, would, would.*

She scanned the remaining two messages. The medical examiner's office had called. The Farr autopsy wasn't even scheduled yet. Big surprise. The cat lady never got priority in life. She sure wouldn't get it in death. The last message was a reminder from her dentist's office about a routine cleaning the next day.

Claudia picked up the phone. The job couldn't take priority over everything in her life, but the dentist? No contest. She rescheduled for the next month.

John Simpson Raynor held the record for the number of complaints filed against Wanda Farr. Claudia wasn't surprised to learn that; Raynor's trailer was about eighty yards from Farr's, making him her nearest neighbor. Still, thirty-two complaints in eighteen months—twenty-one to animal control, the rest directly to the police department—that was a lot, and it more than suggested he didn't hold a fond spot for her in his heart.

Farr clearly hated him right back. She'd called in fourteen complaints on Raynor herself—and might have made more if calling didn't mean a long walk to the nearest phone booth, which was just shy of a mile away.

Claudia learned all that and more during a visit to Delilah Glasser, a wiry woman at the animal control department who smelled vaguely of dog. She fielded complaints and dispatched animal control officers in a voice made raspy by years of talking above the din of the pound, situated in the back of the same building. Claudia didn't know how Glasser could stand it. The racket made her want to retreat to the police station, where Booey was still feasting on databases.

"So what'd Raynor do?" Glasser asked Claudia after they finished with introductions. She fanned herself with the complaint file she'd pulled. "He shoot her and throw her in the tub? That's what some of the boys were speculating."

It always fascinated Claudia, the Indian Run grapevine. "We don't know that Raynor did anything," she said. "I'm just trying to tie up loose ends, finish up my report. Tracing the history of complaints between two neighbors—that's a routine part of it."

"And *neighbors* is a nice word for those two," Glasser said. "You want to know the truth about Raynor and Farr? Think Hatfield and McCoy. Think *Deliverance*. Think—"

"Was it just the cats that created problems between them?"

"Hah! The cats, they were only half of the problem. The other half was Raynor's dogs. You didn't know about them?"

Claudia shook her head. "One of your officers told me Raynor had a few dogs, but he didn't indicate they were a problem."

"Yeah, that'd be Bob, no doubt. He's on the quiet side. Methodical and objective, which just means he understates everything. Anyway, Raynor's got a bunch of dogs, and he trained every one of them to be as mean as he is. Couple of Dobermans, a shepherd or two, and three or four pit bulls. The Farr woman—" Glasser stopped abruptly, rolled her eyes. Something had set off the animals in back.

Claudia waited out the noise with her, then leaned forward when Glasser started speaking again. "Farr claimed he set the dogs on her cats at every opportunity. And you know? She might've been cranky—and maybe even as nuts as everyone says—but I believed her about that." The woman thumped the complaint file. "They both aggravated me on a regular basis, but if one of them had to go, I'd just as soon it had been Raynor."

"I'm surprised I didn't hear his dogs when I was at Farr's trailer," Claudia said.

"Oh, you wouldn't've. You know how some people crop their dogs' ears?"

"Yes?"

"Raynor cropped his dogs' vocal chords."

"Excuse me?"

"They make noise, but it's not a bark. Matter of fact, it's not like anything you ever heard. That man—he silenced them, if not like that, then somehow else."

A flash of unease shot up Claudia's spine, but it passed so quickly she felt foolish for even acknowledging it. She hid a smile. The propensity for exaggeration among Indian Run's residents ran so deeply, so exhaustively, that it was like a virus.

"You don't believe it," Glasser said. "I can see it in your eyes. Well, doesn't matter to me." Obviously it did, though. She took a look at her wristwatch, as if she suddenly had a hot date. "What else can I tell you, Detective?"

"I didn't mean any offense," Claudia said. "Sorry. I have just one more question. Does Raynor live alone?"

Glasser stood. "He does if you discount the dogs. But if you're planning on visiting him, you might do well to regard them as kin." She pursed her lips. "Believe that."

When Claudia got back to the station, Booey was still on her computer. He was on the phone, too, the receiver cradled between his ear and neck, and his eyes on the monitor while he typed at a speed Claudia never would have imagined humanly possible. She watched for a minute, then retreated to the desk she'd occupied earlier in the multipurpose room. Except for the indistinct murmur of Booey's voice and sporadic background chatter from Sally's communications desk, the station was as quiet as an insurance office.

Claudia sighed. Now and then, and never for long, she yearned to be back on the job in Cleveland. The days were brutal. The departmental politics were crippling. But you could count on someone manning the front desk twenty-four hours a day. No one would ask you to hold down the fort because the dispatcher needed a pee break. There were rooms for every purpose, procedures that never varied; and if someone went on vacation, it didn't represent a crisis in staffing.

She gazed around at the handful of desks. This . . . it was the police equivalent of a one-room schoolhouse. She picked up a stained coffee mug that someone had left on the desk and read the inscription: "Indian Run Police Department—To Serve and Protect." The print was beginning to flake around the edges. She frowned, wondering if Suggs rightly worried that Flagg County would eventually absorb the department. Indian Run had just fourteen sworn officers to spread over three shifts—only marginally enough to serve the town's eight thousand residents. Add to that a couple of civilian workers, some of them only part-time, and it didn't take a leap of imagination to see what the chief saw. If Flagg decided to—

Claudia abruptly set the mug down, annoyed. She'd walked herself right into Suggs's head. It was the last place she wanted to be.

"Boy, talk about being lost in thought." Sally stood a few feet away, her eyes speculative. "What do you want first, the good news or the bad news?"

"Dealer's choice, Sally. Give it to me any way you want."

"All right." She handed Claudia several sheets of paper. "The good news is that our fax machine is working again. Flagg S.O. just sent that over."

The crime-scene report. "Thanks," Claudia said, already beginning to scan the pages.

"Don't get too settled in just yet." Sally waited until she had the detective's attention again. "At least that's how I interpret the bad news."

Claudia shrugged. "Go ahead, Sally. Make my day."

"Wish I could, but this isn't gonna do it. The chief just radioed in. He said—and I quote—'Tell Hershey to put Booey in her pocket so she don't forget him and then get her tail over to the No-Name Pond ASAP.'"

"Terrific. What's up?"

"We got ourselves a"—Sally glanced at a scrap of paper in her hand—"a Code 26." She looked up expectantly, but Claudia was already brushing past her, aiming for Booey, aiming for the pond.

CHAPTER 4

THE NO-NAME POND wasn't a pond at all. It was part of a complex state canal system that meandered into and out of Lake Okeechobee to the south, a liquid highway carved from the ground for water management and used for just about everything else. But because canals in the system weren't designed for aesthetic reasons, most ran in tediously straight lines, their banks as parallel as railroad tracks. Not so with the No-Name Pond, which was far too distinguished by its crescent shape, wide girth, and surprising depth to be regarded as a canal, at least not by the locals who were aware of its existence.

Claudia had heard various stories about the No-Name, her favorite being that the fabled Florida Skunk Ape had been spotted near it on several occasions. What nobody could tell her, though, was why the pond—the canal, whatever—was called "No-Name." It just was. As for its irregular contours, speculation held that the canal's shape represented a thoughtful and respectful accommodation for an immense camphor tree situated on its south bank. Given that the state had built the canal system, that made no sense to Claudia whatsoever, but she was willing to go along.

Unfortunately, the camphor tree, a beauty with a canopy that would dwarf most houses, was rarely seen by anyone. Or at least it wasn't supposed to be. Too many accidental drownings had prompted the town to seal off the No-Name eight years earlier with chain-link fencing. The fence curved around both sides of the No-Name, then continued east and west along the narrow portion of the canal for a quarter mile. That barricade alone would not have stopped persistent visitors—indeed, it was repeatedly punctured by trespassers—but unchecked growth of prickly shrubs and tall grasses eventually discouraged most human company. Besides, a golf course serving the exclusive Feather Ridge development had been built just beyond the fringe of wild vegetation, on the north bank. To get to the No-Name meant trespassing across the golf course and then negotiating the fence and scrub. An approach to the No-Name from the south held its own challenges. An abandoned train track ran parallel to the canal, the far side of it shielded by a berm and the fence, the pond side by more nasty brush.

All in all, the No-Name Pond was just too hard to get to for most people to bother trying. There were other places to fish or picnic.

Someone had visited the No-Name recently, though. A body floated facedown on the surface, in the shade of the camphor.

Claudia stood on the north bank and peered over at it, a hushed Booey at her side. To the west, a narrow wooden footbridge optimistically built of two-by-fours during the No-Name's heyday connected the banks, but time and weather had badly eroded it. It bowed in the middle, and its boards were brittle—too brittle, she thought, to safely sustain much weight.

Suggs stood a short distance away with three patrol officers. She felt his eyes on her, but he said nothing, giving her a moment to lock the grim image in her mind. When she finally looked up, he broke from the others and walked over. He gave his nephew a distracted smile. "Hey, Boo."

"Hey, Uncle Mac," Booey said, his voice small.

Suggs turned to Claudia. "It's gotta be Becker," he said quietly. "According to Moody, he never did wander home this time. Our guys looked for him—even poked around here as late as last night—but I guess he didn't pop to the surface till now."

Claudia nodded.

"'Course, we'll do what we have to for an official identification, but I put my money on this being him. Poor old guy."

"How come the wife didn't call him in missing until yesterday?"

Suggs shrugged. "There was some kind of screwup in communication between the wife and a woman who looked after the old man when the wife was out of town. The wife thought this woman was with Becker. The woman thought the wife was."

A fish splashed across the way, drawing their attention back to the body. It moved gently with a slight current, but it wasn't going anywhere. Claudia pulled at her shirt. She'd remembered to leave her jacket in the car this time, but the forethought was of small consequence in the afternoon heat.

"The No-Name used to be real popular," Suggs said. "Now it's a bitch to get to." He jerked a thumb at the patrol officers. "We had to take an old access road to where the canal just starts to widen, crawl through a hole in the fence, then scratch our way past the weeds and shit. I'll be pickin' spurs out of my socks for the rest of the day. Where'd you park?"

Claudia gestured behind her. "On the edge of the golf course."

"Wait—you drove over it to get here?"

"I didn't see any other way to get here fast."

Suggs leaned in toward Claudia, out of Booey's earshot. "See, now that's just the kind of thing about you what irritates me, Hershey. You don't see the big picture in this town, or maybe you just refuse to. These Feather Ridge people? They have a lot of weight with the town council, which calls the shots for our scrawny little police department. I bet someone in that development is calling the mayor right now, raisin' a stink about you tearin' up their private damned golf course."

"The message was a Code 26. We have a drowning victim."

"Yeah, well, in case you didn't notice, he's been dead for a while. We're not exactly talkin' about a situation that calls for lights and sirens."

Claudia let it go. He'd started the day aggravated with her, and clearly he would finish it the same way. She watched him grapple with a Tums roll and pop two of the tablets into his mouth. Maybe it was just his stomach acting up.

"Lieutenant?" said Booey, his eyes still on the body. "Excuse me, but even upside down, he doesn't look . . . right. How long do you think he's been in the water?"

"Hard to know, Booey, but at least a few days. Bodies don't usually float to the surface—"

"They don't come up for a while, son," Suggs interrupted. "They sink first and stay down till their gases make them rise, all bloated up and . . . nasty. That's somethin' you need to learn about if you're gonna be in law enforcement." He turned to Claudia. "And before you even ask, Hershey, I already called Flagg for crime scene and the medical examiner." He grunted and lowered his voice again. "This may surprise you, but I *do* know what's what with procedure on somethin' like this—isolated area, no obvious witnesses, etcetera, etcetera."

"I didn't say you didn't."

"No, but you were thinkin' it."

For the second time in as many minutes, Claudia bit back a response. She looked at Booey. His face had paled, though less than it had in the Farr trailer. "Listen, you still carrying a digital camera in that bag of yours?" she asked.

"Sure, absolutely. I bring it everywhere."

"Good. When crime scene gets here, they'll photograph everything, but—"

"Standard ops," Suggs said.

"Right," said Claudia, inwardly rolling her eyes. "Anyway, Booey, they'll take pictures, but we won't get them back right away. Think you could get some shots for us now?"

He brightened and snapped his fingers. "That fast, no kidding. I'll be back in a second, maybe even faster." He pivoted and started to jog off.

"Hey! Booey! Watch where you step," Claudia called sternly. "Take exactly the path we took coming in." She kept an eye on him briefly, then nodded to herself.

"So, Hershey, the point of that busywork would be . . . what?" Suggs pulled a handkerchief from a pocket, wiped his face. "I ask because from where I stand, it looks like just one more way you're tryin' to keep my nephew in the backseat."

Claudia shook her head. "Then you're standing in the wrong place. Look, if we get digital shots, he can load them on the computer. We can look at them right away. Also, he needed something to do. He's seeing his second dead body in two days. That's a load for anyone."

"Don't you baby that boy, Hershey," Suggs snapped. "I told you he needs some toughening up. I put him with you for that reason."

"You put him with me because you're buying down a debt."

"Both."

The patrol officers looked over. Suggs lowered his voice. "Just this once, Hershey, go my way. I'm not foolin' with you now." He swept an arm toward the pond. "Do it with this, and do it with Booey."

Claudia met his eyes. "Believe it or not, I'm trying—on both counts." She paused. "Anything else?"

"Yeah. On this Becker thing, just in case you don't take my meaning, what I'm saying is, do what you gotta do out here, but do *not* make a federal case out of things." He stuffed his handkerchief back in his pocket. "I'm headin' back now. Make a point of keepin' me apprised."

Booey stood where Claudia told him to stand. He shot the pictures she told him to get. And for every step he took, he walked as if the ground were made of glass and might crack. Try as she might, she could barely picture him as a grown man, never mind a cop. Still, there was something about his persistence she admired, not to mention his extraordinary attention to detail.

On the drive to the No-Name, he'd told her what he'd learned about Wanda Farr. As Claudia listened to his rendition, his voice rising and falling with drama, she knew he was embellishing some, weaving facts with supposition. But she didn't stop him. In remarkably short order, he'd done what no one else had been able to do, or maybe just hadn't cared to do. Driven by single-minded purpose, he'd plowed through databases and made a swift succession of phone calls, undeterred by voice-mail loops and disinterested bureaucrats. Of course, his pseudo-police status didn't hurt in speeding the process. But even so, and quite on his own, he assembled a background for the cat lady that gave her texture and dimension, that elevated her beyond the cardboard persona she'd acquired in Indian Run. Ultimately, the history might not matter. The person did.

Wanda Farr, Booey related, had been born in Pittsburgh as Wanda Joy Harrimond, a name she forfeited for a marriage that produced two children by the time she was nineteen. Her husband, Robert, worked in the steel mills. Wanda worked as a waitress. Their babies, boys born eleven months apart, were shunted around while their parents navigated graveyard shifts and overtime schedules that left them exhausted and still somehow perpetually behind on their bills. Like so many who had come before them and would come still, they decided that a better destiny lay in Florida, where, if they could just get away from killer winters, they would find good jobs and marital harmony, which somehow never took hold in Pittsburgh.

Their aging Plymouth got the couple and their babies as far as Jacksonville before it died. Neither Robert nor Wanda despaired about that, though. Jacksonville's streets positively sparkled compared to those in Pittsburgh, where the curbs seemed perpetually stained from traffic and old snow. And the palm trees! Wanda had never seen them except in pictures; here, they stood like elegant ornaments in every neighborhood. People seemed friendly and, of course, there were beaches. They would get work. They would visit every tourist attraction. They would save up to buy one of those one-story houses with the red-tiled roofs.

They were wrong about everything. Robert scrabbled to find jobs that, once obtained, never seemed to last. He started drinking. Wanda held out longer, but waitressing in Florida wasn't any different than waitressing in Pittsburgh. In fact, she made less money; and of that, what didn't go to raising her babies seemed to go down Robert's throat in a whiskey habit that sometimes turned him mean. Eventually, she went the same way. The babies—toddlers by now—received less and less attention and ultimately wound up as temporary wards of the state. Robert didn't seem to care, or perhaps he just didn't notice. Wanda cared, but she couldn't stay sober long enough to be persuasive. When the kids were four and five, Robert and Wanda formally relinquished all parental rights. Before long, it was as if they'd never had children at all.

The couple never divorced. Robert spared Wanda the expense and aggravation of that process by getting himself killed in a bar fight over a perky young woman who reminded him of his wife before she'd gotten herself all worn out and ill-tempered. There was no evidence to suggest that she ever remarried. Indeed, her history grew spotty as the years unfolded. She didn't work regularly—at least not on the books—though what work she did report showed a twenty-year pattern of wandering that eventually brought her to Indian Run. At first, her interest in the town seemed more a flirtation than a commitment. She stayed; she left. She stayed; she left. Finally, she took a job at a diner, where, despite a sullen demeanor, she remained for a surprising four years—and might have remained longer if a gas fire hadn't reduced the diner to rubble. What happened after that wasn't documented, though it seemed certain that Wanda must have taken to the streets for years—jobless, loveless, and homeless.

Booey apologetically told Claudia that he'd been unable to learn when Farr's obsession with cats began. During his endless round of phone calls, he turned up one old man who vaguely recalled seeing her about a year after the diner burned down, feeding cats—and herself—from Dumpster pickings. She wound up in church shelters during inclement weather and, occasionally, as a guest of the jail on charges of vagrancy. How she survived wasn't clear. But then she got lucky—more or less. During a brief but ambitious state-driven campaign to rehabilitate homeless drifters, she was among five recipients awarded free housing in Indian Run.

"The trailer?" Claudia asked.

Booey nodded vigorously. "She *owned* it, free and clear. The state donated the trailer, hers and four others. The town donated the land. All she had to pay for was utilities. Someone must've shown her how to collect Social Security, because that's what she lived on. And can you believe this—she lived in that trailer for twenty-two years!"

"What I can't believe is that the trailer is still standing," Claudia said, thinking back to the dismal structure.

"Guess what else?"

"What?"

"She wasn't a hundred years old. She was only seventy-two."

Claudia said nothing to that. What was there to say? The chief had been right. Farr lived her life hard. It showed.

"Is there any surviving next of kin?" she asked.

"I couldn't find any. Her father was listed as 'unknown' on her birth certificate, and her mother died when she was fifteen. There were no brothers or sisters. She had the two little boys, but they stopped being hers a long time ago." He sighed. "I guess she just had her cats."

They hadn't spoken for the remainder of the ride to the No-Name, further discussion blotted by the thought of what lay ahead. Drowning deaths in the elderly were not common, but neither were they unheard of.

As Claudia watched Booey angle for another shot on the bank of the No-Name, she hoped she could wrap this one up quickly. No one seemed to be grieving for Wanda Farr, but a woman who didn't know she was a widow yet waited anxiously for news of the man in the pond.

"All right, Booey," Claudia called out. "That should do it. I'm going to call in and see what's keeping the crime-scene unit. Just sit tight."

"Want my cell phone?" he yelled back.

Claudia smiled. "No. The radio's fine." The point was moot, anyway. No sooner were the words out of her mouth than she heard car doors slam in the distance.

Five minutes later a team of crime-scene technicians strode into view. A burly man in civilian dress barked orders at the others, then turned to Claudia. He introduced himself as James Rigg. "What've we got?" he asked.

Claudia gestured at the body in the water. "Best we can figure, this is an old guy named Henry Becker, who had a history of wandering off." She told him what little she knew, then walked the bank with him for a bit.

"You think he fell in trying to cross the bridge?"

"Possible. It'll hold human weight, but for how much longer I don't know. The thing is shaky, and there's not much handrail left to grab hold of."

"Handrail! There's not much *bridge*, period. What's left looks like it's held together with toothpicks. You try it?"

She nodded. After Suggs left she'd reluctantly crossed once, slowly, half afraid to breathe for fear of making the structure sway more than necessary. It wasn't something she intended to attempt again. But then, a man whose ability to reason had long passed might not have given it another thought. Claudia told Rigg as much.

"You got a point, Lieutenant." He shaded his eyes against the sun and slowly surveyed the area. "All right. We'll get started. The M.E. is about an hour behind us, but we should be wrapped up before dark. Anything in particular you want us to look for?"

Claudia glanced at her notes. Rigg's crew would make detailed drawings, but she had her own rough sketch as well. Between that and Booey's digital pictures, she probably had as much as she would likely take away from the scene for the moment. There weren't any witnesses to interview, no fingerprints to lift, nor was there evidence of a scuffle to suggest anything but an unfortunate accident. Later, she would talk to the man's doctor, and she'd talk to the man's wife. Beyond that, it looked like the chief could put aside his concerns about a federal case. This wasn't one of them.

Rigg slapped at an insect. "Yes? No?"

"Sorry. No. I'll hang around, but nothing strikes me right now."

"Okay. By the way, who's the carrottop over there?"

"Chief's nephew. He's . . . sort of an intern."

Rigg laughed. "Aren't you the lucky one. The kid looks like he stepped off the pages of an old *Archie* comic book."

"Some of those comics are worth a lot of money now," she said.

"Yep. Probably more than the kid."

"Actually, probably not," said Claudia. She left Rigg standing there and walked away to smoke a cigarette.

Claudia never wanted to own a cell phone. Robin called her a technophobe, but it wasn't that. Fax machines, computers, voice mail . . . even if she didn't exactly embrace them, she used them all, understood their value. But cell phones? From what she could see, more people used them to clarify shopping lists from grocery stores than for emergencies. Fine. They saved a buck a pound on veal with a quick call to the spouse. They spent forty bucks a month for the convenience.

Right now, though, with darkness descending and one more miserable place to go, Claudia reluctantly asked Booey if she could borrow his. They had just settled into her car, though she hadn't started it yet; and as she watched him fumble for the phone, she fought a snap of irritation. His eagerness to please was just so damned cloying. She mumbled a "thank you" when he handed it over, then she stepped out of the car and leaned against the hood to dial.

Robin answered on the third ring—late for her—and chirped a hello.

"Hey, hon, it's me," Claudia said. "I'm running late. Probably won't be home for another hour or so. Everything all right?" *Meaning: Is Brian still there?*

"Yeah, everything's cool. Dad just ordered a pizza."

"Terrific," Claudia said. She closed her eyes and listened to the crickets for a beat. "Save me a piece?" Her daughter's response was muffled, and then Claudia heard Brian's deep laugh in the background. "Robin? Hon?" she said.

"Sure. I said sure, we'll save you a piece."

Claudia wanted to ask what was so funny. She asked about the kitten instead.

"Oh, Mom, he's just so cute. Dad gave him a paper bag, and he must've played with it for maybe an hour. Dad said he likes him because he doesn't have to run out and buy batteries to keep him going."

Yeah. Like "Dad" knew anything about buying batteries.

"You'll need to come up with a name for him," Claudia said.

"I know, I know. I've been bouncing around a few ideas. Dad's got some ideas, too."

"I have a few thoughts myself," Claudia lied quickly.

Robin groaned. "Puh-leese don't tell me 'Radar' or 'Bandit.'"

"Nope. Nothing cop-like." *What was wrong with Radar or Bandit?* "I'll tell you when I get home." She heard more muffled laughter, then her daughter's voice again, telling her she had to go. By the time Claudia got a good-bye out, Robin had already hung up.

People reacted to the news of tragic death differently. Most often, their eyes widened in disbelief, then shock, then horror. They wept, nearly all of them. Some screamed. Some shook so violently and unremittingly that they literally had to be carried off. Others, no matter the depth of their love for the victim, showed almost nothing at all.

Barbara Becker fell somewhere in the middle. When Claudia quietly confirmed that the police believed an elderly gentleman found dead in the pond was her husband, she nodded once, twice, then briefly closed her eyes and cried so quietly that only her tears gave her away. They stood just inside the dimly lit foyer of the Becker house, as far as they'd made it before Mrs. Becker guessed why Claudia and Booey had knocked on the door.

"I'm so very sorry," Claudia said. She put a sturdy hand on the woman's arm. Mrs. Becker leaned on a cane, but in the low light Claudia couldn't see her expression adequately enough to gauge how well she was holding up. She worried that the elderly woman might pass out. She'd seen it happen. "Would you like to sit down?"

"I'm all right," Mrs. Becker replied hollowly. "But thank you." She played with a pearl necklace that rested in two thick loops against her sweater, momentarily lost in her own thoughts.

Claudia dropped her hand but inched closer, just in case. The woman was nearly as tall as she was, but she appeared shorter, stooped as she was on the cane. Claudia couldn't quite place her age. She might've been sixty—or seventy-five. Her makeup was heavily applied, though artfully so, and Claudia idly wondered whether she'd benefited from a facelift or two; her chin was firm, her flesh tight. Then again, perhaps her appearance was merely flattered by the low light and feathery hair expertly styled to frame her face.

"As you might imagine, Detective, your news is not completely . . . unexpected. I guess it couldn't be. But . . . my husband, my Henry—he was found in a pond? And there's no doubt that it really is Henry?"

Claudia nodded. "We have no reason to think otherwise, Mrs. Becker. We'll still need a formal identification, but the body matched the description we'd been given when you reported your husband missing. The officers on the scene also found a wallet with a photo ID in his pocket."

She gave Mrs. Becker a minute to absorb the information, then presented a brief accounting of the discovery. She didn't gloss over details, but neither did she offer specifics that could only be upsetting. Booey stood solemnly to the side, his own face so drawn that Claudia feared he might begin crying himself. She needed to cut this short.

"Mrs. Becker, do you have children? Or anyone else I can call for you? A friend? Maybe a brother or sister? It's not a good idea to be alone after something like this."

Mrs. Becker seemed to consider that. She pushed an errant strand of auburn hair behind an ear, then shook her head. "That won't be necessary. I have someone who . . . well, never mind. Frankly, I think that right now, just at this moment, I'd rather be by myself. You know, Henry and I, we were so close, so. . . ."

Claudia waited.

"Did you know that after he retired he developed a passion for model railways? No, I don't suppose you'd know that. Of course not." The woman smiled briefly. "He'd spent his whole career with trains—buying them, selling them, negotiating deals for them in the U.K., Australia, and, of course, the United States. But it was his job, a career; and although we were rewarded with a handsome lifestyle because of it, it was really only after he retired that he could enjoy them." Her face clouded over. "Then it seemed like he'd no more than started to find that passion when he began to experience moments of forgetfulness and, sometimes, odd behavior. I guess that's when the Alzheimer's began to show. It's, well, it's a. . . ." She couldn't continue, and Claudia tensed.

Mrs. Becker wiped at a tear. "I'm sorry. I'm all right. Really." She drew in a breath and smiled. "One day, I'll show you his trains, his models. They're really quite something."

Claudia murmured that she was sure they were, that she wished she had found an opportunity to meet Mr. Becker, said that she'd always loved trains herself—found them soothing, romantic. After that, there seemed little else to add. For a minute, she could hear them all breathing in the still of the foyer.

"Mrs. Becker, it's late now and I know you have a lot to absorb. Unfortunately, I still need to go over a few points, ask you some questions. They're just routine, questions that are standard in a situation like this, but—you know, why don't I just come back tomorrow? It won't take a lot of your time."

The woman tiredly waved a hand. "I'm not sure I understand, but I know that Henry would. He would give you a brisk nod and . . . well. Please call before you come. I imagine I'll have to see to funeral details and . . . that sort of thing. Where have they taken Henry?"

Claudia hated this part. "He's been moved to the morgue," she said as gently as she could. "I'm afraid that's standard."

"The morgue! Oh, Detective, I assume you're not going to let them leave him there! Surely he can be moved to a funeral home. We haven't lived here that long, but I know there's one in town. Give me a minute. I'll just go look up the number and—"

"I'm sorry, Mrs. Becker." Claudia winced. "I'm afraid there needs to be an autopsy first. It's procedure."

The woman's mouth opened to respond, but she said nothing. She merely looked at Claudia, swayed briefly, and slumped toward the floor. Claudia got an arm around her just in time.

CHAPTER 5

THE PIZZA WAS LONG PAST ITS PRIME by the time Claudia got home, but someone had wrapped two slices with tin foil and left them on a paper plate for her. She perched on a stool at the counter and devoured both pieces. The force of her appetite surprised her. It had been a lousy day—Becker in the pond, Suggs on the warpath, Farr on her mind, Brian in the house. *Still* in the house.

The TV played quietly in the living room, sending random showers of blue and white light toward the kitchen. Claudia crumpled the foil and tossed it in the trash. She didn't want to go in there. Brian lay stretched out on the couch asleep. Or maybe he was faking, trying to avoid her as much as she was avoiding him. In the last days of their marriage, that's what they did. But now they had to talk, because this business about taking Robin for the summer. . . .

Claudia poured herself a glass of wine and pushed herself into motion. Brian must have heard her in the kitchen, because he was up now, stretching his arms and yawning. He blinked in her direction, then squinted at his wristwatch and said, "Still keeping late hours, huh?"

"Not normally," said Claudia.

"Got any more of that?" He nodded toward her wine glass.

"Help yourself."

Brian disappeared into the kitchen. When he returned, he held up his own glass and the wine bottle. "It'll save us a return trip."

"Where's Robin?" Claudia asked. She eased into an armchair, watched Brian take his place on the couch again.

He laughed lightly. "Better you should ask where the kitten is. She's become joined at the hip with him." He sipped his wine. "They're both in bed asleep. I don't think she was planning that, but the kitten's like a narcotic. I moved the stereo to her room, and he fell asleep on her chest while she was listening to music. She was out like a light a second later."

Claudia picked up the remote control and aimed it at the TV. She pressed the MUTE button but didn't turn it off. Her hands felt clammy.

"You used to do that when we were married," Brian said.

"Do what?"

"Turn off the sound, leave the picture on, as if you couldn't bear the thought of being alone with me."

"It's just a habit, Brian. Don't read things into it."

They fell silent again. Claudia turned her eyes to the screen, weighing how best to say what she had to say. For him to take Robin for the summer—unthinkable. "We didn't get a chance to talk yesterday," she said at length. "The kitten, the store . . . time just got away from us."

"Yeah. And I know I came at you from left field. I'm sorry for that."

"Why, Brian? Why now? What's changed in your life that you want to spend time with Robin? We've been divorced for almost eight years, and in all that time you've visited her—what? A dozen times? You've missed every single thing that's been important to her since she was seven. But now, here you are, wanting her for the entire summer. I don't get it."

Brian went to fill their glasses. Claudia put a hand out. "No. Tell me what's going on."

He leaned back into the couch. "What's going on," Brian repeated softly. He tilted his head to the side. "Funny thing is, Claudia, nothing is going on. There's no great story here. I'm not dying of a fatal disease. I'm not having a midlife crisis. But good things have been happening in my life—good things that are steady, good things that matter—and for the first time ever, I feel like maybe I have something to offer her. I feel like I can hold my head up in front of her. Whatever I've shown, or not shown, I've wanted that for a long time."

Claudia bit back a response. Brian's tone was persuasive, but then, it almost always had been. She nodded for him to continue, studying him as he talked.

The years had been good to him. Clearly, he wasn't leaving a lot of hair on the bathroom floor. It remained as thick as ever and still radiated a complicated blend of sandy tones that could never be duplicated by even the best hairstylists. He'd put on perhaps five or six pounds, and minute wrinkles fanned out from the corners of eyes so blue they looked like a trick of light. But if anything, the cumulative effect merely enhanced the casual good looks he'd always and effortlessly possessed. She wondered if he even wore reading glasses. She wondered how often he slept around.

He told her that he now lived in Arlington, Virginia, commuting regularly to Washington, D.C., where he played piano at charity banquets, political events, fund-raisers. He described a foreign-affairs dinner hosted by the President, where he played a medley of classics by American and European composers. He told her about back-to-back engagements over Memorial Day weekend.

"There's magic going on, Claudia," he said simply, almost wonderingly. "I don't know how else to describe it, but they love me. I'm sought after. It's crazy. It's insane. I've traded blue jeans and smoky nightclubs for a tux and ballrooms. Me. Who'd'a thunk it, right?"

He swirled wine in his glass, then took the last swallow. "The pay is terrific. And it's *regular* work, Claudia—what you always wanted, what I was sure I never did. You weren't right about everything, but you were right about that. And now I'm hooked. I'm booked, too, from now through next February."

He was electrified, more animated than Claudia had seen him since the first years of their marriage. And what he said, what he described—it all had the ring of truth. Could that be? She filled her glass, hesitated, then filled his.

"Thanks. Can you understand now?" he asked. "Can you see why I want to show Robin my life? Why I want to share it?"

Claudia wanted a cigarette in the worst way. She smiled ruefully, at that, at him, at them . . . at what might have been.

"I've got photos in the car. I can show you some of these events." Brian chuckled. "Listen to me. I sound like one of your perps sweating it out during an interrogation." Then he sobered. "You haven't said a word."

Claudia searched his eyes. "Bring me the pictures."

They negotiated over another bottle of wine, Brian's glossy eight-by-tens spread across the coffee table and backlit by the silent TV. Once, they left to raid the refrigerator. Brian built sandwiches with tomatoes and old cheese on top of hamburger buns. Claudia watched for a minute, then went to peek in on Robin. She lay on her side, her mouth slightly open and her hands tucked beneath her pillow. The kitten was curled into the hollow of her knees. It stirred, but Robin never moved.

What a gift this girl was. Claudia bent down and kissed her forehead. She'd freak if she knew, and Claudia smiled to think of it. She pulled the covers higher up on her, then quietly backed out of the room.

Brian had returned to the coffee table. She joined him and they ate silently. She imagined he was mentally celebrating, for he'd won most of what he wanted. Robin would leave with him the next day, not for the whole summer, but for three weeks. He would perform at the historic Fourth of July celebration in Washington, their daughter witness to a talent rescued from the same stubborn pride that trampled their marriage. Funny how life worked out.

"Claudia?"

"Hmm."

"Play your oboe for me."

"Look, it's—"

"Don't say no. Please. I know you still have it. Robin told me you play every night before you go to sleep."

"It's nothing, Brian. Just my version of reading in bed."

"Then read to me, Claudia. Please."

No one had asked her to play in a long, long time. Of course, almost no one knew that she played, that she was nearly as good with the oboe as Brian was on the piano. He knew, though. He'd always known. His piano had been the moth to her oboe, or maybe it was the other way around.

Claudia shook her head. "I can't, Brian. There's no point. Not to mention that it's late."

"Music doesn't need a point. Come on. Five minutes? I'll be gone in the morning, and you probably won't see me for the next decade." He smiled and quickly added, "Just kidding."

She shouldn't. But . . . no one had asked in a long time. "Four minutes, tops. And I *will* be counting." She stood and headed for her room to retrieve the instrument. She flicked on a small bedside lamp and eased the oboe from its case. When she turned around to go back, Brian was there, leaning against the door frame.

He nodded. "Just pretend I'm not here," he whispered.

Claudia looked at him for a long moment. Then she moved to the window, looked out at the dark, and lifted the oboe to her lips. She closed her eyes and began to play softly, choosing a complex piece weighted with tones both melancholy and hopeful. She could not pretend he wasn't there, though; in her mind, the gentlest of notes from his piano strayed into the background, urging her own music into a dimension that flooded her senses. She rode every note, pulling nuance from one, then drama from the next, her fingers gliding as effortlessly across the keys as a surf against the shore. When the piece drew to its conclusion, she held the final note for as long as her breath would allow. Finally, she let the oboe hang loose at her side, a faint echo of music still in her ears.

Brian stood behind her now, his breath on her neck as light as an eyelash against her cheek. If she turned, his lips would be there to meet hers. Neither of them spoke; there was no language for what passed between them. They lingered like that for a full minute—maybe more—and then she did turn.

His arms went around her at the same moment their lips met. For a moment they merely nuzzled, finding each other all over again. Then Brian's lips pressed more urgently and began to explore, finding the crevice in the front of her neck, then the soft place just below her ear. Claudia felt his hands sliding slowly down her back, fingertips tugging at her shirt. She let it happen. She let his hands roam to the front, gasping when they first made contact with her flesh. Sensation washed over her and caught in her throat. The oboe dropped soundlessly to the carpet.

She didn't know when he closed the door, but he had; and when he guided her toward the bed, she let him take her there without protest. That would come tomorrow, she knew, but for one rash sliver of time she was content to let her body make decisions. She watched him turn off the lamp as she made room for him beside her.

Brian had always been a good lover—an extraordinary lover—and aging had not changed that. He traced a finger along her arm, studied her face, then leaned over her, a lock of hair falling gracelessly against her forehead. She reached up and touched it, then let it fall loose once more.

"It's good to see you smile," he whispered, his lips a hair-trigger from her lips again.

"I was smiling?" she murmured. "You must be confusing me with someone else."

They chuckled together, then Brian grew serious. "I've missed you, Claudia."

She put a finger to his lip. "Shhh. Don't talk."

His hands traveled up, then down. They lingered here, then there. And finally, with a touch almost elegant, he slid her clothes from her body, piece by piece, until she was covered with nothing but darkness and the goose bumps he created.

Claudia inhaled sharply. He was doing something at her feet now, something exotic and new and . . . she grabbed a handful of sheet and held on, willing him to stop, willing him to continue. A few seconds later he edged back up; and when he did, she seized on the moment to try and think, because this could come to no good. She groped for the pragmatic side that had gone underground, sternly reminded herself that he was the hateful ex—or if not that, then at least a man who had no further business in her life, certainly not the intimate part of it, anyway.

To her surprise, her own hands began to move instead. She grappled with his clothes, shrugging them off and tossing them to the side. This wasn't her. This was some animal, and she wanted no part of it. But her hands stayed busy. His stayed busy. When he knocked she let him in. They locked themselves together and remained that way until they had exhausted all invention and sleep sneaked up on them both.

CHAPTER 6

IF JOHN SIMPSON RAYNOR WAS A SMART MAN, which Claudia doubted, he would do his best to show some respect when she and Booey approached him. He would have his dogs chained to a fence and in full view. He would answer her questions promptly, courteously, and truthfully. If he was a smart man, he would do all of that and more, because she was loaded for bear. Claudia didn't like clichés, and she didn't know the origins of "loaded for bear," but she knew that it suited her on a late-June morning that looked a lot better than she did when it dawned.

She logged off the computer, stood and stretched, then took another look at the crime-scene report from Farr's trailer. Interesting. Not conclusive, but interesting. She checked her weapon and slid it into her holster. Her notepad was filled. She grabbed another and dropped it into the pocket of her jacket, the black one she favored when she wanted to show she meant business. After a final glance at her desk, she stepped into the multipurpose room.

"Everything all right, Lieutenant?"

Claudia looked left. "Hey, Mitch."

"You seem a little . . . distracted."

Mitch Moody. Solid man. By-the-book officer. Sensitive. Open. Right now, she could clobber him. She hated people asking her how she was. Even more, she hated that her moods were more transparent than she thought. Then again, this was Mitch. Maybe they only showed to him.

"I'm fine, Mitch," she said. "I'm just a little tired."

He smiled. "I won't ask you what you're tired of."

"Probably a good idea."

This time they both smiled.

"By the way," Mitch said, "Booey told me where you're going. If you want some backup out there, just give a holler."

"Count on it."

He started to leave, but Claudia stopped him. "Mitch, quick question. I want to put a wrap on this Becker case as fast as I can. The widow's a wreck, and I don't want to upset her any more than I have to. Maybe you can help me avoid being in her face."

"I heard she passed out on you last night. Booey says you caught her just before she almost became a fatality herself. 'Just in the nick of time' is how he put it."

"Yeah, well, she would've been hard to miss. I was about two inches from her." Claudia shrugged. "She came to before the paramedics arrived. She let them look her over but refused the ambulance."

"Tougher than she looks, huh?" Moody said.

"In shock, is more like it. Anyway, you're the one who talked to her when she called in the missing persons report, right?"

"That's right."

"This woman she mentioned, some caregiver, do you happen to have her name and phone number?"

Moody colored slightly. "Truth is, I didn't think to ask. Mrs. Becker mentioned her, said there was a miscommunication, but . . . well, she was so upset that I didn't pursue it. I just, you know, got some guys out with me to start looking for him."

Claudia sighed. "Well, never mind. I'll catch up with Mrs. Becker later today, maybe talk to the caregiver, too. If I'm lucky I'll be able to put a bow on this package and be done with it by tomorrow." She saw a flash of red out of the corner of her eye. "Booey! Come on. Let's go."

Booey turned from the direction of the men's room, showed a wide grin, and hefted his backpack to his shoulder. He hurried toward her.

"Boy, that kid's really stuck on you," Moody said.

Claudia gave him a look and headed for the door, Booey struggling to catch up.

If sunlight had ever touched Raynor's property, it had been a long time ago. Towering Australian pines and oak trees with limbs thicker than a man's waist blocked all but the most fleeting rays, their roots erupting across the ground like snakes on the move. His trailer was wedged so tightly among them that Claudia spotted it only at the last minute. She braked abruptly, sending a jolt through the car when it bounced over a rock.

Booey grunted and grabbed the dashboard.

Claudia glanced at him. "Still got your kidneys?"

"I think so," he said. He straightened in his seat and looked out the window. "Wow. Dante's *Inferno*. You remember the passage about—"

"Later, Booey. Let's go talk to Mr. Raynor." She began to unbuckle her seat belt, then glanced over. Booey was sorting through his backpack. "What are you doing?"

"Looking for my camera and—"

"Forget it. Just leave your stuff and let's go."

They stepped out of the car, Claudia's eyes scanning left and right. The trailer stood about forty feet from the car. It listed slightly to the right, so wedged between trees and shrouded in shadow that it was hard to know where it began and where it ended. In front of the trailer on one end was an old metal tub and, next to that, a small stack of tinder. An assortment of old tires lay abandoned on the other end. But no dogs. No vehicle. She put a hand on Booey's shoulder when he started forward. "Hey, hold up a minute. I don't want you straying from me, understand?"

He nodded earnestly.

"Good. Raynor's not likely to be happy when he sees us. He might get edgy, and edgy people sometimes overreact."

"It doesn't even look like he's home."

"I'm sure that's what he'd like us to believe." Claudia reached beneath her jacket and loosened the snap on her holster. "Come on." She led Booey to the trailer door, nudged him behind her and rapped hard, then called out, "Mr. Raynor! Detective Lieutenant Claudia Hershey, police department. Please step outside. I'd like to talk to you." She gave it a minute, then rapped again and repeated herself, more loudly this time.

Silence.

"It's kind of creepy here," Booey whispered.

"Shhh."

"I don't even hear—"

Claudia wheeled around, simultaneously shielding Booey and whipping out her revolver. Raynor stood at the side of the trailer, a shotgun trained on them, four white dogs tensed at his side. Their mouths curled back, showing teeth, but they made no sound. Raynor lowered his weapon first.

"You don't look like thieves and you don't look like in-laws," he said. "I guess I won't shoot you today. You plannin' on shootin' me?"

Claudia found her voice, surprised that it sounded as steady as it did. Slowly, she lowered her own gun, but she didn't put it away. "I'm Detective Lieutenant—"

"Ain't nothin' wrong with my ears. I heard you the first time, but I got no window in my door. That's why I came out the back and around the side, to check you out. You just can't be too trusting these days. Who's that boy with you?"

"Put your weapon on the ground, Mr. Raynor."

"It's legal."

"Put it down. Now."

Raynor chuckled. "Ain't even loaded, Miss." But he rested it against the side of the trailer.

"Now get rid of the dogs."

He looked at her, amused, then turned to the dogs and clapped his hands three times. They tore behind the trailer, kicking up a small cloud of dust. "Nice pups," he said. "I don't know why everyone is so durned afraid of them." He folded his arms across his chest. "I hear the witch next door is dead. If you're takin' up a collection for her, count me out."

"Why don't we go inside and talk," Claudia said. Her heart had almost settled into a normal rhythm again. She hoped Booey's had.

"Suit yourself," Raynor said. He brushed past Claudia and opened the door. "Don't mind the dust. It's the maid's day off." He started to lead them in, then abruptly pivoted toward Booey. "Boo!"

Raynor laughed when the boy jumped, then he held the door wide. "That hair of yours is so red it looks painful, boy."

Booey blushed furiously.

"All right, enough," Claudia said irritably. She closed the door behind them and paused while her eyes adjusted to the trailer's gloomy interior. It looked just like Farr's and was nearly as cluttered. No cat odor, though. Just dog. Lots of it.

"Coffee?" Raynor asked. He grinned, beginning to enjoy himself. "This here's a fully stocked kitchen. For the grownups I got decaf and regular. For the little guy there . . . hmm, might be I could make some Kool-Aid. Would that suit you, boy?"

Booey cleared his throat. "I'm not—"

Claudia stopped Booey with a slight shake of her head. "We won't be here long enough for your hospitality, Mr. Raynor," she said smoothly.

Raynor threw back his head and laughed. "Oh, sure you will. And long's okay. I got nothin' much else to occupy my time, and I'm makin' coffee either way. Have a seat." He gestured at some chairs around his kitchen table, then busied himself at a stainless steel sink, measuring coffee into a filter.

Claudia and Booey scraped back chairs and sat. She watched Raynor open a cupboard and move a filmy glass out of the way, reaching for mugs behind them. Even through the gloom of the trailer, she could see they were filthy. She shuddered to think of touching them, never mind putting one to her lips. She caught a flash of the glass again when he closed the cupboard, and she smiled grimly. As bad as the mugs looked, it was entirely possible the glass was more lethal yet.

"No surprise you're here," Raynor said. "Anytime a rabbit farts in the woods, someone sends a posse." He blew dust from one of the mugs, then set them on the counter.

Claudia quietly secured her weapon but kept an eye on him while he poured water into the carafe. Raynor was of average height and weight, and he looked about sixty years old. Three or four days' growth of whiskers covered his face, except where a jagged scar ran from his left ear to his chin. He was scratching at it, as if aware she was examining him. He turned on the coffeepot, then sat at the table and leaned back in his chair, balancing it on two legs.

"Okay," he said. "Let's get right to it, shall we? Wanda Farr. Dead in her bathtub. That's what I hear, and it don't surprise me one iota. It don't depress me, neither. She was a blight on the face of the earth, her and those scrawny cats of hers."

"You had a lot of run-ins with her over the years, Mr. Raynor."

"Yup. And I mighta eventually got around to killing her myself if she didn't do me the favor of drowning first." He slammed forward in his chair. "That why you're here? You think I sneaked into her trailer and held her head underwater until her face turned blue?"

Claudia held his eyes. "Did you?"

"Nope." Raynor hooted. "There ain't a thing in the world that woulda ever possessed me to be in a situation where I'd have to see that old bat naked. Just imaginin' her without clothes is enough to give me a heart attack. Nope. If I was gonna kill her, I'd shoot her or set my dogs on her. Truth be told, drowning was too good for her."

"That's sick!" Booey said suddenly. The second the words were out, his eyes widened, registering surprise at his own outburst.

Raynor sneered and leaned in close to him, showing a mouthful of yellow teeth. "What's 'sick,' son, is that she ever got born at all."

"All right, enough." Claudia glared at Booey briefly, then turned her attention back to Raynor. "Look, let's get back on track here. Tell me where you've been and what you've been up to in the last couple of days. Try not to make anything up."

"This is just conversation, right?"

"Unless you think it needs to be something more."

Raynor tilted back on his chair again, seemed to consider that. "Nah. I got nothin' to hide." He pursed his lips, stared at the ceiling. "Last couple of days? I been here. Couple of days before that? Here again. Today? Still here. I got an old truck out back, but unless I need to stock up on anything, it don't go nowhere and neither do I. The dogs are all the company I need."

"You've had no occasion to be at Wanda Farr's trailer?"
"Nope."
"Not outside it? Not inside it?"
"Nope."
"Not ever?"
"Nope."
"Not even for a neighborly drink?"
"Hah! Good one! But nope to that, too."
"No reason to chase any of her cats back to her place?"
"Nope."
"Did you see anyone in the area who doesn't belong?"
"Nope."
"So I guess you just aren't in a position to be very helpful, are you, Mr. Raynor?"
"It's startin' to sound that way."
"Okay." Claudia stood to go.
"Aw, you're really leavin' so soon? I haven't even poured the coffee yet."
"I told you we wouldn't be staying. But maybe another time." She smiled thinly. "Maybe soon."

Side by side, she and Booey walked a straight line to the car, the eyes of the silent dogs on them the whole way.

CHAPTER 7

THE OVERNIGHT COMPLAINTS were blessedly routine. No deaths. No arrests. Claudia sipped coffee and thumbed through the reports while she waited for Carella and Moody to come in off the road, quickly calculating which reports might require follow-up. The smashed window? No. Loud stereo? No. The stolen cable converter box—likely; there'd been a rash of them lately. Overturned garbage cans along Pine Grove Avenue? No. Husband-wife dispute called in by a neighbor? Probably not, at least not this time. The responding officer noted that the couple were lip-locked and cooing at each other by the time he arrived.

Claudia put a fingertip to her lips and thought darkly about Brian. That groping, that grappling . . . it had to be the wine. Of course. The wine, the stress of an absurd day, the music—all of it conspired against her, left her vulnerable, just vulnerable enough to long for a soft touch, a physical release, a. . . .

Yeah. Right.

She shoved the reports to the side of her desk. Robin didn't know. That's all that mattered. She and Brian were already dressed and at the kitchen table when she woke up, and if Robin had anything on her mind at all, it was the kitten, which she scooped into her arms the moment she surfaced. She looked at the kitten's food bowl, then at Claudia.

"You didn't even feed it yet," she said accusingly. "How could you forget?"

"I didn't forget. Look. There's still some dry food in his bowl."

"You're supposed to top it off." Robin scowled and muttered something undecipherable, then busied herself at the bowl, the kitten winding around her legs.

Brian took over then, smoothly stepping in to tell Robin about the vacation he and Claudia had worked out. Robin shook a triumphant fist in the air. "Yes!" she said. "Yes!" She threw her arms around Brian, and then, a little uncertainly, around her mother.

Claudia realized with a pang that Robin already knew. Oh, she didn't know the details, but she knew, or at least she wasn't surprised. Had Brian drawn her into a conspiracy? Would he stoop that low? Or had he just dropped hints?

Robin pleaded to take the kitten with them, and Claudia won a small measure of satisfaction watching Brian play the heavy, telling her no, it just wasn't practical, not for them or the kitten. For a minute, it looked like Robin might decline going at all—Claudia could practically *feel* her waver, hoped desperately that she would—but finally she relented and turned her attention to her mother once more, with a lecture on how best to take care of the kitten.

"Please don't give him a name while I'm gone, all right?"

"I won't."

"Promise? The thing is, kittens learn names fast and I want to be the one to teach him one." Robin's voice softened. "Is that all right, Mom?"

Claudia pushed a lock of hair from her daughter's face. "It's more than all right. He's all yours. I'll just keep him healthy and safe for you. Promise."

There wasn't much else to say, nor was there time. Claudia had to go to work, leaving Brian and Robin to pack and lock up. They'd probably drive as far as Tallahassee and then stop for the night. Good road trip, the kind she would've enjoyed making herself.

Laughter in the multipurpose room jarred her from her musings. Carella and Moody were in and high-fiving about something at the coffeepot. Carella turned when he spotted her walking toward them.

"Hey, Lieutenant. Sally radioed us, spewed some codes I couldn't figure out and said you needed us for something?"

She nodded. "Let's get with the chief. He's expecting us." They waited while she refilled her own coffee cup, then followed her to Suggs's office.

The chief waved them to chairs. "Where's Booey, Hershey?"

"I don't know. He told Sally he had an errand to run. I was on the phone. Didn't talk to him myself."

Suggs grunted. "All right, what's on your mind that you needed us all together in the middle of a shift?"

"Wanda Farr."

"Now, why am I not surprised?"

"It's looking more and more like she didn't drown on her own."

"Uh-huh. We don't even have an autopsy yet, but you know that for a fact?"

"Not for a fact. Not yet."

"Then why are we here?"

"Because the crime-scene report shows that John Raynor's fingerprints are all over the glass that was on the edge of Farr's bathtub. Because I saw a glass just like it in his own cupboard."

Claudia watched Suggs's facial muscles working while he absorbed what she'd said. She took the opportunity to bring Moody and Carella up to speed, pleased to see them take detailed notes. She was almost finished recounting her visit to Raynor's trailer when the chief interrupted.

"I don't get it," he said. "Raynor's a lowlife. I'll give you that. And he hated Farr—that's no secret—but nothin' in his history shows this man to be a killer." Suggs scratched at his head. "We're forever hearin' that he puts together cockfights—rumor is he's workin' to arrange one now—but cockfights aren't exactly a high priority, and he stays away from anything that *would* be a high priority. So what've we actually got on him over the years that could stick? A couple bar fights? A drunk and disorderly?"

"That's about right," said Claudia. She scanned her notes. "He's kept animal control plenty busy—and yeah, we've been out to his place with some regularity—but he hasn't butted heads with us in any really serious way for several years."

"That's what I don't get, because it sounds like what you're tellin' me is that a guy who's been nothin' but your basic schoolyard bully has suddenly turned into a bona fide killer. He wakes up one day and— What? What are you shakin' your head for?"

"I wish it were that simple." Claudia leafed through her file and pulled out the crime-scene report. "Personally, I think Raynor's more than a bully, and to me he looks better than most for Farr's murder—"

"*If* it was a murder," said Suggs.

"Right. *If*. But it might not have been him at all. And if it was, then he might not have been acting alone." She slid the report across the desk to Suggs. "There were three sets of fingerprints on the glass. Farr's, Raynor's, and an unknown. Routine analysis didn't pull enough detail on the third print to give us a name. They could belong to someone who just doesn't have prints on file. Or they could belong to an ax murderer. Either way, we're screwed on identity."

Suggs glanced at the report, then leaned back in his chair. "So this would be another of your 'incongruities,' huh?"

"That's right," Claudia said evenly. "It's enough of one to merit more investigation. That's why I wanted Mitch and Emory here. If Farr was murdered, then we're already moving way too slow. I need them to talk to the other people who live out by Farr and Raynor. We need to learn more about Wanda Farr's last couple of days alive—who she saw, where she went, what she did."

"Lieutenant?"

Claudia looked to Moody. "Isn't it possible that Farr had some company over? What if someone else came by with a bottle of booze and poured her a shot? And Raynor's glass—she could've come by that a couple of different ways. Right?"

"Damn good questions," Suggs muttered.

"Agreed," Claudia said. "And that's the point. We have more assumptions than we do facts. We can't shift the balance if we don't pick at her lifestyle. That takes questions."

Carella snorted. "Yeah, like for starters, what's up with that old woman taking a bath in the first place? Don't get me wrong. It was sad, what with her plowing through garbage cans and all, but she wasn't exactly a sympathetic character, and she most definitely wasn't particular about hygiene."

They hammered at the case for another thirty minutes, splitting up assignments and working out a schedule that wouldn't cripple regular patrol duties. On the books, the case remained a suspicious death, not a homicide. That suited Claudia fine. For now, anyway, it would get the same investigative treatment, and if they were wrong—if *she* was wrong—then backing off would be easier for Suggs to explain to a critical town council.

As they filed out of Suggs's office, the chief stopped her for a second. "So, Hershey, here we go again, eh? I'm back out on a limb with you, just like last year."

Claudia sighed. She was about to give him her take on metaphors when he suddenly grimaced and doubled over, clutching at the side of his desk. Papers cascaded from the top, jarring her into action. She got to his side a heartbeat before he straightened again and irritably waved her off.

"Whoa," she said. "What *was* that? Are you okay?"

"I'm all right, I'm all right," he said thickly.

"You sure? Because you really *don't* look all right. Your color's off and—"

"I said I'm all right. Just somethin' bad I ate."

"Yeah, but it might not hurt you to see a doctor. You've—"

"Back off," he snapped. "I already got a wife."

Perspiration beaded the chief's forehead, but he was slowly pinking up again. Claudia nodded. "On the Farr case, I'll keep you posted on a daily basis," she said, then turned and headed outside for a quick cigarette. She bet he was fanning himself with a file folder the second her back was turned.

***

Booey was at Claudia's desk when she returned. He didn't say where he'd gone and she didn't ask. But she did fill him in on the meeting he'd missed, then left him at her computer to check a few files while she settled into an outside desk to make calls. He seemed uncharacteristically quiet; but of course, his world had been turned upside down in just a few days. Maybe he would decide to cut short his stint with her. Claudia thought about that. Booey was all right, more or less, but she couldn't say she'd miss him if he decided to bail. No, she couldn't say that.

She picked up the phone and dialed Barbara Becker's house. When she had tried earlier, no one picked up. This time she let it ring a long time. Mrs. Becker was slowed by arthritis, and getting to the phone might take herculean effort. But even after a dozen rings, no one responded and Claudia gave it up.

She looked at her notes and tried the medical examiner's office next. No surprise there; the Farr autopsy still wasn't scheduled. As for the Becker autopsy, they'd let her know.

Claudia drummed her fingers on the desktop. There came a time during any investigation when time stood so still you could watch dust settle. People weren't home. No one answered phones. Computers were down. The world would not be rushed.

Then again, there was someone she could almost always find at home—Dennis. He lived there. He worked there. He didn't filter incoming calls. Claudia felt a rush of by-now-familiar guilt as she began to dial.

Don't think about Brian, about what you did.

She paused midway through dialing and hung up. She shook her head and doodled on a file cover for a second, then irritably snatched the phone again and punched in his number—all of it. The line was busy.

Enough. Claudia stood and stretched, fidgety. She gathered her files and went to collect Booey. "You involved in anything that can't wait?" she asked.

"Not really. NCIC just went down and—"

"Good. Let's go. We'll grab some lunch and swing by Barbara Becker's house. On the way there—and I can hardly believe I'm thinking this at all—but on the way over, I might just lose my mind and run into Radio Shack to pick up a cell phone." She smiled. "I suspect I happen to know someone who could help me pick out a decent model and teach me how to use it."

"Sure!" Booey brightened. "And actually? If you don't want to wait on this person, I could probably show you myself."

Claudia just looked at him. "Booey, Booey, Booey. . . ."

They headed out, Booey's "What? What?" setting cadence to their footsteps all the way to the car.

CHAPTER 8

IN THE LIGHT OF DAY, the Becker house showed off an imposing structure which had been obscured by shadow the night before. Claudia remembered steering past a fountain that rose from the middle of the Beckers' circular driveway, but the fountain had been turned off and she'd paid it scant attention. Now, with water springing from it in an intricate display of choreography, she slowed the car to get a better look.

"Do you know what kind of amazing electronics must be behind that thing?" Booey said, immediately scrambling for his digital camera. "It's awesome!"

"I don't know about electronics, but I can guess at what kind of amazing money," Claudia replied. "Put that thing away, Booey. This isn't a field trip."

"Sorry."

She pulled up to the house—estate, really—and parked behind a Jaguar. Claudia had tested her new cell phone by trying to reach Barbara Becker on the drive over, still with no results. She hoped the Jag signaled that the widow was in now.

"Look at the size of this place!" Booey said, loping beside her to the front door. "It must be, like, eight-thousand square feet—maybe even ten."

There was no point in telling him not to gush. His expression registered his thoughts before they ever reached his mouth. Claudia ignored him and rang the bell. She heard it chime inside and stood back a foot to make herself clearly visible through the peephole. A few moments later the door opened to reveal a tall, bearded man in jeans and a rumpled sports jacket. His hair was dark and pulled back in a tight ponytail. She couldn't see his eyes, which were concealed by sunglasses with a dark purple tint. He didn't say "Hello." He didn't say "Can I help you?" He just stood there. Claudia identified herself and introduced Booey, then asked for Mrs. Becker.

"She's not taking calls or seeing visitors today," the man said.

"I'm here on official business. We won't be here long."

"I'll let her know you came by. She'll call you later."

"I'm sorry, but I need to see her now."

The man shrugged. "Can't help you."

"And you are—?"

Before he could answer, Claudia saw Mrs. Becker coming up behind him.

"It's all right, Aaron. Let them in," she said. "I should've mentioned they might be stopping by."

The man gave her a dubious look, then held the door open for Claudia and Booey to enter. As she had done the night before, Mrs. Becker leaned lightly on a cane, but she looked rested and spoke in a clear voice when she greeted them. Claudia felt heartened. Perhaps they could get this over quickly.

"Aaron's been a real sweetheart," Mrs. Becker said. She patted his arm. "He's my neighbor's son, and I've had him running errands. He's quite wonderful."

Somehow, her tone made it sound like Aaron was just an overgrown high school boy. Claudia put him in his mid-thirties and calculated his height at six-five or six-six. She hoped he wasn't already angling for a piece of the widow's pie.

"I'll be all right now," Mrs. Becker reassured him. "Really. You don't need to stick around any longer." They stepped to the side and spoke quietly for a minute, then Aaron nodded coolly at Claudia and left.

"I hope he didn't sound too abrupt," the woman said. "He's so protective of me. And he absolutely dotes on Henry." She paused, catching herself. "He did," she added softly.

"I'm sorry, Mrs. Becker," Claudia said.

"That's all right, dear, though I appreciate your expression of concern." She turned to Booey. "Would you like to see my husband's model trains? If I'm not mistaken, I promised to show them to you last night."

Booey yipped his enthusiasm before Claudia could tell her that a tour of Henry Becker's model railways wouldn't be necessary. She frowned at his back while Mrs. Becker led them out of the foyer and into what once must have been regarded as the "grand room." Claudia heard Booey gasp. She was pretty sure she did, too.

An elaborate web of camouflaged scaffolding and plywood throughout the room supported hundreds of toy trains in painstakingly detailed settings that mimicked real life. There were farm towns and bustling cities, beachfronts and rocky shores, flatlands and mountain regions. The support structure ran from one end of the room to the other and crisscrossed diagonally at various points, with dips and curves that put some layouts above Claudia's shoulders and others nearly at her feet. Everything had been carefully arranged to depict the topographical realities of each scene.

She stared, momentarily speechless. Not a thing had been left to chance. From the tiniest shrub to the most majestic summit, the display evidenced a meticulous attention that suggested both a labor of love and an obsession. Even the walls boasted canvases painted to reflect the scenes they were nearest to.

"It's incredible, Mrs. Becker," Claudia said.

"You should see it when the lights are out and the trains are running," she said softly. "Henry used some sort of projection system to put a twinkle of stars on the ceiling. It's astonishing. *He* was astonishing. Right up until the end, he was working on this, though obviously less and less as the disease took hold of him."

Booey had not yet found his voice. He stood rooted in place, as spellbound as a toddler seeing snow for the first time.

"What will you do with it?" Claudia asked.

"I'm not sure. I haven't thought that far. There's another display out in the garden, only with much larger model trains. When Henry had all of this set up back home, he'd open it to the public once a year, right around the holiday time. Museums clamored for it. But I don't know, now that he's gone . . . well, I suppose I might sell it. As much as I respected his passion for model railroading, it's not a hobby we shared." She smiled. "Tennis was my passion, at least until my arthritis began kicking up in a serious way, mostly in my hip."

"I wish I'd brought my camera in," Booey said wistfully. "Mr. Becker must have every HO-scale train ever made. I can't tell if these are from Lionel or American Flyer—there weren't many of them to begin with—or maybe someone else, but they're just beautiful. The whole thing, it's just, it's just . . . I don't even have a word for it."

"Well, young man, if you have a camera in the car, by all means feel free to go get it. Henry would've insisted."

Claudia firmly shook her head. "Thank you, Mrs. Becker, but this isn't the time or place for—"

"Nonsense! Henry would've been very flattered by the young man's interest. Besides, while he's snapping pictures, you and I will have a chance to talk. Please. Indulge an old lady."

"All right," Claudia said politely. She would kill Booey later, and he must have sensed it. When she gestured for him to retrieve the camera from the car, he sidled out without looking at her. "Mrs. Becker, would you like to sit down while we talk? You've been on your feet quite a while now."

"Actually, I would. When your young man gets back, I'll take you into the kitchen. We'll have some coffee."

When Booey returned, Claudia whispered stern instructions for him to join them in the kitchen when he was finished taking pictures. She hissed at him to hurry up and, for heaven's sake, to not knock anything over. She knew nothing about model trains but suspected that any one of the displays could rival a year of her salary.

"Boys and their toys," Mrs. Becker clucked as she led Claudia across an acre of tile and toward the kitchen. "Henry would have liked your Booey."

"Someone needs to," she said, too low for the woman to hear. And then she put Booey and the trains out of her mind. She needed to get down to business.

While Mrs. Becker made coffee over her protest, Claudia idly examined the kitchen. Stainless steel everything, and all of it gleaming and spotless. She couldn't help but contrast it to the kitchenettes in Farr's and Raynor's trailers. There were the haves and the have-nots. Mrs. Becker was a have; and eventually, when her husband's will was probated, she would glide into a have-even-more category. Claudia didn't resent the woman's good fortune, but hoped that instead of selling the model railways she would donate them to a museum or charity, maybe make some kids happy.

Finally Mrs. Becker set their coffee on the table and gingerly eased herself into a chair. She rested her cane against the table and folded her hands in her lap, making idle chitchat while she got settled. Claudia pulled discreetly at her jacket. Although the house was clearly air-conditioned, she guessed it was set to eighty; hotter than hell, at any event. She didn't know how Mrs. Becker could stand to wear a sweater, although she supposed that being chronically chilled was just one more concession people had to make when they aged.

"Mrs. Becker," she began, "the officer who originally talked to you when you reported your husband missing said there'd been some sort of communication mix-up between you and a caregiver. Can you tell me what that was about? It'll really help me close the file on this."

Mrs. Becker shook her head. "Stupid, stupid, stupid. Not the caregiver—me." She shuddered briefly. "Henry and I have lived down here almost eight months. We moved here from Chicago because the doctors advised us that a quiet town and more temperate weather could be beneficial for Henry. You see, he wasn't bad off yet—most days you'd never even know anything was wrong with him—but Alzheimer's is a progressive disease, and we were quick to take advantage of every possibility that might forestall it, even a little."

"Go on," Claudia encouraged.

"Well, prior to moving, I met with a lovely young woman who was trained in caring for Alzheimer's patients. Henry needed virtually no help at the time, but I knew that one day he would, so I hired her to be with him on a part-time basis. Actually, I'm not even sure you could call it part-time. I probably only had her in six or seven hours a week, just long enough for Henry to get used to the idea of having someone besides me around."

Mrs. Becker grew silent and her eyes misted over. She pulled a tissue from the sleeve of her sweater and dabbed at them. "I'm sorry, Detective."

"Take your time, Mrs. Becker," Claudia said. "I know this is hard."

"Thank you." She pushed the tissue back up her sleeve and put her hands in her lap again. "Anyway, Henry took to the woman instantly. She was gentle. She was kind. She didn't seem to mind listening to his endless stories about railroading."

"What's her name, this woman?"

"Oh, I'm sorry. Her name is Barbara Kensington. We simply called her 'Babs,' though, mostly so Henry wouldn't get confused with two Barbaras in the same house."

"Makes sense," Claudia said. She wrote it down, wondering whether Barbara Kensington minded the nickname, which to her ears sounded almost as childish as "Booey."

"Henry quickly grew to love Babs, almost as if she were his own daughter." Mrs. Becker laughed lightly. "In fact, she looks like she *could* be. No one would confuse our ages or our energy levels, but she has the same build that I do and similar features. At least I think she does, though that might be the wishful thinking of an old lady who never had her own children." Mrs. Becker sighed and said softly, "But that's another story."

Claudia stole a look at her watch. "This . . . Miss Kensington, she moved down with you?"

"Not right away. She had other obligations, and frankly, I thought I could handle Henry on my own for a while longer. What I didn't count on was how . . . restrictive our new lifestyle would be. Henry, well, he was content to putter with his trains. He was content to take walks. Indeed, there were times I thought he really might rally here." She shook her head. "It's a vicious, heartless disease, Detective. I wouldn't wish it on my worst enemy."

"So it got worse and you asked Miss Kensington to come down?"

"Well, as I said, I didn't right away. But I realized that if I was to be any good for Henry, then I needed a break now and then. I longed for my friends. I longed for conversation that had nothing to do with disease and treatments."

"So. . . ?"

"I'm rambling. Forgive me."

Claudia told her it was all right, though she yearned to get through the interview and be on her way.

"To make a long story short, I invited Babs down to live with us. I'll be honest; as much as I know she sincerely loved us both, I'm not sure she would've come if I hadn't induced her with a great deal of money and the assurance that Henry didn't need a full-time babysitter. Even to the end, he could still be left alone for hours—at least that's what I thought, though in retrospect I obviously underestimated the stage he was in. Or perhaps I was in denial. I don't know, and for that matter, Henry himself mightily resisted being treated like an infant who needed someone at his side all the time. I knew that day would come, but I genuinely didn't think it was here yet." Mrs. Becker shuddered and pulled her sweater more tightly around her neck. "I told Babs she would largely be free to come and go here as she pleased."

"So what happened?"

"Everything worked out beautifully. Henry had his Barbara and he had his Babs. I continued to take care of him, of course—doctor visits and so forth—but now I had someone who could pinch-hit for me on those occasions when I just had to get away. Now and then, I'd take a two- or three-day visit to Chicago to visit friends and check on our house there. I haven't gotten around to selling it yet, so of course I have to see that it's maintained. At any event, Babs was always here in my absence. And it worked in reverse as well. She had freedom to come and go, to make her own visits back up north. One way or another, we were looking after Henry."

Claudia flexed her fingers, trying to shake off writer's cramp. She'd filled three pages with tightly scripted notes.

"More coffee, Detective? I'm going to refill my own cup, anyway." She braced her hands on the edge of the table, beginning to rise.

"I . . . sure. Why not?" Claudia reached to hand over her cup, inadvertently knocking the woman's cane toward the floor. She fumbled for it, but Mrs. Becker pivoted and snagged it in the second before it landed. She pooh-poohed Claudia's apology and made her way to the sink.

While Mrs. Becker refilled their cups, Claudia thought about

Booey, hoped like hell he wasn't fooling around in the train room. She'd have to kill him twice.

Mrs. Becker picked up her narrative the moment she settled back into her chair. Claudia blew on her coffee and sipped as quickly as the steaming brew would allow. The woman had to be getting tired. They both needed to move this interview along.

"This communication 'mix-up' that we had, I . . . well, I blame myself. I'd gone back to Chicago for a visit. My intention was to be gone just two days, but then I decided to stay longer. I called the house. No one answered, so I left a message on the answering machine. I'd delayed a return one time before, and on that occasion I'd also left a message, assuming that Babs would call me if my change in plans presented a problem. It didn't then, and it didn't this time—or at least that's what I thought."

"So you didn't talk to her again?"

Mrs. Becker shook her head, looked down at the table. "I didn't, no. And it was . . . a fatal mistake."

"What happened?"

"Babs didn't get the message. She didn't check for it, and the next morning, she left."

Claudia straightened in her chair. "Wait a minute. She didn't *check* the machine? And she just—"

"I know, I know. It sounds terribly irresponsible. But Babs was tremendously excited about a trip she was planning on making herself. In a short period of time, she'd saved a great deal of money and she had plans to close on a pleasant little house just outside Chicago. It would be her first. And, though she didn't specifically say as much, I got the impression she was getting back together with an old boyfriend. Perhaps they were making a commitment to each other."

"Still."

"Yes. Well, Babs knew—or *thought* she knew—that I'd be returning the next morning." Mrs. Becker choked back a sob. "She left. She wrote a note to me and left just a few hours before she expected I would be walking back in the door."

Claudia seethed. *Outrageous.* Deal or no deal, boyfriend or no boyfriend, for a caregiver to abandon an old man in Henry Becker's condition screamed of a thoughtlessness so complete, so arrogant that it needed a whole new vocabulary.

Mrs. Becker put a hand on Claudia's. "I can see what you're thinking. If I didn't know Babs as well as I did, I would think it myself. But you have to remember that it seemed to me a minimal risk to leave Henry unattended for a few hours here and there. Nothing ever happened and—"

"But, Mrs. Becker," said Claudia, "you yourself had reported him missing on a few occasions. You *must* have known the risk was greater than minimal. You *must* have expressed that to Miss Kensington."

"On those occasions, I overreacted. I *thought* I was overreacting, and truthfully, your own officers seemed just as convinced. As you must know, Henry would inevitably show up almost as soon as I'd put in a call. He wasn't lost. He was merely . . . dawdling. He— You don't know much about Alzheimer's, do you?"

"I . . . no."

"Well, as much as the disease gets progressively worse, it's very difficult to predict behavior with any accuracy. Henry could go for days without exhibiting symptoms, or at least not serious symptoms. He was certainly far from being at the point where he didn't know my name—or his own. And oh, he loved his walks! To deny him that small pleasure or *cling* to him would be to deprive him of a dignity that he already *understood* he was slowly having to surrender. Don't you see how painful it would be to have that kind of knowledge about yourself?" She pursed her lips, her eyes steady on Claudia. "There's a balancing act, Detective, and I would challenge anyone who claimed they had it down perfectly."

Claudia tried to put herself in the same situation, tried to imagine how she might react. She couldn't, and waited out an uncomfortable silence that she suspected Mrs. Becker thought she should fill with an apology.

The woman sighed. "If Babs had checked the answering machine, this wouldn't have happened. I've thought about that, of course. Certainly Babs has too. I told her it wasn't her fault, at least not—"

"She's back? You've talked to her?"

"Just this morning, early. She's still in the Chicago area, but she called to say hello and see how Henry was doing. Telling her what had happened was probably the hardest thing I've ever had to do. We cried together for twenty minutes." Mrs. Becker repositioned herself in the chair, groaning lightly. "I hope she gets . . . I don't know, maybe some counseling. She's too young to feel the weight of this kind of guilt."

"So she's not coming back?"

"What? Oh, sure. She'll be returning, probably in time for Henry's funeral. But truthfully? I told her not to rush the closing, or whatever other personal matters she's seeing to. What would be the point? Henry is . . . dead. Recriminations won't bring him back."

Claudia shook her head. "I'm not sure I could have such a generous spirit about this. Do you have a number for Miss Kensington?"

"I'm sorry, no. I didn't even think to ask. We were both rattled." She leaned forward. "You know, Detective, what you have to remember is that this isn't just about Babs—what Babs did or failed to do. Henry was my husband, and yet . . . *I didn't even think to call back.* I failed to make sure my message had been received. I was so concerned with myself that I didn't give Henry *or* Babs another thought."

Claudia scribbled a note, then looked up. "In the end, you thought Miss Kensington would be here. She thought you would be here. It's as simple as that?"

Mrs. Becker nodded. "It's as *tragic* as that," she said, so quietly that Claudia had to strain to hear. "It's a mistake I will live with for the rest of my life."

On the ride back to the station, Booey was as animated as Claudia was depressed. The camera dangling from a cord wrapped around his wrist, and his face radiant with excitement, he had found her in the kitchen just as she was standing to leave. Even now, oblivious to her mood, he chattered about Henry Becker's model railways and about the digital photos he'd taken. He couldn't wait to load them into the computer. He wanted to print some out on photo-quality paper. Did she know how important it was to have the right kind of paper for digital pictures? Because he could show her, if she wanted. He could teach her how to crop photos right on the screen, how to bring out highlights.

Claudia tuned him out. She had the note that "Babs" Kensington had scrawled for Mrs. Becker. She had the answering machine tape with Mrs. Becker's message. The widow gave both up freely, and why not? They were what they were: *A fatal mistake. A tragic miscommunication.*

The traffic light that Claudia always seemed to catch at Hoop Road turned red. She braked and silently cursed. If she told the chief she wanted to close the books on the Becker drowning now, he'd be fine with it. More than fine. And it was tempting. It was also tempting to simply comply with Mrs. Becker's renewed request to forego the autopsy and just let Henry Becker rest in peace.

Detective, let him have just that little bit of dignity, please. . . .

The widow's parting words echoed in Claudia's mind.

Just that little bit of dignity.

Strictly speaking, it wasn't up to her. The circumstances mandated an autopsy. But canning the procedure . . . it could be done. No one would fight her.

A car behind her beeped impatiently. Green again. Claudia glared into the rearview mirror, then moved her foot to the gas pedal and continued down the road. All right. She'd give it another day—two at the most. Barbara Kensington was expected to call Mrs. Becker any time now. Claudia had extracted a promise from the older woman to put her in touch the moment the call came through. She figured that if she still hadn't managed to personally talk to the caregiver by Friday morning, she'd think about arranging for Becker's physician to sign off on the death certificate. Mrs. Becker had jotted down the doctor's number for her. It wouldn't take much more than a quick phone call to put things in motion. It was done all the time.

Claudia wheeled into the police station parking lot and turned off the engine. She realized that Booey hadn't shut up once—and wasn't shutting up now. Something about Becker's train display in the garden.

"Whoa, whoa, whoa, Booey. You went into the garden?"

"Oh, it was so unbelievable. Mr. Becker had nothing but G-scale trains. *G-scale!* It's all set up near the pool and almost perfectly laid out. The tracks wind around some dwarf gardenia and fern—artillery fern, I think it's called—and I'm pretty sure he used dwarf mondo grass, too. Blew me away, and that's before I saw that he'd built a trestle out of redwood! *Had* to be redwood. That's just so—"

"Wait a minute." Claudia thumped the steering wheel. "Who the *hell* gave you permission to go into the garden?"

Booey froze in place, one hand still gripping his seat belt.

"I asked you, who gave you permission."

"I . . . no one."

"So you simply wandered the place as free as could be."

"No, not like that. I was looking for the kitchen."

"Obviously you didn't find it in the garden."

"I, uh, I got . . . distracted."

Claudia leaned toward Booey so close that if he'd been wearing glasses they would have fogged. "You listen to me," she said. "You're here because you want to be a cop, but you keep acting like a kid on vacation. Now either grow up or *get out*. Got that?"

He nodded miserably, unable to meet her eyes. "I'm sorry." Then he mumbled something so quietly that she had to ask him to repeat it. He did, but he still would not look at her. "My uncle, he said . . . he told me I needed to get some . . . balls. He said I. . . ."

His voice faded and Claudia shook her head. There was nothing to say to any of that. She hurtled out of the car and left Booey to think, act, play—whatever. She had work to do.

CHAPTER 9

THE KITTEN DIDN'T OWN A CORNER OF CLAUDIA'S MIND, not yet. In fact, though she would never confess it to Robin, she had forgotten about it altogether. She didn't know what kind of person that made her, but she hoped that if found out, she might actually be forgiven when her forgetfulness was viewed in context of everything else she had to remember at the end of another miserable day. She especially hoped she might be forgiven when her failure to remember put her on a collision course with the kitten the moment she stepped through the front door. It was there. She was there. Both went on a sprawl, she harder than it, her arms pinwheeling and her briefcase skimming across the floor like a sled on packed snow.

On her way down, she rapped her elbow on the edge of a bookcase. Tears shot to her eyes. She cursed and clamped a hand around her elbow while she found her feet and frantically scanned the floor. The kitten, the kitten . . . had she stepped on it? Did she crush it?

Except for a preposterously long wooden hallway that led from the living room to the bedrooms, Claudia had never regarded the house as big. She did now. There were a thousand rooms to explore, a million dark corners to investigate, and somewhere in one of them a kitten had to be hiding. She moved from room to room, turning on lights as she went, crooning gibberish in a voice intended to sound reassuring. She hoped the kitten's silence meant only that it was frightened, not that it was dead or dying or incapable of sound because she'd crushed its throat with a shoe that must have appeared the size of Montana when it was coming down. She looked under beds and in open closets first. Then she looked in places she hadn't thought of since she and Robin had moved in. She scored a missing earring, a quarter and two nickels, a button, and a fountain pen that Dennis had given her and which she'd never used. She also unearthed enough dust bunnies to crochet an afghan, prompting a quick vow to vacuum over the weekend.

The kitten was under one of the beds, after all—hers, no less.

Claudia spotted it on her second sweep. It cowered against the wall at the headboard, right in the middle, and it wanted nothing to do with her. She couldn't blame it, but she also couldn't leave it there. The thing was trembling and as wide-eyed as it had been the night she'd coaxed it from the backseat of her car. She didn't think it was hurt. But she didn't know for sure, and she wouldn't until she got it out. Claudia wished it had a name. If it had a name, maybe it would at least meet her halfway. It wasn't responding to "kitty, kitty, kitty."

She leaned against the wall beside the bed. If she brought in a bowl of food and quietly thumbed through the case file right here, would the kitten come out? She thought about it, liking the idea that maybe—just maybe—her unobtrusive presence could be productive in two ways. Worth a shot.

Ten minutes later she tiptoed back, unsteadily carrying the food bowl, her briefcase, a mug of steaming coffee, and a throw pillow to cushion her back against the wall. There wasn't a lot of space between the bed and the dresser, but it would do. She set the bowl just outside the bed and, as casually as possible, removed folders and notepads from the briefcase.

"It's you and me, kitty." She sighed, missing Robin. "Come on out. I won't name you. I won't step on you. I won't even try to make you like me. Kitty? Kitty?"

Nothing.

Claudia gave it up and opened the Farr folder.

Despite their thoroughness, Moody and Carella's efforts to learn anything from Farr and Raynor's neighbors yielded no new insights. They hadn't noticed any suspicious people in the area, nor had they heard any noises that might have signaled a disturbance around the time of the cat lady's death. They did refute Raynor's claims that he stayed away from Farr's trailer, but Claudia hardly viewed that bit of news as a revelation. She knew Raynor was lying, and he probably knew that she did. That could mean two things. He freely lied because he had nothing to do with the woman's death but found perverse pleasure in putting the police through hoops, or he lied because he had killed Farr and hoped not to be found out, or possibly even expected that he wouldn't be.

Of course, the unidentified fingerprints on the whiskey glass remained a problem. Whoever else had touched that glass didn't touch anything else in the trailer, or at least not that the crime-scene technicians had found. If she presumed that the glass came from Raynor's trailer, a buddy of his might've touched it there. Later, somehow, that glass wound up on the edge of a dead woman's bathtub. Farr might've found it on the ground at some point, claimed it as her own, began using it. Could be. Their trailers weren't close, but . . . could be. It could also be that she'd taken a liking to whiskey, had acquired some without a bottle, poured it into a glass she happened to find that happened to belong to Raynor, then took the first bath she'd had in a very long time and, along the way, happened to knock herself silly on the bathtub faucet and drowned as a result.

Could be. Anything could be.

For another twenty minutes Claudia sipped coffee and thumbed through the file, studying interview notes and official documents. She reread reports by social workers who stopped by Farr's trailer to check on her. They didn't come often. They didn't stay long. One way or another, their reports said the same thing that Farr's neighbors did: the woman had no friends, no visitors. And if she'd had service people in—a plumber, an electrician—Moody and Carella hadn't been able to find them. Claudia stretched her legs and tried to shift to a more comfortable position. Everything she considered took her in loops that inevitably brought her back to Raynor. Even if it didn't end with him, it began with him. His glass. His fingerprints. His lies.

Claudia closed her eyes. She didn't intend to drift off, but when she opened them again, another half hour had passed. She knew she should get on her feet, eat dinner, make phone calls. Her legs had stiffened from being locked in place, and she craved a cigarette. But the kitten had come out. The stupid thing slept on the open case file on top of her lap. She put a finger against his head and tentatively petted him, half expecting him to bolt. He didn't. He purred instead, so she petted him again, watching his little body rise and fall with every contented breath. She decided to stay put for just a little longer, wryly acknowledging that the kitten had crossed some sort of threshold, morphing from an "it" to a "he" in the process.

Damn.

Dennis Heath sounded glad to hear from her, but Claudia noticed that he didn't exactly enthuse when he picked up the phone. There was none of that "This must be my favorite Hershey Kiss," a lover's term she thought ridiculous, but right now felt like a rabbit punch to the gut for its absence.

She got right to the point. "I've been a thoughtless shit, Dennis. I'm sorry. I should've returned your calls." She waited into the silence, one eye on the lemon-Dijon chicken breast she was frying, another on a pan of rice.

"You sound like you're calling from a tunnel," he said at length.

"I bought a cell phone. I'm trying it out."

"Ah."

"Dennis, look—"

"You don't have to explain."

People never meant that. Claudia flipped the chicken and said, "I'd like to, though. You probably thought I'd fallen off the edge of the earth."

He didn't laugh.

"It's felt a little like that lately."

"Rough week on the job, huh?"

It wasn't exactly a sympathy vote, but at least it was an opening. Claudia rushed to fill it. She glossed over the work stuff and told him about Brian's unexpected appearance, how he'd bought Robin the stereo she intended to buy, how he whisked her off to Washington, how he claimed he was a new man. She didn't tell him how she'd allowed him into her bed.

"I guess you just described the proverbial week from hell," Dennis said when she was done. He paused. "I guess I would've wanted to crawl into a hole, too."

"But you wouldn't have, Dennis. That's the difference between us. I brood. You don't. I'm a jerk. You're not."

"I hope you're not expecting me to debate you on the point," he said, but his tone was lighter, and they both laughed. "All right. You're off the hook, Hershey. Now, what are you doing that you can't come over?"

The chicken was done. The rice was overdone. Claudia salivated for them both, but. . . . "Can you give me ten minutes?" she said.

"Given your recent history, how about I give you fifteen?"

"You have an absurdly generous spirit. You know that, don't you?"

"Fifteen minutes. My eye's on the clock."

"Done deal."

Claudia fumbled with the tiny cell phone buttons and disconnected the call. She dropped the phone into her purse, then looked longingly at the stove. Dennis liked her chicken, or claimed that he did. She shoveled the food into a casserole dish and headed for the door. She didn't know if she was about to break a relationship or fix it. What she couldn't do was pretend it didn't need one or the other.

When the cell phone rang a mile from Dennis's house, Claudia nearly ran off the road at the unexpected intrusion. She swerved to the shoulder and braked hard beside a row of cabbage palms, her heart quaking in her throat.

Who the hell could be calling?

She fumbled to retrieve the phone from her purse, simultaneously furious for buying it and dismayed to see that the sudden stop had turned her casserole dish into a projectile. The chicken and rice lay in a sodden mess in the well of the passenger side. All this, and no doubt for a misdial.

The phone had a cheerful ring, which made Claudia hate it all the more while she stabbed at the "receive" button. "Yes," she hissed. "Hershey."

"Lieutenant-it's-Booey-and-I'm-in-trouble."

"What?"

"*Booey. It's Booey. I'm in trouble.*"

"Booey? Either you're whispering, or I'm getting a weak signal on this phone, because I can hardly hear you."

"*It's not the phone. I'm trying to keep my voice down.*"

Claudia thumped the phone with the heel of her hand. "Say again?"

"*I SAID I CAN'T TALK LOUD.*"

This time she made him out and felt a flutter of unease at his urgent tone. "Tell me what's going on." She pressed the phone tighter against her ear and used her free hand to block the other. "Try to speak up."

"*I need help.*"

"Why? Where are you calling from, Booey?" She thought she heard rustling, and then his voice came back on: "I'm on my cell phone. I'm at Mr. Raynor's, in a tree. There are dogs everywhere."

CHAPTER 10

THE DOGS WEREN'T EVERYWHERE. They were in one spot, restlessly pawing at the base of the tree like wolves anticipating a kill. In the dark, with only Claudia's headlights for illumination, they looked even more fierce than before. And there were more of them. As she drove slowly past Booey's VW and approached them, she counted the shadowy figures. Seven. Seven that she could see.

She shuddered. He'd made it back from Raynor's trailer as far as the tree, something broad and so tall that its top blended with the dark. Another eight yards and he would've made it to his car.

Giving the dogs wide berth, she inched by them. Her cell phone connection with Booey was still open and she could hear him breathing. She whispered a reassurance and told him she'd be back, then continued another twenty yards beyond, to Raynor's trailer. To her surprise, the dogs did not follow. But then, why should they? Their prey was in a tree, visible and vulnerable. She was not.

Raynor's trailer was dark and quiet. If Booey was to be believed, it had been that way since he arrived thirty minutes earlier and foolishly decided to get out of his car and knock on the door. Claudia wondered why the dogs had not gone after him immediately, why they'd waited until he'd almost made it back to his vehicle. Training? Some kind of pack mentality? She gave a short laugh. Up until now, she'd thought her biggest challenge would be the kitten.

What about Raynor's truck? Was it parked behind the trailer? Claudia's high beams pierced the gloom. She sought access through the trees, so densely nestled that it was hard to know where one stopped and another began. How did Raynor get through the wooded curtain? Or did he have another route that accessed the trailer from the back, bypassing the front altogether? She wished she'd paid more attention on her earlier visit.

She maneuvered the car forty-five degrees, letting her headlights sweep the other end of the trailer. There appeared to be a gap between two trees that she might be able to navigate. But she didn't like it, didn't like not knowing what she might encounter on the other side, didn't like knowing that she might have to back the car out to return. And of course, just as with the dark house, even if Raynor's truck was gone, it didn't mean *he* was. Too many unknowns. Not enough time.

Claudia turned around and headed back to Booey's tree, this time pulling close but driving slowly to avoid alarming the dogs. They edged away at her approach, but just barely, their mouths pulled back in snarls and their thick bodies rigid with deadly anticipation. She put the car in park a foot away but kept the engine running. Two or three of the dogs restlessly circled the Cavalier. The others resumed their post at the tree.

She sat ramrod straight in the car, nervously drumming her fingers on the steering wheel and weighing options. She hadn't called for backup, partly because Booey pleaded with her not to, terrified of his uncle's reaction. But more than that, she feared an overreaction all around. With a boy in a tree, mean dogs on the ground, and a man with a shotgun possibly lurking in the shadows, the prospect of calling in inexperienced officers who never saw real action seemed the larger threat. It didn't take much to turn one tense moment into a blistering Waco.

Claudia cracked her window a few inches. Except for the scuffling of their paws along the ground, the dogs made no sound—or almost no sound. Then, as her ears grew accustomed to the environment, she picked up on a low, throaty noise over the idle of the engine, a scratchy sound almost like static. It scared her more than the dogs' teeth.

"How're you doing, Booey?" she said into her phone, keeping her voice as low and even as possible.

"All right, I think." He feigned a laugh. "I'm a banquet for the bugs, though."

She wasn't worried about the bugs. She was worried that his muscles would give out on him, that he would fall. Athletic he wasn't, and he'd been clinging to tree branches going on forty minutes now. Why he was there—why he was on Raynor's property at all—none of that mattered at the moment. She needed to get him down.

"Listen, do me a favor, huh? Don't scratch. Just hang in there a little longer while I figure this out."

"Okay . . . Lieutenant?"

"What?"

"Did you know this is a camphor tree?" His voice caught, as if he were shivering. "It's just like the one at the No-Name Pond. Not as big, but the branches are sturdy. You can find them almost anywhere in the state." His voice hitched again. "Beautiful, aren't they?"

"It's all right, Booey," she said gently. "I'm going to get you down."

Claudia could barely see him from her position, but she judged him to be about twelve, maybe fifteen feet up. Theoretically, he could drop to the top of her car and they might be able to spin away before the dogs could react. She dismissed the idea as too risky before it was entirely formed. She dismissed her next idea, too—using herself as a lure. Stepping out of the car would be suicidal for both of them.

That left her gun. If she had to, she could shoot the dogs—or some of them. It was a last resort, for reasons both philosophical and practical. Claudia was hardly an animal activist, but clearly the animals were doing what came either naturally or by training. They didn't deserve to die for that. Besides, her .38 Colt Special was at home. The silver-plated .22 in her purse might take down a few of them, but even with a true aim she wouldn't stop them all. Indeed, the effort might bring on a far more dangerous opponent: Raynor.

Claudia eyed the chicken breast and rice on the floor. She fantasized flinging the chicken out the window and watching the dogs tear each other apart in a competition for the choice meat while Booey scrambled down and got into the car. . . .

Right. One lousy piece of chicken. Probably one bite for a single dog. Mere perfume for the rest. She either needed seven chickens or—

"Booey," she said into the phone, "where are your car keys?"

"In my pocket."

"Good. Is your car locked?"

"No."

"Good. How fast can you get down that tree if you have to? Don't answer until you think it through." She waited.

"Fast?" he said.

"What's 'fast,' Booey? I need something concrete. Think."

"I . . . maybe ten seconds? Fifteen?"

Claudia paused, automatically doubling his estimate, then doubling that, thinking about the timing, calculating the odds. It could work.

She told Booey what to do, what she would be doing. When she was sure he understood, she closed her eyes for a minute and ran the scenario through her mind one last time. Finally, she took her .22 from her purse, set it close beside her, groped in her purse again, this time for a pocketknife, and then began unbuttoning her shirt.

The summer before Robin was conceived, Claudia and Brian had found cheap flights to Mexico. Claudia's interest was in the culture—the Mayan ruins, the Folkloric Ballet, the silver mines. Brian wanted to see a bullfight. She didn't want to go, but neither did she want to duel over their itinerary. So they went. While they settled into their seats, Brian nattered about the long history of the fights and flung terms at her that he pulled from a brochure. Claudia barely listened. All she could hear was the blood lust of the crowd, thousands of people waiting in eager anticipation for the fights to begin. After the first, watching the bull taunted into savagery, watching the matador make the kill, she got up and left. She found a concession stand and drank bad coffee until the fights were finished. Weeks later, when Brian suggested they plan a trip to Spain for the running of the bulls, she told him no with such swiftness that he never brought it up again.

The images swam to Claudia's mind as she rolled down her window just far enough to toss a chunk of chicken at the dogs. It took them a few seconds to react, and when they did, they seemed more confused than anything else. Then a squat brown dog—a pit bull, she guessed—thrust its nose into the ground. He snatched the trophy and downed it in a gulp.

By then the other dogs understood. They pushed at him, darting in and out, snapping at him. Claudia threw another piece, just off to the side. The dogs dove at it, as if they'd never eaten. It was gone in an instant; she didn't see which one got it. Agitated, they pushed against each other and snuffled at the ground, some of them turning in furious circles.

Claudia backed the car up slowly. This time, she threw two morsels at once, one of them wrapped in a piece of her shirt, which she'd torn and thoroughly rubbed with the meat. Midway in flight, the chicken popped out of the fabric. Neither piece of meat landed as far from the tree as she hoped, but the dogs moved swiftly to claim them, and the animals fell on the cloth as if it were just as edible. And now they understood.

They looked toward the car and stared at its occupant. Claudia felt her heart hammer. They were deciding something, she was sure of it. She barely had time to throw out another shirt-wrapped piece of chicken before they lunged.

She flinched, then accelerated backwards, almost dropping the last piece in her hand before she could throw it out, too. It stalled them just long enough for her to drape the rest of the shirt from the window and roll it up with shaking hands, clamping it to the frame. She couldn't hear their snarls, but she felt the car rock when they threw themselves against it.

She backed up with reckless speed, her hands slick from the chicken. The dogs tore at the shirt, battering the car and snapping at each other. Claudia glanced in the rearview mirror. If she didn't brake now, she would ram Raynor's trailer.

"Now, Booey! Go!" she shouted at her cell phone. She counted to ten, her eyes on the dogs, then cracked the window long enough for them to wrest the shirt entirely free. For a second, they forgot her. They ripped and pulled on the shirt in a frenzy, their bodies quaking with rage. Claudia seized precious seconds to chuck a fistful of rice out the window. It cascaded onto some of the dogs, turning them into targets for the others. She threw another, and then another, until she had none left.

She caught her breath and looked over the dashboard, squinting into the path cut by her headlights. She looked for Booey, couldn't spot him, glanced down at the dogs. They were beginning to break up, their ears perked. She reached for her .22 . . . and stopped. She heard what the dogs heard—Booey's car starting up.

Claudia sent up a silent prayer of thanks, shifted into drive, and got the hell out of there.

She'd told him to meet her in the parking lot of the Git-Go, a small convenience store that was convenient only until nine o'clock at night. It was nine-thirty now, and the parking lot was vacant except for Booey's VW. He sat on the ground, leaning against the car until he saw her headlights. Then he rose unsteadily to his feet.

Claudia almost didn't care if he saw her in her bra or not, but she told him to look away as she got out of her car. She flicked sticky rice from her left arm and retrieved her parka from the trunk. She felt queasy and took a few deep breaths. She wondered how he was doing, and asked.

"Well, I didn't wet my pants," he said shakily. "That's something."

It caught her off guard. She threw back her head and laughed. At that moment, she liked him more than she ever had and more than she probably would again.

He laughed uncertainly with her, then both fell into silence for a minute.

"How are the bug bites?" she finally said.

"Bad. But I'll live."

"Too bad tree climbing isn't an Olympic event. I don't know how fast you went up it, but it didn't take you long to come down. I gather you didn't break any bones in the process?"

He shook his head. "I knocked my left ankle hard somewhere along the line—I'm not even sure if it was going up or coming down—but it's all right. I'm all right. Other than being stupid."

Claudia nodded. "What's the story, Booey? What were you doing out there?"

He told her then, too rattled to tell it neatly, but the gist of it was that somewhere on Raynor's property he'd lost his PalmPilot and he'd gone back to get it. He didn't find it. Didn't have time before the dogs came out from beneath the trailer.

"It had my whole contact list in it," he said, as if that explained everything. "I probably have three hundred names and addresses. The minute I meet someone I add them to it. At least I used to. Now, I imagine it's become a chew-toy for the dogs. . . ." His voice trailed off.

"Give me a minute, Booey," Claudia said. She went back to her car and rooted through her purse for cigarettes. She lit up and came back. Booey had dropped back to the ground again. She joined him there.

"Why'd you go alone?" she asked. "You knew what kind of man Raynor is. You knew about the dogs."

Booey played with a shoelace. "I thought I could handle it. And I thought—I've read this—that if you don't show fear to dogs, they'll leave you alone. Then they didn't even seem to be around. I must've sat in my car for a good five minutes, just to see. So I knocked on Raynor's door. When he didn't answer, I headed back for my car. I wasn't far from it when the dogs came out."

Claudia pulled on her cigarette, then asked, "What I don't understand is why you parked so far from the trailer. You could've pulled right up to the door, or just about."

"I . . . to show I wasn't afraid." He looked at Claudia. "You wouldn't be. Uncle Mac wouldn't be."

"Booey," she said gently, "we both carry guns. We both have years of experience and even then, we—"

"No!"

He spoke so suddenly, so passionately, that Claudia almost dropped her cigarette.

"It's *not* that simple!" He grabbed a fistful of his hair and yanked on it, hard. "I . . . do you know what it's like to have hair like, like . . . *this?* To have a name like mine? It defines you, it *defines* how people see you. They don't care whether you're smart. They don't care if you're friendly. They only care about the package. *Look* at my package, Lieutenant! *Look at it!*" He began to sob. "They see a nerd, a goofball, a . . . a clown. And they're right. They're. . . ."

Claudia stared at him, speechless. With Robin, she'd know what to do. She'd grab her, hold her, murmur reassurances, let her cry it out. But this . . . man-child. She was too tired, too rattled to ferret out a response—the right response, if there was one—in the middle of a convenience store parking lot. She crushed out the cigarette with her shoe and waited for him to come around, thinking.

"Done?" she asked.

He nodded miserably, too embarrassed to look at her.

"All right, here's what's going to happen, Booey. Tomorrow, I don't want you in the station. In—"

"I understand," he mumbled to the ground. "I'll type up a . . . what? Letter of resignation. Yeah. I can drop it off or put it in the mail or—"

"Shut up, Booey." Claudia slapped at a mosquito. "I didn't say I don't want you in the station forever. I said I don't want you there tomorrow. You need a break. *We* need a break. You can work on your computer at home. Think things through. "

Booey sat upright. "You're not throwing me out?"

"Not yet. Pull another bonehead stunt like tonight, and I will. That's a sure bet." She lowered her head, forcing eye contact. "I don't give a damn about your fear, or about your red hair, or your stupid name. It is what it is. You are what you are. Get over it." She paused, then added, "I've heard every tall joke in the book, and I've lived with a lot of people calling me Claude because they think they're so clever. Guess what? I'm never going to be shorter and my name isn't going to change."

It began to sprinkle, rain so light and feathery that it was little more than a mist. But that could change in a heartbeat, and Claudia pushed herself off the ground. "Long night, Booey," she said. "Let's go home."

He stood quickly. "Thank you. I—"

She waved her hand, cutting him off.

"What should I tell my uncle? He'll ask why I'm not going in tomorrow."

"Tell him whatever you think is appropriate for the circumstances," she said tiredly. "You're on your own with that." She turned to go, telling him she'd touch base in the morning. She was almost to her car when he called her back.

"I forgot something," he said. He thumped the side of his head with a hand. "I don't know if this is important, but just after you got the dogs to follow your car, I saw a light wobbling from the direction of Wanda Farr's trailer. It looked like a flashlight. I put it out of my mind because I had to think about getting down the tree."

Claudia looked at him. She smiled slowly. "Interesting. Score yourself a brownie point."

"Think it was Raynor?"

"I'll talk to you tomorrow, Booey. Put some lotion on those bug bites."

She got in her car and started up the engine. Rain was beginning to dance off the windshield. She turned on the wipers, wondering if the cell phone had enough charge left to call Dennis.

CHAPTER 11

MORE SLEEP WOULD HAVE BEEN NICE. Claudia stifled a yawn and leaned against a desk in the multipurpose room. She studied the six officers assembled in front of her, all of them freshly shaved and sipping coffee, hooting over a joke one of them got off the Internet the night before. Except for Moody and Carella, she didn't know them well. Most were young, using Indian Run as a stepping-stone to larger departments. Made sense.

She rapped on the edge of her desk to get their attention. She hated leading roll call, but she had no choice. Chief Suggs was out again—or maybe just not in yet—and Sergeant Peters was still cashing in on vacation time.

"All right," she said, "let's get started." She called off the roll and ran down a summary of activity from the previous shift, which she'd barely had time to review herself. Not much to talk about: no arrests, no significant complaints. Keeping the peace in Indian Run hadn't taken any muscle.

"Hey, Lieutenant," said an officer, "you hear about the ex-nun who just signed up with some little police department north of Orlando? Sixty years old—the nun, not the town."

"Hurley, what'd you drink last night to bring on hallucinations like that, man?" This from a lean officer whose hair was still damp from a morning shower. "Whatever it was, I want some."

"I swear," Hurley said. "I read it in the paper. Town's got like two thousand people. Bet someone's already writing a screenplay based on it."

Claudia gave the officers a minute to play out the nun thing, then rapped on the desk again. "All right, all right. Anybody have anything else?"

Moody gave a half wave. "In the good-news department, we got a call just before roll call. Gorman's Eldorado surfaced in Daytona. Two guys on a drunk wrapped it around a stop sign after they took down a couple mailboxes in a residential area. Naturally, they claim they didn't boost it. Said they bought it from another guy, thought it was legit. Daytona's processing it now."

"Gorman will be pleased," said Claudia.

"I doubt it. Daytona says the car's banged up good, but not totaled. Gorman's going to be looking at a lot of body work. He'll probably take a loss when he sells it."

"Okay. Well, let him know what's going on so he can get in touch with his insurance people. Are the bad guys anyone we know?"

"Nope. Daytona's boys. Daytona's headaches."

"Good. Finish up the details, Mitch. You know the drill."

"Got it."

"Anything else?" Claudia asked the group.

An officer with a cherubic face told her he had a court appearance on a disputed traffic stop and would have to bail from the shift at noon. Another groused about the new computers. Carella asked about the chief; Claudia had no answer. Then Hurley started with the nun again.

"Okay, okay," she said. "Let's give the nun a rest, all right?" She waited for the officers to settle back down, then gave them a thumbnail of the Farr investigation. "Moody and Carella are working with me on this, but I need all of you to keep your ears open. You're on the streets. You talk to a lot of people. See what they're saying, what they're speculating. You never know what might come out. But keep everything low-key. We don't even know for sure that we have a murder yet. All we *do* know for sure is we don't have a crazed killer on our hands, and we don't need anyone thinking we do."

A few of the officers had questions. With a patience she didn't feel, she took them in order, then concluded the briefing. The officers began to file out. Claudia watched them leave. She wondered if the story about the nun was true.

"Lieutenant?"

Claudia looked up from the paperwork on her desk. She'd been wrestling with administrative forms for an hour, debating whether she could shuffle them off on anyone without ruffling Suggs. Anyone could put in an order for No. 2 pencils. "Hey, Sally," she said. "What's up?"

"I got the M.E.'s office on the phone. They're looking for a Lieutenant Claude."

"Ha ha." *See, Booey?*

"No, really. I think the guy's serious. Says he's got 'Lieutenant Claude' on the Farr autopsy request."

"Obviously I need to make myself better known in Flagg," Claudia muttered. "All right. Put the call through."

She gave her full name and title when the phone rang on her desk a minute later. "I'm the 'Claude' on the Farr case," she added.

"Oh. Sorry about that," the caller replied. He identified himself as Dirk Lorren.

"Please tell me you're calling because you finally have Farr scheduled for the table."

Lorren sounded confused. "No . . . I'm calling with a verbal on the results."

"What! Your office told me yesterday she wasn't even scheduled yet! I was planning on being there."

"I don't know anything about that. I'm just a grunt here. Morrison had a family emergency. He left, told me to give you the verbal. He'd fax a report later."

Son of a bitch. It wasn't the first time the medical examiner's office had crossed signals with her. But Morrison was a decent M.E. She'd take what she could get.

"All right. Let's hear it," Claudia said. She clicked a pen open and reached for her pad. "Any surprises?"

"There usually aren't in drownings, and that's what this was—a garden variety drowning. Toxicology showed she had alcohol in her system. Morrison says it could've been a contributing factor. She also had a head injury at the base of her skull, which would be consistent with her banging the bottom of her head on the faucet."

"Any defensive injuries?"

"Uh-uh. No unusual cuts. Nothing under her nails."

"So she had too much to drink, stepped into the tub, slipped and cracked her head on the faucet, and then she drowned. That it?"

"Well, she had a nasty contusion on the front of her head, right side, just above the hairline; but Morrison says, don't make too much of that. The bruising looks to be older than the skull injury, so it probably happened earlier."

"Big bruise? Little bruise? What're we talking?"

Lorren sighed. "Little, Lieutenant. And not enough to kill her."

"All right. Time of death?"

"Last Thursday night, maybe Friday morning. Morrison says he can't pin it down any more than that."

"Lovely. You can tell me cause of death, but you can't give me manner of death. Am I right?"

"Morrison's leaning toward accidental."

"He's *leaning*? Meaning what? He's not sure?"

"Meaning, it's impossible to say. He told me to tell you 'pending' for now, but that's only because he knows you've got the case listed as 'suspicious.'"

"What—he's banking on me to help him finish the paperwork?"

"Hey, he's giving you a break, Lieutenant. He's buying you a little time. But absent of other evidence—and soon—he'll finalize his report with 'accidental.'"

"So that's it, then?"

"Look, I'm reading off notes. Like I said, he'll send a full report later."

"All right, thanks. Tell Morrison thanks. And listen, while I got you on the horn, any clue when the autopsy for Henry Becker is scheduled?"

"Who?"

"Becker. Old guy with Alzheimer's. He was brought in on the 27th, late, the day after Farr."

"Oh, right. The No-Name Pond."

"That's the one."

"I don't know when he's scheduled, but don't hold your breath, not with Morrison out now. We got bodies stacked to the ceiling—and that's only a small exaggeration."

"Probably just as well. I'm getting pressure to let Becker's physician sign off."

"I doubt Morrison would fight you."

"Yeah, well. Can you check the calendar? Let me know what's what?"

"You got it. I'll call you back."

Claudia hung up. *Pending.* Great. She needed to shake something from the trees fast. She sorted through the Farr case file and dug out Raynor's number. His phone rang half a dozen times before he answered with a gruff "yeah."

"Well, hello, Mr. Raynor," she said. She identified herself and said pleasantly, "Remember me?"

"Like I could forget. You're the tall gal with the redheaded sidekick. You lookin' for that cup of coffee now?"

Claudia eyed the mug on her desk. "No, but thanks. What I'm thinking is, maybe you've had time to ponder our conversation the other day. Maybe you remembered something that didn't occur to you at the time?"

"Nope. Can't say that I do." Smug. Confident.

"You sure?"

"As sure as a bat pickin' off bugs in the dark."

"Speaking of the dark, did you find what you were looking for last night?"

Raynor paused. "Say what?"

"Did you find what you were looking for last night?"

"I don't follow you." Careful now. Wary.

"Sure you do. Last night. I came by, but you weren't home. I thought I saw a light in the woods. By Farr's trailer."

"Maybe you saw a firefly, because me, I'm a damned hard sleeper, Lieutenant. You shoulda knocked like you meant it. I was home all night."

"This wasn't that late. Maybe nine-ish."

"I'm an old country boy. I hunker down early."

"Hmm. So you didn't even walk your dogs?"

"They practically take care of themselves. Maybe you noticed."

"Then you weren't out last night?"

"Seems to me like that's what I just said."

"Ah. My mistake then."

"Must be."

"Well, if anything strikes you, anything you want to talk about, you just give me a call, all right?"

"You'll be the first."

"See you later, Mr. Raynor."

"Hey, that invitation for coffee, it ain't good forever."

"It won't be forever." Before Raynor could respond, Claudia hung up. She slipped her jacket on and headed for the door, stopping just long enough to coordinate tasks with Moody and Carella. She could do more on her feet than she could at a desk.

CHAPTER 12

THE GOURMET GROCERY STORE IN FEATHER RIDGE reminded Claudia of one she and Robin visited in Boca Raton a few months after settling in Indian Run. The Boca stop was part of Claudia's campaign to show Robin all of the Sunshine State, to persuade her that relocating to Florida had been a good move—an adventure, even—and that just because they lived in Indian Run didn't mean they had to be isolated. She rented comfortable cars for each journey, most of which involved weekend stays at pricey hotels that played hell with her budget at the end of every month. But they did it all. They toured the Everglades and on the same day stopped at Parrot Jungle. They visited Disney World and Sea World. They hit Busch Gardens. They educated themselves at St. Augustine and Cape Canaveral. They drove the west coast and then the east coast, frying themselves at beaches and swinging through ritzy malls that offered valet parking outside and numbing inducements to spend inside. Robin seemed to enjoy most of the excursions, though in the end the campaign was a bust, serving only to reinforce Indian Run's limitations by comparison. No beaches here. No malls. No exotic animals or larger-than-life fantasy characters to woo tourists.

"Give it a rest, Mom," Robin finally said. It was a week night, and Claudia was poring over a state map, trying to plan their next visit. "I know you're trying. You want me to like it here, which I don't see happening in my lifetime, no matter what. But I'm getting used to it, and you don't have to worry that you've . . . I don't know . . . maimed me in the head or something. Anyway, I'm sick of packing and unpacking. Admit it. You are too."

Claudia regarded her daughter thoughtfully, then sighed. "I could weep with relief at just the idea of putting my suitcase back in the closet and leaving it there."

"A no-brainer. Now let's go get a pizza and celebrate going nowhere."

Claudia smiled now, thinking of their exchange. She looked around the Feather Ridge gourmet grocery store. The one in Boca didn't have anything on it. Self-help glass bins, containing everything from exotic spices to chocolate-covered pretzels, lined both sides of two aisles. She examined labels on the bins, astonished at the varieties of rice alone. She counted seven, recognized only four. Booey, she thought, would know them all.

She wandered further, getting hungry, letting her nose lead her to the produce section, where she developed a sudden and rare hankering for a salad. Rows of pristine lettuce, broccoli, eggplant, and asparagus beckoned from displays so artfully presented they looked like still-life paintings. She lingered for a minute, then reluctantly moved on.

A few minutes later, after her circuit of the store was complete, she went in search of the manager. His name was Milo Aggastino, and he emerged from behind the deli section, beaming and wiping his hands on a stained apron that barely covered his girth. He exchanged hearty greetings, pumped her hand, and—all without taking a breath—remarked that he remembered seeing her on TV but didn't believe he'd ever seen her in the store before. Could that be?

It was impossible not to like him. He effervesced with good nature, which would be grating if not for its genuineness. She found herself grinning back, then told him she was only in the store on business.

"Business!" said Aggastino. "But it's the lunch hour! How about I personally make you a sandwich—it won't take long—and we can talk while you eat?" He wheeled around before Claudia could answer and called out, "Bruce! Brush off some counter space for me!" He turned back. "You like provolone, Detective?"

"I . . . sure."

She stood to the side of the deli counter and waited while Aggastino built a fat sandwich on sesame wheat bread. When it was complete, a pickle harpooned to the middle with a toothpick, he swept it onto a paper plate and beckoned for her to follow. She accompanied him to a cramped office that had none of the luster of the store itself. He gestured for her to sit behind his desk, then poured coffee before she could say no. Finally, he sat across from her in a folding chair that she worried would collapse beneath his weight.

"That coffee, it's the finest Colombian you'll ever find. No filler in that, I guarantee you," he said. "Eat, eat."

Claudia ate. Between bites, she asked him whether he was familiar with Wanda Farr. He shook his head until she described her.

"Ah! The cat lady! Yes, sure, I know her. Well, wait—I *should* say, I know her to the extent that anyone can know someone who doesn't talk to them. Anyway, she's a regular, here a couple times a week." He dropped his voice. "She doesn't actually come *into* the store, only around to the back—"

"The Dumpster."

"Yes." Aggastino shrugged. "She picks out sandwiches or other food she can eat, expired lots that get tossed, that sort of thing. Once in a while I put out something specifically for her. That's only if I'm not busy, if I happen to think of it. Either way, she won't take anything if she sees me watching—probably thinks I'll chase her off—but she *does* take whatever's there the minute I'm not. She's an odd sort of— Wait a minute. Something's wrong with her. You wouldn't be asking about her otherwise. What's happened?"

Claudia swallowed the bite in her mouth and told Aggastino that Farr had been found dead in her tub, drowned.

"I can't believe it," Aggastino said slowly. "I mean, I never imagined her to be in *good* health, exactly, but she was so . . . *steady*. Her and her cats, they. . . ." He looked at Claudia. "I don't understand. Are you here because . . . you think it was a bad sandwich I gave her? That it made her sick or so weak that she drowned?"

"What? Oh, no. No, no, no . . . nothing like that," Claudia said quickly.

"But you think she was murdered?"

"I'm just tying up loose ends."

Aggastino gazed at her thoughtfully, then shook his head. "That's what a politician might answer, not a homicide detective."

Claudia ignored the rebuke and wrapped the remainder of her sandwich in a napkin. "There are always loose ends when someone dies unattended. An investigation is routine. That's all."

"You're not going to finish?" Aggastino pointed to her sandwich. "You don't like it?"

"It's great, really. I'll finish it later in the car. Mr. Aggastino, do you remember the last time you saw Wanda Farr?"

The grocer sighed and looked at the ceiling. "Honestly, I don't know. Let's see . . . this is Thursday. I know I didn't see her yesterday. I was off the day before. I'm not sure about Monday, but . . . I don't believe I saw her then, either. We had roast beef on special, a ton of it; my mistake, I ordered too much. I put a half pound out for her. It didn't go."

"What about the week before?"

"The week before!" Aggastino's eyes widened. "In this business, a week ago is a lifetime. I can't remember which part-timers I had on last week, never mind an old woman who rooted through the Dumpster. I'm sorry."

"How about anyone else? You ever see anyone with her? Maybe following her?"

He shook his head. "And anyway, why would someone follow her? She had no wealth. I don't think she probably had any friends. I can't imagine why someone would kill her. For what possible gain?"

Claudia stood. "I appreciate your taking time to see me, Mr. Aggastino. And the sandwich, it was wonderful." She dug through her purse for money, but the grocer refused payment. He labored to get out of the chair, then escorted Claudia to her car.

"You want me to ask around about her? Discreetly, that is?"

"That won't be necessary. Of course, if conversation *does* happen to come up. . . ."

"I'm on it."

She smiled and got in the car. She could still see the grocer in her rearview mirror when she pulled out of the parking lot. A nice man. Why couldn't Suggs be more like him? Why—

The screech of her portable radio yanked her from her musings. Sally's voice crackled to life.

"What is it, Sally?" Claudia asked. She eyed the rest of her sandwich on the passenger seat.

"What's your 10-20?"

Claudia rolled her eyes. She'd created a monster. "I'm just leaving the gourmet grocery store at Feather Ridge."

"Can you, uh, 10-45 me?"

"Can I— Sure, Sally. Give me two minutes to pull off the road." Claudia tossed the radio next to her sandwich and coasted to the shoulder. She pulled out her cell phone and dialed. "All right, what's up?" she said when Sally picked up.

"Hey, got to love this new technology, huh?"

"Yeah, yeah, what've you got?"

"Don't tell me *you're* going to be cranky, too. I can't take you and the chief all in one day."

"He's in?"

"About a half hour ago."

"He wants to see me?"

"No. I raised you because you had a phone call I thought you'd want to know about. I've learned a thing or two, you know, and one thing is not to blab names and phone numbers over the radio."

"Good point. So who called?"

"Barbara Becker."

"And?"

"And she said to tell you that some other lady—a Babs Kensington?—she's at the Becker house now."

"She's *here*? In town?"

"That's what Mrs. Becker said. I'm supposed to tell you that if you can swing by in the next hour or so, you can catch her. After that, I guess she's going out. Or something."

"Well, hot damn," said Claudia. Good. Maybe she could get the Becker thing off her desk before the day was over.

"Glad you're happy, Lieutenant. Stay that way, all right?"

"Oh, hey, Sally. That's a big 10-4. And thanks. I'm heading over there now."

"Is it all right to just plain say 'good-bye' when we're talking on the phone?"

"Yeah. That works."

"You sure? I don't want to be breaking some kind of police telephone protocol."

"Smart-ass. Yeah, I'm sure."

"Well, then—bye-bye."

Claudia laughed out loud. "Bye, yourself, Sally." She disconnected, wolfed down the rest of the sandwich, and turned the car back toward Feather Ridge.

CHAPTER 13

BARBARA "BABS" KENSINGTON WASN'T EVEN REMOTELY CLOSE to what Claudia expected. She expected someone plain—maybe even dowdy—someone with a reticent demeanor, someone who had trouble making eye contact. Somehow, that was the impression Mrs. Becker had left her with, but that wasn't this woman. This woman, the one who escorted her into the kitchen and poured a scotch over ice as if it were a reflex motion, this woman boomed laughter and radiated energy like a live wire. Indeed, from the plunging neckline of her blouse to a tightly wrapped skirt worn mid-thigh, she practically screamed "Look at me!" Claudia suspected that most people did.

True enough, there was a physical resemblance between Kensington and Mrs. Becker, just as the older woman had described, but even with that, Claudia didn't know how anyone could mistake this . . . Babs as the daughter of Henry and Barbara Becker. She also didn't know why Mrs. Becker would want anyone to. The women were from different planets. It seemed inconceivable that both orbited around Henry Becker.

Kensington turned suddenly from the sink counter. Her drink sloshed over the glass in her hand. "Did Barbara tell you she had to go out? She should be back in an hour or two, if you don't mind waiting." She licked at her fingers. "Sure you don't want a drink?"

"No, thank you," Claudia said. "I was under the impression that Mrs. Becker would be here, but it doesn't matter. I got her statement earlier. I just need yours now."

"Fire away!" Kensington said as she scraped back a kitchen chair and joined Claudia at the table. She laughed heartily and added, "Not literally, of course. I know all you police officers carry guns. You tuck yours up in your bra somewhere?"

Right then, Claudia gave up trying to like the woman. She didn't like her singsong way of talking, she didn't like her flamboyance, and she certainly didn't like her jokes. And now that the woman was in closer proximity, she realized she didn't like her perfume either. She sat back in her chair, wrinkling her nose at the heavy, woodsy scent.

"I won't keep you long, Miss Kensington," she said. She flipped her notepad open to a fresh sheet.

"Just call me Babs."

"Miss Kensington is fine, thanks. Now, if you don't mind, tell me how it was that you and Mrs. Becker missed connections."

"Didn't Barbara already explain?"

"She did, yes. But because you were both responsible for Mr. Becker's care, I'd like to hear your own description of events."

"Hmm. Let me see how I can put this." She tapped her fingers against her glass, took a long swallow, then sighed impatiently. "You want to know what happened? What happened is, we screwed up. Very simple. I fell down on the job. She fell down on the job. We botched things." She shrugged. "No point trying to paint a rosy picture of it."

"Be specific."

"Specific? All right. Barbara went to Chicago on a Monday evening—"

"June 19th?"

"What? I don't know. If the 19th was a Monday, then it was the 19th. Anyway, she was supposed to be back on Thursday morning, somewhere around ten or eleven. Now me, I already had plans to leave on Thursday, because I was heading to the Chicago area myself."

"And Mrs. Becker knew that?"

"Of course she knew. We talked about it before she left. It didn't look like a problem because, like I said, she'd be back just about the time I'd be leaving. We did this kind of thing all the time."

"Go on."

"Well, she decided to stay a little longer in Chicago. That's where we blew it, because she apparently called and left a message on the answering machine, but I didn't see it."

"You didn't see it, or you didn't look?"

"I didn't look." Kensington shrugged. "Dumb, dumb, dumb, I know. Normally I do make a point of checking for messages, but I had Chicago on the brain. I'm getting a house up there, and I have a man there to go with it"—she winked—"and I guess I wasn't as together as I normally would be."

Claudia doubted Kensington had ever demonstrated a truly together moment in her life, which looked to be about thirty-five years long. "So you took off before Mrs. Becker got home?"

"I did leave a note, you know," she replied defensively. "I'm sure Barbara explained that much. I felt a little bad, leaving Henry and all, but I had a two-thirty flight and I had to boogie no later than eleven to make it. It's not like the airport's next door, and anyway, I thought she'd be back within a few minutes of me leaving."

Dipshit. Irresponsible dipshit.

"What was Mr. Becker doing when you took off?"

"Well, he'd already had breakfast, but I left out a plate of crackers and cheese for him to snack on, and got him settled in front of the TV. He loved CNN, and he could watch for hours, so that's what he was doing when I left. He *wasn't* as far gone as you might think. He had memory glitches now and then, sure, but it's not like he was in diapers yet or needed someone to wipe drool from his lips."

"Apparently he was 'gone' far enough to wander clear across the golf course and drown in the canal."

"But he strolled over there all the time! There *and* other places! I used to joke with him, called him the 'traveling man.' He loved that. *No* one could make that old goat get a little fire in his eyes like I could." Kensington threw back her head and laughed. "Jeez, he was something, Henry was. Him and his toy trains . . . did you see them?"

Claudia nodded.

"Yeah, well, that's not the *only* thing he liked, old or not, Alzheimer's or not." She winked conspiratorially. "I think that's why Barbara kept me around, you want to know the truth."

"What are you saying? That you *slept* with him?"

"No! Don't be ridiculous. I mean, sorry, but . . . no. Not *that!* But I *would* let him play a little peekaboo. That kind of thing."

"And that was okay with Mrs. Becker? She knew?"

"Well, we didn't exactly discuss it, but she must have. She sure didn't keep me around just because of my nursing skills."

"But my understanding is that you'd had experience with Alzheimer's patients."

Kensington rolled her eyes. "Yeah—to the extent that I worked as an aide in a nursing home for two months, which is as much as I could stand. Barbara knew that. What mattered more was that *Henry liked me.* He *adored* me. And as long as he was adoring me and didn't need a high level of care yet, it was a situation that worked all around."

"How did you and Mrs. Becker happen to meet?"

"Aren't we really off the subject now?" Kensington looked at her watch. "No offense, but I have a ton of stuff to do this afternoon."

"How'd you two meet?"

Kensington sighed dramatically. "At the nursing home. She didn't know squat about Henry's condition yet and had brought him in for a visit. I guess she wanted to get a feel for the home and see how Henry reacted just in case he wound up there. One of the staff people grabbed me to give the grand tour. Well, Henry *hated* the nursing home, but he loved the hell out of me. He flirted shamelessly—you know, like old men do—and I flirted right back. Barbara called me a couple weeks later and offered me a job. As the saying goes, it was too good to pass up."

"So your job with the Beckers, it was all a money thing?"

"Mostly, sure. It's not cheap to buy a house, and the job paid more than I'd make anywhere else with my skills. But I liked Henry all right, and Barbara too. I wouldn't have stayed when he hit the babble stage—I'm not the kind who can handle that—but as long as I only had to keep the old guy company, why not?"

Claudia closed her notebook. "Miss Kensington, will you be available if I have any follow-up questions?"

"I'll be in and out."

"But reachable?"

"Sure. Barbara can always get me."

"All right. Thanks." Claudia stood.

Kensington hooked her fingers around the glass of scotch and pushed away from the table. The ice tinkled like wind chimes. "Look, I hope you don't think I'm just some kind of bloodsucking, money-grubbing insect, what with all I've told you. I *did* like Henry, and I'm truly, truly sorry that he's dead." She set the glass on the table and walked Claudia to the front door. "I know he couldn't have been long for the world, but . . . well, I miss him. He was a good guy."

"You don't need to persuade me of your good intentions, Miss Kensington. I just needed to clarify some points."

"All right. Give a jangle if you need anything else."

"I'll do that. And tell Mrs. Becker I'm sorry I missed her."

Kensington sang out what sounded to Claudia like "toodle-loo," which gave her one more thing to dislike about the woman. She got in her car and followed the circular driveway around the fountain, then took a left onto the road. The Jag she'd seen before was just pulling into the Becker estate, and she gave a half wave. If the driver saw her—Adam, Alan, Aaron, something like that—he made no acknowledgement. Claudia sighed. Barbara Becker seemed like a bright enough woman, but evidently she was clueless when it came to picking friends.

Dark clouds were building in the east. Claudia stopped for a traffic light and debated whether to go straight to the station or swing by Farr's trailer on a hunch. Most cops treated hunches with quiet reverence. An author, whose name she didn't recall, had even written a book about them, drawing some kind of parallel between hunches and instincts. She vaguely remembered the author's argument that human instincts weren't dead—not exactly—but that they'd gone underground in direct proportion to technological and sociological advancements. Why sniff the air for danger when you could punch a code to set your alarm system at night? The book included helpful tips on how to flog instinct back to the surface, at which point Claudia stopped reading. Still, when the light turned green she headed toward Farr's trailer. A half hour more on the road wouldn't make her or break her.

Ten minutes later she pulled into the small clearing and got out of the car. She half expected to see cats skulking around, but either animal control truly had captured them all, or the felines were smart enough to know their meal ticket was gone forever. The crime-scene tape was still in place, which didn't surprise her. If Raynor had come back to look for his glass or anything else, disturbing it would have raised a red flag. Even so, Claudia felt a tug of disappointment. She wanted clues. Clues the size of shoeboxes. Clues obvious enough that a rookie cop would recognize them.

Methodically, she made her way around the trailer, looking for anything, looking for nothing. Vague scuff marks on the ground might have been footprints, but the previous night's rain rendered them too indistinct to know with any certainty. She turned and looked toward the woods. Raynor's trailer wasn't visible through the trees, but she knew it was an easy walk between the two homes, and she had half a mind to cross the distance herself. Those silent dogs, though. . . .

He'd been here, she knew it. *Knew it.* Even if Booey hadn't seen the flicker of a flashlight, it was in Raynor's voice on the phone. He'd been here. He was looking for something.

Claudia gazed around the clearing once more, then turned back to her car. She smiled ruefully. Whatever it was that had pulled her to the trailer felt a lot less like instinct or a hunch now, and a whole lot more like wishful thinking. Maybe she should write her own book.

CHAPTER 14

FOR THE FIRST TIME IN DAYS, laughter boomed from the chief's office. Claudia hesitated outside his door, hand poised to knock, and watched him for a second. The door was open, but Suggs was on the phone, his chair turned to the wall so that all she could see was his back. Interrupting his phone call didn't bother her. Knowing she would be the one to cripple his good mood did. She glanced once at the page of notes in her hand and rapped twice. Suggs swiveled in his chair and waved her in.

"Yeah . . . yeah," he said into the phone. "Just remember what I said about protection." He laughed again, playfully rolled his eyes toward Claudia, then said to the caller, "Look, I gotta go. I'll talk to you later. Uh-huh. You too."

He hung up and chuckled. "That was Boo. I was gonna give him hell this morning when he said he was taking a personal day, but he *is* wicked with bug bites." Suggs leaned into his desk, his voice confidential and his eyes twinkling. "The boy won't say much except that he and some woman were 'talking' in a parking lot last night, but you know what I think? I think there was a little more than talk goin' on. He turned red as his hair when I asked him was he sure all those bites were just from insects."

Claudia offered a noncommittal smile.

The chief laughed again and shook his head. "I had my doubts, but maybe young Boo is from the same tree as the rest of us Suggs men. So, Hershey, what brings you into the lion's lair today? Jeez, you look like hell."

"Well, I—"

"You eat yet?"

"What? Actually, yes."

"Too bad. I was gonna buy you a hot dog at the bowling alley." Suggs leaned back in his chair and patted his stomach. "Feelin' pretty good today, Hershey."

Claudia looked at the bottle of Maalox on his desk. "Good. Good to hear it."

"Yeah. So what's up?"

"I just talked to the M.E.'s office, a Dirk Lorren over there."

"I know, I know . . . Farr's 'pending,' but that could change if you shag ass and bring in some real evidence. I got my own sources, you know."

"That pending thing, that was from the first time I talked to him. This was a call-back. The message he left was 'don't shoot the messenger.'"

Suggs grinned, playing. "Ah. So what's the word now? Farr ain't dead at all?"

Claudia leaned into the desk and slid the Maalox closer to Suggs. "This isn't about Farr. It's about Henry Becker. They went ahead and did his autopsy, too."

"What!" Suggs abruptly sat forward. "I thought we were maybe gonna nix it, let the doctor sign off. You led me to believe that's how you were leanin'. How'd this happen, Hershey?" He waved a finger at her. "I told you I wanted to be fully informed, but—"

"They screwed up," she said swiftly. "Actually, they screwed up twice." She told him about the mix-up over her name with the Farr autopsy, how Morrison had to leave on a family emergency, and finally, how an assistant medical examiner moved ahead with the Becker autopsy, trying to score points with his boss by assuming some of the caseload that Morrison had left sitting. "What it comes down to," she said, "is that one hand didn't know what the other hand was doing."

Suggs pushed to his feet. "Aw, man, this is worse than a plague of locusts," he said. "It's, it's. . . ." He sighed and idly began straightening the fish mounted on the wall behind his desk, a leering twelve-pound bass with its mouth open. Then he turned back to her. "I didn't tell you this before, Hershey—didn't want to see your lips curl the way they do when you're pissed—but . . . well, I talked to Mrs. Becker earlier, told her we had to go through the motions but that the chance of an autopsy actually happening was just about nil."

"You *told* her that—"

"See? Already, there goes your lip, Hershey. But our own communication, right now that's not the real problem. The real problem is—"

"The real problem is that Henry Becker was murdered."

Suggs slapped the back of his chair. "Damn it, Hershey, don't interrupt, all right? Just once, I'd like to . . . hold on, hold on—what did you say? Just now. What did you say?"

"You heard right."

She gave him a second to take it in, discreetly looking away when he reached for the Maalox, chugged some down, then burped silently into his hand.

"Well. That's . . . a real showstopper, Hershey. You're sure?"

Claudia shrugged. "The M.E.'s office is."

"What's the story?" Suggs settled heavily back into his chair.

"Becker drowned. But here's the twist—he didn't drown in the No-Name."

"Say again?"

"He had minute bits of pond debris in his mouth, but none in his lungs. If he'd drowned in the pond, he would've sucked in a lot of water from it. Algae, bits of vegetation, sedimentation—it would've shown up. It didn't. His lungs were clean, or at least too clean to be consistent with drowning in the No-Name, which means he went in there when he was already dead."

Suggs thought about that. "They know where he *did* drown?"

"Uh-uh. They're guessing a pool, but not all of the toxicology tests are in yet. When we get those, maybe we'll know more."

"I just can't . . . how hard did the M.E. really look? Did the old guy have any other problems? Maybe a bum heart? Like that?"

"Mild hypertension. That was it. Lorren said that, physically, Becker was in terrific condition for his age. He was drowned, Chief. It is what it is."

Suggs inhaled, then released a whoosh of air. "Shit, Hershey. What kind of time frame they give us on this thing?"

"They think last Thursday, maybe Friday. We're looking at about a week ago."

"So we're late gettin' into it."

"Very."

"Who looks good to you on this?"

"Off the top, it's what you'd think. We've got to look at the wife. We've got to look at the caregiver. They have to be first."

"The caregiver—what's her name again?"

"Barbara Kensington."

"She was the last one with him, right?"

"That's the story."

"You don't buy it."

"I don't know *what* to buy now. We're at square one."

"Nothin' random about this, huh?"

"Not a chance, Chief. Someone wanted to make it appear like Becker drowned in the No-Name, like he wandered over there in an addled state and fell in, maybe off that rickety footbridge. It fits with the Alzheimer's profile. Very believable."

"Which is why the wife didn't want an autopsy."

"Could be. Or it could be like she said, that she didn't want the indignity of an autopsy."

Suggs brushed at his computer keyboard with a finger, shifting dust around, mulling things over. "Here's another little Catch-22 for you, Hershey. I'm not the only one Mrs. Becker talked to. She got on the horn with the mayor's office at some point and raised a stink about how unsafe the No-Name is, wonderin' how it was that such a hazardous place could be so accessible to the general public."

"Did she threaten a lawsuit?"

"Not yet. But she persuaded the mayor to yank that wispy little bridge the rest of the way down. Took a crew of four no more than two hours to do that, less than forty minutes more to put up some no-trespassing signs."

"So it's gone. Potential evidence was removed."

"No one knew we had anything but an accidental drowning. Public safety looked to be the only issue. So what are our next moves?"

"I'm going to need Moody and Carella full-time now, Chief. I can't half-step on two homicide investigations."

"You still don't know about Farr, for sure." He made a sour face and eyed the Maalox bottle.

"If you want to bag it, that's your call. But it would be a mistake."

"Says you."

"Says Wanda Farr," she replied softly.

Suggs grunted and picked up his phone. He buzzed Sally and told her to find Carella and Moody. Then he called Booey and told him to get his tail in, bug bites or not. He hung up and said, "All right, Hershey. The troops have been summoned. Let's meet again in an hour. That oughta give you plenty of time to figure out new ways to club me over the head."

She started to protest, but he motioned her off, and this time he closed the door behind her.

If you set your mind to it, you could do a lot in an hour. Claudia did, beginning with Dennis. They hadn't spoken since Booey's shimmy up a tree. Dennis wouldn't pick up when she tried to call him afterward, and he hadn't picked up since. Now they were playing stubborn with each other. He wouldn't call. He wouldn't answer. She wouldn't leave a message on his machine. Someone had to budge. An hour, she thought, an hour was enough time for her to be the adult.

His car was in the driveway. She looked it over, a vintage Mustang that had brought them together when she backed into it at Philby's grocery store. Good. Unless he refused to open the door, he had to see her. They could sort this thing out.

Lizards scattered from the walkway at her approach. She'd grown so accustomed to seeing them dart around that she didn't even notice. Her eyes were on the front door and, a minute later, on Dennis's face when he opened it to her knock. He didn't say anything, just stood there for a second, and then finally stepped back and gestured for her to come in.

"Something came up the other night, Dennis," she said.

"Not even a preamble, huh?"

"It was an emergency."

"It always is."

He'd been working out lately—not a lot, but enough to tighten the slight paunch around his middle. He looked good, she thought, resisting an impulse to touch his tawny hair. It was thinning, but as soft as the hazel eyes that sometimes arrested her in mid-sentence. But he was already turning away, and Claudia brushed past him, toward the kitchen. "Got anything cold to drink?" she asked.

She could feel his eyes on her back when he said "help yourself," just a little more sarcastically than she thought necessary. She sorted through the refrigerator and pulled out a can of Diet Pepsi, then closed the door and leaned against it. "Look, I'm sorry, Dennis. I really am."

"You always are." He stood near the sink, eight feet away. A variety of paint brushes rested in the drain board, which was perpetually stained with colors. "That, I can handle—your emergencies, your apologies. What I *can't* handle is everything in between."

"Meaning?"

"Meaning that before your latest 'emergency,' you weren't exactly making yourself available. No calls. No returns on mine."

"Dennis, it was only a few days. I was—"

"Busy. And not for the first time, at least not lately."

Claudia popped the tab on the Pepsi. She took a long swallow, felt it burn down her throat. He had a smudge on his cheek—paint, probably—and she wanted to go to him and wipe it off, make contact, make whatever had come up between them vanish. *Poof.* Just like in the movies.

"You know, Claudia, I see you standing there, eyeing me. And what I see is someone who doesn't know what she wants, who wishes it was me—*tries* to make it me, but who can't quite pull it off. That's the sense I have, what I've been picking up for a while now." He wiped at his cheek, missing the smudge. A faint rosebud appeared where his fingers had been. "How am I doing, Claudia?" he said softly. "Pretty accurate read on the situation, isn't it." Not a question now. A statement.

"I think. . . ." *What? What did* she think? She began again, her own voice as soft as his. "I think, Dennis, that . . . I can understand where you might think that. I can—"

"Oh, come on, Claudia. You're good at a lot of things, but sidestepping an issue isn't one of them." He paused, then said, "We've been seeing each other for eight months. Guess what? I fell in love with you, pretty damned fast and pretty damned hard. Whoosh! Rockets! Cannons! Sparkles! You . . . well, you only fell in *like* with me."

"That's crazy." She felt a flutter of panic. "I'm nuts about you, Dennis! I *adore* you."

"Adore is good," he said. He smiled dolefully. "It's just not enough. It took me forever to see it, but I do now. I'm surprised you don't. Or won't."

"You're right I won't." The soda can felt slick in Claudia's hand, and too cold. She clutched it more tightly, afraid it would slip loose. "Rockets go off for me, too," she said, hearing the automation in her tone, knowing he heard it as well.

"Claudia, it's all right. I'm making it easy for both of us. Come look."

She followed him into the living room, which he'd converted into a studio for his work. At no small cost, he'd hired a contractor to widen two windows and build a skylight into the roof. He tinkered with wood well enough to erect a handsome and complicated series of shelves to hold his art tools. All told, the remodeling work took nearly two months; and when it was done, the room began to blossom with canvases in various stages of completion. He did some paintings for personal pleasure, but most were freelance jobs—artwork destined to become book covers, or backdrops for modeling studios—what Dennis called "mini stages" for jewelry displays and hand lotions. There were few places where she could cast aside a bad day as swiftly as she could in Dennis's studio. They made love there more often than in his bedroom. But it was all gone now, the room bare except for boxes sealed with tape.

"I don't understand," Claudia said, though of course she did.

"Well, it seems my talents are wanted in California. A set designer I know, a friend, he hooked me into a deal to do backdrops for a film producer. It's just on a one-year contract, but it sounds good. Could lead to other things."

Claudia walked to the shelves and ran a finger along the inside of one. He'd already wiped it down. "I— When did all of this happen?"

"When you weren't looking," he answered gently. "My friend's been after me for a few months. I'd been putting him off. But recently, it started to sound . . . right."

"But I thought you loved it here."

"I do. It's just that I never intended to stay." He waved a hand around. "I'd only come here to close the house after my aunt died and left it for me. She . . . well, you know the history on that, so I'll fast forward. I came, I met a woman, I fell in love, I stayed. The woman didn't love me back. It's time to go."

"Dennis—"

"Don't, Claudia. Please."

By now, both of their voices wobbled, hers as much as his. "When?" she asked.

"Saturday."

"*This* Saturday?"

He nodded.

"That's . . . fast."

"It had to be. If I wavered, you might've talked me out of it."

"I wish you'd given me the chance."

"I did. I tried." He shrugged. "All those calls that went unanswered? That was me, Claudia, looking for a thread to hang onto."

She looked around the room, feeling the first tears threatening at the corners of her eyes, blurring her view. She took off her glasses and jabbed at the tears, as if she could push them back. How could she have not seen this coming?

Dennis moved toward her, took one of her hands in both of his. "What we've had, it was good. It—"

"It *was* love. *Is* love."

"No. Shhh. For me, it's love. For you, it's the *idea* of love." He lifted her hand and kissed it. Then he smiled. "We'll try it again when we're old and gray, huh?"

She pushed her face into his shirt, letting it blot the mist from her eyes, inhaling his scent. Dennis gently pushed her off, then tilted her head and put his lips to hers. They swayed together in a melancholy embrace. Long seconds later, he breathed a good-bye into her hair and let her go.

She got back to the station with five minutes to spare, long enough to hit the ladies' room and fill her mug with coffee. That someone had thoughtfully bothered to brew a fresh pot escaped her. She gathered files and a notepad, then dragged a chair into the chief's office a beat behind the others. Carella and Moody edged sideways, trying to make room.

"Boy, Hershey," said Suggs. "You looked lousy an hour ago. You look worse now, like you just swallowed battery acid. Hope whatever I got ain't catchin'."

"I'm sure it's not," she said absently, already thumbing through a folder. She looked up, feeling the heat of five people pressing in. Booey fidgeted at his bites. He quit when her gaze stopped at him. "Let's get started," she said. "You already know about the Farr case. We're nowhere with it, and now we have another situation."

Suggs snorted. "Spoken like only the queen of understatement could speak it. Tell 'em straight up, Hershey."

She nodded and stepped them through details of the Becker autopsy, waiting out a chorus of gasps before she described her interviews with Barbara Becker and Babs Kensington. They couldn't shake it, the concept that Henry Becker's watery death had nothing to do with a misfire in the symmetry of his brain and everything to do with cold calculation in the brain of someone else.

"Barbara Becker seems such an unlikely candidate to kill someone," Moody said at length. "Sure, she's going to inherit her husband's money, but it's not like she's tried to hide the fact."

"Not only that," Carella added, "but why take the risk? Becker was a sick man. Why kill him when he would be dead soon enough, anyway?"

Claudia was about to respond when she caught Booey out of the corner of her eye, his arm throttling the air. "Go, Booey," she said.

"Actually, unless he had some kind of complicating disease or infirmity, Mr. Becker could've lived another decade, maybe more. Alzheimer's isn't a death sentence, not in the strictest medical terms. It's more like a . . . a. . . ."

"Life sentence," Suggs said quietly. "My granddaddy went that way, with Alzheimer's. Boo, you were too young to even know him, but the poor man got kicked around by that disease for fifteen, sixteen years. It was awful, watchin' a man who'd been proud all his life forget where he lived." Suggs pulled nail clippers from a pocket and opened them up. In the next second he seemed to remember where he was and tucked them away again. "Thing is, up till the last couple of years, he was in good shape, physically. He'd been tough all his life. That man *never* sat, *never* stopped moving. You shoulda seen him. He . . . anyway, even after retirement his ticker was strong. Lungs were good, too. But eventually he forgot how to use his body—I guess that was it, really—and he stopped moving. He took to sittin' a lot, starin' a lot, lookin' out at nothing, really. In the end, he just . . . drained away."

Booey mumbled something, and then a respectful quiet filled the room. Claudia wished she could think of something to say. She glanced around; Moody and Carella were looking at their feet.

Suggs spared them all by breaking the silence himself, growling that he was just trying to illustrate a point and for everyone to, damn it, get back on track. They weren't at a wake. They were at a murder investigation.

"Putting aside the widow for a minute," he said to Claudia, "you got any motives that jump out at you on the Kensington woman?"

"I wish," she replied. She turned to Moody. "Mitch, see what kind of background you can get on our Babs Kensington. Who was she before she came into Henry Becker's life? Who's she friends with? What about her family? All we know right now is what she's told us, and that isn't much."

"You got it," said Moody, "down to the color of her underwear."

"Sure, give *him* the looker," Carella quipped.

"Don't you worry, Emory," Claudia said. "She's not your type."

"Oh, yeah? What *is* my type, Lieutenant?"

"Your wife."

Carella laughed. "Minor detail."

"Not to her, I bet."

"Can't argue with the truth," he said, affection for his wife evident in his tone. "The woman centers me. I ever mention that?"

Suggs grunted. "About a hundred times a day."

"Okay, okay," said Claudia. "Look, Emory, while Mitch is getting acquainted with Kensington, you and Booey take the paperwork trail. Do whatever it takes to get a grip on Becker's estate. See how Mrs. Becker is really going to make out—down to the dime. See what kind of investments he had. Take a walk through his business life, too. He's been officially retired for a long time, but that doesn't mean he wasn't recently or even still dabbling in something. Oh. And find out whether there might even be a possibility that his passion for model railroading could've set someone off—another hobbyist, or maybe a collector with a keen eye for his displays—that sort of thing. You never know."

They kicked the Becker case around for a while, trying out theories, refining investigative strategies, making lists, assigning tasks.

"So, Hershey," said Suggs, "it ain't like I don't have plenty to do right here, but if you got anything in particular that would take some higher-level muscle, you just say the word and—"

"Word."

"What?"

"I have something." Claudia shifted to face him squarely. "It would be a huge advantage if you could keep a lid on the M.E.'s conclusions for as long as possible. Let Barbara Becker continue assuming that the doctor is going to sign off on the death. Stall everything. Stall the M.E.'s office on releasing the body. Stall her on funeral arrangements. Be sympathetic, but . . . stall."

"Whoa. I said I got higher-level muscle. I didn't say I could move heaven and earth."

"We need this."

"I . . . yeah. All right." Suggs looked grimly at his phone, as if it might ring any moment, with Mrs. Becker on the other end. "I'll give it my best shot."

"Good." Claudia began to gather her files and notes. "Then that's all—"

"What about the Farr case?" Moody asked.

She looked from him to the others, then settled back in her chair. "We're staying with it. I wasn't going to bring this up yet, but I suppose now is better than later because I think it's just about time to squeeze Raynor." She looked at Suggs. "I think I know how we can do it."

"Somethin' tells me I should fasten my seat belt," Suggs groused. "But go on, Hershey. Make it good."

She laid out a plan, talked them through the questions, then stood up and smiled. What she had in mind was routine—routine anywhere else, anyway. Here, though . . . she could see the doubt in their faces. "Come on," she said. "Think about it. What we're going to do will be interesting. Maybe even fun."

Suggs groaned. "Hershey, sex is fun. Fishin' is fun. Moonshine on a hot summer night—even that's fun if you don't think about the next mornin'. What you're talkin' about? *Fun* is not the first word that springs to mind." He sighed. "But it just might work." He aimed a finger at her. "*Might.* Now, I got things to do, so get on out of here, all of you—and take those stupid extra chairs with you. They're cluttering up the place."

CHAPTER 15

ALMOST MIDNIGHT OF DAY TWO WITHOUT ROBIN. Day Two without worrying about a proper meal, dishes, skirmishes over chores, or what to watch on TV. Claudia didn't miss any of it, but she ached for the company of her daughter and felt the silence of her house as if it were a tomb. Of course, there was the kitten. Though not yet named, it had begun to demonstrate actual moments of affection, but the distraction lacked staying power.

Nothing—not the freedom, not the wine, not the oboe—nothing could fend off a long night weighted with loss. Her daughter was in Washington with her ex-husband, with whom she had slept for all the wrong reasons. The boyfriend with whom she had slept for all the right reasons, or so she'd thought, was packing for California. Claudia felt the creep of loneliness press in.

She settled onto the couch, put her bare feet up on the coffee table, and flicked on HBO, not caring that a Mel Gibson movie she'd never seen was already half over. She refused to open the case files again—had intentionally left them on the dining room table—but banishing them from her thoughts was something else altogether. The Becker case didn't bother her. Oh, it wouldn't be open and shut, but the components were comfortably familiar: wealthy man killed, wife to inherit, brazen young woman in the background. It would take legwork, but not a lot of creativity. The Farr drowning, though. . . . Claudia shook her head. Suggs better do his part. He better have the network he claimed he did. Raynor better have the greed she thought he did.

The cordless telephone was on the table beside her. She picked it up and pressed the "talk" button. She'd spoken to Robin two hours earlier. Was it too late to call again? She started to dial, then set the phone down. Of course it was. What was she thinking? For as good a time as Robin was having (and she was; Claudia could hear it in her voice), she sounded tired, too. How could she not? A long drive, bonding with her daddy, the kitten she'd left behind . . . the poor kid's world had shifted on its axis in little more than seventy-two hours. Her daughter needed sleep, and Claudia hoped Brian had enough parental brain cells to make sure she got it.

She yawned, tired herself, but restless. Two murders. Two murders in tiny little Indian Run, both made to look like accidents. She wondered whether it had occurred to Suggs that other murders masquerading as tragic mishaps might well have slipped by him over the years. Easy enough to happen, once you began to make assumptions, to take things for granted. Claudia irritably pushed off the couch and aimed for the kitchen. She'd almost done it herself with Becker. There was a . . . a *mind-set* here, a small-town mentality of invincibility. And really, hadn't she moved to Indian Run partly for that very reason? For that seductive notion that bad things—really, really bad things—just would not—*could* not—happen here? Life happened quietly here. Except for the murder last year, death happened quietly, too. Or so it would appear.

She paused with her hand on the refrigerator, Henry Becker's swollen face abruptly intruding in her mind. Why had the Beckers moved to Indian Run? Was it Barbara Becker's idea? Did she imagine that Indian Run would be an ideal place in which to go unnoticed? In which to orchestrate an accident? Was the woman *that* clever? *That* calculating? Claudia opened the door and rummaged for a piece of cheese. Maybe she was. Maybe she was smart enough for that, and smarter still to bring in a flighty young woman to serve as an unwitting accomplice.

The kitten wound around Claudia's ankles. She broke off a small piece of cheese and dropped it for him. Robin would probably disapprove, but she was curious to see if he'd go for it. He did, and she smiled. A relationship without complications.

The Raynor thing wouldn't go down until Saturday, but by Friday morning Claudia's team had developed at least a little information on the Becker case. She wasn't sure any of the information qualified as a lead, but it showed promise. For one thing, Moody had learned that Barbara Kensington had a record. In the scheme of things, it was so minor that it hardly counted—a juvenile shoplifting bust and half a dozen bad-check charges eight years old—but Moody hoped the information might lead him to something else or someone else who could tell him more about the caregiver.

More immediately intriguing, though, was Carella's news: Barbara Becker wasn't merely going to become rich with her husband's death; she was destined to become filthy rich. Becker's estate, trains and all, was worth a cool eight million dollars. She wouldn't get it all, though. A last-minute codicil to Becker's will provided a hundred thousand dollars to the "current and primary caregiver of Henry Becker, excluding his wife, Barbara Becker."

"I never heard of such a thing," Carella told Claudia. He'd waylaid her behind the station, where she was resentfully having a smoke beside the Dumpster. "The will doesn't name an individual. It leaves it open to whoever happens to be in Becker's employ at the time of his death—which of course happens to be one Babs Kensington." He flapped her smoke away with a sheaf of papers. "You should've quit when I did. That thing's gonna kill you."

"Never mind," said Claudia. "Whose idea was the codicil?" she asked.

"You'll love it. According to the attorney who tacked on the provision, a Frederick Montgomery in Flagg, it was Barbara's idea, although Becker didn't seem to object. This was within two months of their moving down here from Chicago."

"And Montgomery didn't question it? Didn't ask for clarification on the language, anything like that?"

"Uh-uh. But get this: Montgomery only saw the Beckers twice. It was a walk-in job, and he admitted he didn't ask a lot of questions. He said Mrs. Becker doubled his fee for him to draw up the papers and have everything done in no more than ten days. He got half up front, the other half before the ink was dry on the final papers. Everything was in cash."

Claudia took a drag. "The will's not even probated yet, Emory. How'd you find Montgomery?"

"Wish I could take credit, but it was Booey. Got to love that kid. He plowed through real estate records yesterday afternoon and turned up a Chicago attorney's name. I called the guy, and although he had nothing to do with drawing up the will, he's golfing buddies with the lawyer who did—"

"Small club," Claudia said.

"You got that right, and we should be grateful. He gave me the name of the original estate lawyer, who told me he hadn't been in touch with the Beckers since before they moved, but he'd recently gotten a phone call from—"

"Your Mr. Montgomery."

"Yup. Mrs. Becker gave Montgomery the Chicago name so he could touch base and get the paperwork expedited."

"What's your take on this Montgomery?"

"Washed out. The guy looks to be about sixty, and like maybe a heavy drinker. Red face, tired eyes, veins popping out around his nose. I don't know; maybe he was good once, but he's definitely not at the top of his game now. He works solo in a beat-up office between one of those 'instant' loan companies and a mom-and-pop hardware store. It's not the kind of place you'd expect the Beckers to even set foot in. I mean, this guy had an artificial plant on his desk that looked dead."

"And he *showed* you the codicil?"

"Better than that. The guy was wonderfully free of ethics. Or maybe he just figured it would be less trouble to play nice with a cop in his face than to deal with Mrs. Becker later. I don't know which, but he made a photocopy of the whole will, which, as you can see, is fatter than our phone book. Once you strip out the gobbledygook from all those pages, what it comes down to is, the wife gets everything. Well, all except that hundred grand."

"Smarmy lawyer."

"He shrugged it off. 'Gonna be probated soon enough,' is what he said to me. And anyway, I told him it was just routine, me asking questions on an 'accidental' death. He never pushed a question back at me—not one. Maybe that's why Mrs. Becker picked him."

Claudia kicked at a bottle cap on the ground, sent it skittering. It binged off the Dumpster and rolled in a tight little circle before coming to a stop back at her shoe. "Montgomery say anything about Henry Becker?" she asked. "Anything about how he . . . appeared?"

"Not really. Montgomery said Becker mostly sat there, quiet as a stone. Mrs. Becker did all the talking, and when they followed up on signatures a week later, it was the same thing."

"I don't suppose Kensington was conveniently with the Beckers when they visited Montgomery's office."

"Now you're pushing your luck."

"Yeah." Claudia took a final drag on the cigarette, then crushed it with her shoe.

"You just going to leave that there?"

"Hey. Since when did you become so high and mighty?" Claudia said. She bent down to pluck the butt from the ground and tossed it in the Dumpster.

"Reformed smokers are the worst," Carella replied. "It's because we constantly want what we can't have anymore." He fanned himself with the will. "You want to read this over?"

"Leave it on my desk. I'll probably take it home tonight. I *hate* legalese."

"All right. I'll see if I can catch up with Mitch, too. He's got a good eye for this kind of thing."

Claudia nodded. Moody had dropped out of law school after three years, dismayed at the prospect of waiting years for legal machinery to right injustices. "Good idea, Emory." They headed back to the building. "And look, nice work on this. We now know something that we didn't before. I just wish we knew what it meant. Meanwhile, how about the train angle? Anything there?"

"Don't hold your breath. I'm still looking—correction, Booey and I are still looking—but if there's a lunatic out there who'd kill for Becker's trains, we haven't found him yet, and so far there's nothing to suggest we will."

"About what I thought," said Claudia. "But keep at it. You—"

"—never know."

He feigned alarm at the look she gave him, then laughed and spun off in search of Moody, leaving her to sort things out.

The phone rang six times before someone picked up and a brisk voice said, "Good morning. Dr. Krestler's office."

"Good morning," said Claudia. "This is—"

"Can you hold for a moment?"

"I—"

"Thanks."

Fuzzy music instantly replaced the voice, and Claudia bristled. It didn't matter whether you were ordering a pizza or checking on a car repair. Either you got slammed on hold before you had your name out, or you got shuttled into a recorded "menu of choices" in lieu of a real person altogether. But this, a *doctor's* office! What if she had an emergency? What if—

"Good morning. Dr. Krestler's office. Please—"

"No, I *won't* hold," said Claudia. She barked her name and position, and told the voice what she wanted. A beat later, the voice muttered something indistinct, and put her on hold again. The wait was longer, but this time when the canned music cut off, it was the doctor himself who answered. He identified himself in a tone only slightly less brusque than that of his receptionist.

"Mrs. Becker told me you might be faxing over paperwork on the death certificate," Krestler said. He paused. "I didn't know Henry Becker all that well, but I was sorry to hear about his passing."

Krestler sounded more perfunctory than sorry to Claudia, but she supposed he was accustomed to having patients die on him. "Actually, there's a hitch with the M.E.'s office," she said smoothly. "They got my last name screwed up and then . . . well, I won't take up your time with the annoying details. Point is, it's already Friday and I just wanted to give you a courtesy call, let you know not to look for anything till maybe Monday."

"That wasn't necessary, but thank you. I'll have my—"

"Funny that the Beckers didn't locate a doctor closer to home," she said. "I didn't realize until I looked at the area code and called that you're—what? Over in Palm Beach County?"

"That's right. North Palm Beach, actually."

"That's quite a drive from Indian Run. Two hours or so. I'm surprised you didn't refer her to someone closer."

"As a matter of fact, I'm sure I must have," Krestler said defensively.

Claudia heard him flipping through papers. Becker's medical file, no doubt.

"I'm not sure where she got my name—someone told her about me, I assume, but—yes, here it is. The first time she and her husband visited, I specifically advised her that at some point Henry would need more regular care. I offered to give her the names of specialists closer to her. We were supposed to discuss it on her next visit, but then I didn't see her again, just her daughter."

"Her daughter?"

"Yes, her . . . well, I presume it was her daughter. She looked like a younger version of Mrs. Becker, and she called Mr. Becker 'Daddy.'"

Babs.

"At any event," Krestler continued, "I only saw Mr. Becker a few times. They broke several appointments, so let's see . . . I actually only had Mr. Becker in here four times, to be exact."

"That's all?"

"All things considered, he was in remarkably good health. He had mild hypertension, but we were treating it with diet and exercise." Defensive again. "Look, it's up to the patients and their families to make and *keep* appointments, you know. This is a very busy practice and—"

"When's the last time you saw him?"

"This is starting to sound like more than a courtesy call."

"Not at all," Claudia said. "I just need to dot all the *i*'s and cross all the *t*'s, what with the distance involved and all." She doodled on the margin of her notepad. "You wouldn't believe the form I have to fill out. It's new, the . . . IR 202-DX. You've—"

"Look, what was the question?"

"The last time you saw Mr. Becker."

"Right. Uh . . . May 26th."

"So, a little more than a month ago."

"Yes, and he was fine. No measurable changes. Anything else I can help you with?"

"Can't think of a thing," Claudia said. She could think of a lot of things, but nothing that wouldn't raise questions she wasn't prepared to answer. "I appreciate your time, Dr. Krestler. If I have anything else, I'll give a call. Otherwise, I'll just get the papers over and we'll be done."

She waited for him to say "fine" or "you have my number" or almost anything else that would signal the end of their conversation. When he didn't, she realized he had already hung up. She closed her own connection then and set the phone back in its cradle. Yep. Just like calling in a pizza order, all right.

CHAPTER 16

BABS KENSINGTON DIDN'T SEE THEM COMING, and Claudia was sorely tempted to announce herself, just for the entertaining reaction she was sure it would produce. But if there was anything to be learned, it would be learned by giving the woman a moment to camouflage what she was unknowingly revealing right now.

Claudia put a hand on Booey's arm and a finger at her lips. She tiptoed him backwards until dense shrubbery at the corner of the house concealed them both. It took effort not to laugh aloud at Booey's face, which blazed with embarrassment—and probably something else—over the naked woman in the pool. The something else might have been horrified fascination over the ponytailed man paired in the water with Kensington. He belonged to the Jag out front, and he clearly had more than a neighborly concern over Mrs. Becker's emotional well-being.

Interesting.

"Someone should've answered the phone or door," Booey whispered. He seemed to be having trouble swallowing. "Think we should come back later?"

Claudia shook her head. "Not a chance. We're going to find out what they'll say when they weren't prepared to say anything at all."

The pool was connected to the house through French doors, and it shimmered beneath an immense screened enclosure, one side of which was shaded by trees and included an elaborate garden with a discreet fountain. A cluster of small palms concealed a hot tub and shower on the other side, near the shallow end of the pool. Paradise.

Booey pointed at the garden. "You can't really see them from here, but that's where Mr. Becker's G-scale trains are," he said wistfully. "I bet no one's keeping any of it up now."

"Never mind about the trains," Claudia said. "Come on. Let's back up and make a noisier entrance."

They slipped quietly back to the driveway, where Claudia paused long enough to jot down the license number on the Jaguar, then turned around and retraced their steps to the pool at a leisurely pace. This time, though, Claudia called out "Hello" and "Is anybody home?" in a voice loud enough to stop a pulse.

Their timing couldn't have been better. Kensington and Ponytail had enough time to fumble back into decency, but not enough to appear casual about it. Kensington sat dripping on the edge of the pool beside two hastily abandoned beer bottles, breathing hard and groping behind her neck at the ties for her bikini top. Claudia wondered why she bothered. The bikini had the size and substance of a paper towel. Ponytail wore khaki shorts that he'd forgotten to zip, and he was pushing a long brush against the inside rim of the pool. Neither of them was looking at the other. Claudia knew it would be the moment she would cherish most from the investigation.

"Oh, good," she called out cheerfully to Kensington. "I saw the car out front and figured someone must be home. Glad I caught you." With Booey in her shadow, she walked briskly toward the pool, not stopping until she loomed over the woman from a foot away.

Kensington's sunglasses were on the other side of the pool, nestled together with Ponytail's like lovebirds. She shaded her eyes and looked up. She smiled tightly. "Another minute or two and you would've missed me. I just finished a workout and need to get dressed. I'm going out shortly."

"Well then, I'm *really* glad I caught you," said Claudia. She knew she was enjoying herself way too much, but so what? There weren't a lot of perks in a murder investigation. She turned her attention to the man. "You look familiar," she said. "Didn't I meet you with Mrs. Becker earlier?"

He grunted and said, "Aaron."

"Oh, right, right," she said, this time locking the name in her mind. "The neighbor's son. I knew it began with an *A*. Just couldn't call it up." She looked pointedly at the pool broom in his hand. "Mrs. Becker is lucky to have you. I'm not sure my neighbors would carry my trash can to the curb, never mind clean a pool."

He shrugged. "She's going through a tough time."

"Aren't we all," Kensington said to Claudia's legs. She edged away a little, looking for a comfort zone, and flashed a brilliant smile at Booey. "You must be the police chief's nephew. Booley, right?"

"Booey," he mumbled. He cleared his throat, then jammed his hands in his pockets.

"Booey! That's it! Mrs. Becker told me all about you." She winked at him. "You can call me Babs."

Booey stood frozen in place and nodded mutely. Aaron chuckled.

"I hope you'll tell me where you get your hair colored," Kensington continued. "It's so . . . theatrical!"

Enough. Claudia didn't want Kensington to get too comfortable, so she answered for Booey. "His hair is colored by God. We should all be so lucky." She turned to Aaron and conversationally added, "Incidentally, your fly is open. Thought you'd like to know."

While he pawed at his zipper, she squatted beside Kensington. The woman's breasts dramatically rose and fell with each breath she took. Claudia gazed at the flat water. "Bet you'll be glad to get back to Chicago. When do you actually close on the house?"

Kensington drew circles in the water with a foot. "Soon, I hope."

"I bet. This has to be hard, being down here with a tragedy and all, your boyfriend being up there." She leaned close enough to see Kensington's pores. "This guy"—she jerked her head in Aaron's direction—"just between you and me, don't you find him a little unsettling? He reminds me of that actor who played Lurch on that old TV show . . . what was the name of it?"

"I don't have to like him," Kensington replied stiffly. "Mrs. Becker likes him. That's all that counts."

"I'm sorry. I meant no offense," Claudia said. "I'm sure he's very nice."

"He seems to be, but I don't know him well. I only just met him."

Liar, liar, pants on fire. . . .

"Ah. I thought you might've been introduced when you were living with the Beckers." Claudia shifted her weight. "Well, I—" Her cell phone chirped from inside her purse. The sound still startled her, but it had lost its punch. "Excuse me," she said, rising smoothly. "I'll be right back. Booey, keep Miss Kensington company."

She rooted through her bag for the phone as she walked out of hearing distance. "Yes," she snapped.

"Hershey, it's Suggs. Bad news. I just got a heads-up from the M.E.'s office. Mrs. Becker called this morning, raisin' all kinds of stink 'cause the body hasn't been released and no one will tell her anything. They put her off for now, and I dodged the next call she made, which was to me. But you can forget about stallin' on this anymore. It's gettin' too hot."

"Damn it," Claudia said. She glanced over at Kensington, who had climbed out of the pool and was slowly toweling off, making Booey's life an exquisite hell. "All right. I'm at the Becker estate now. The vixen's here, but it doesn't look like Mrs. Becker is. I'll have to leave a message for her to call me."

"She's probably at the mayor's office," Suggs said glumly.

Claudia rolled her eyes. "Look, do you have connections at the phone company? It'd be handy if we could get a handle on the calling activity at the Becker house."

"There's official channels for that kinda thing, Hershey."

"Yeah. And official channels are slow. So do you have anybody, or not?"

Suggs grunted. "All right, all right. My sister-in-law Estelle works over there. I'll see what I can do. How far back?"

"Since the Beckers moved here."

"Figured that's what you'd say. Anything else?"

"I need a tag run." She reeled off the plate number on the Jag.

"All right. That it?"

"That's it."

Claudia heard Suggs swallow, once, twice. She caught the familiar sound of the bottle cap going back on the Maalox. She waited, resisting a comment.

"How's Booey doin', anyway?" Suggs asked a moment later. "He still scratchin' at those bites?"

"I think they're the last thing on his mind right now."

"Say what?"

"Never mind." She watched Aaron set the pool brush down, say something to Kensington, and leave. "Anything else developing?"

"Moody's been on the phone since you left. I don't know who he's talkin' to, but he's scribbling notes so fast he looks like he's possessed by demons. Maybe he'll come up for air when you get back."

"All right. Good. We'll shake something loose." Claudia said goodbye and ended the connection, then went to pry Kensington away from Booey. He was watching her brush her hair out, mesmerized. Claudia didn't think he'd spoken a word beyond his name since they'd announced their arrival.

"Sorry for the interruption," she said as she approached the pool. "Unfortunately, something's come up and it's urgent that I get in touch with Mrs. Becker. Do you have any idea when she might be home?"

Kensington stopped in mid-stroke. "What do you mean, 'urgent'?"

"It's about Mr. Becker, and I really need to talk to her."

"Just leave a message with me. I'll make sure to pass it along."

"Sorry. It's private."

"She'll only tell me anyway."

"Sorry."

"Oh, come on. What happened?" Kensington looked at Booey and wriggled her eyebrows. Then she turned back to Claudia and giggled outright. "Did old Henry rise from the dead and wander away from the morgue or something?"

Without Aaron around, Kensington had regained her confidence and, thought Claudia, reverted to form. "Just tell Mrs. Becker I need to see her as soon as possible," she said. "Let's go, Booey."

"Oh, for heaven's sake," Kensington said, sighing elaborately. "If it's *that* important, I'll wake her up."

"She's here?"

"I never said she wasn't. You just assumed it." Kensington tossed her hair, which had nearly dried in the hot sun. "You'll need to give her some time, though—fifteen minutes, maybe. Old people move slow, and she's closed up in her bedroom with a migraine."

Claudia checked her watch. Already nearly two. "All right. We'll wait here."

"Suit yourself." Kensington turned to go, tugging at the bottom of her bikini in a contrived show of modesty that Claudia knew was for Booey's benefit. Then she paused and pivoted. "I was planning on going out, but if you want me here, too, I'll be happy to stick around."

"I'm sure you would," Claudia said wryly, "but this is private. If Mrs. Becker chooses to tell you anything later, that's up to her."

Kensington shrugged. "Fine. I'll tell her where to find you." She winked at Booey again. "Toodles." He stuttered a good-bye and murmured that he was pleased to meet her. She laughed and sauntered off.

"She's quite . . . an interesting woman," he said a moment later.

"That she is," said Claudia. She used a corner of her jacket to pluck the beer bottles from the side of the pool, then carefully eased them into her purse. They just fit. "That she is."

Fifteen minutes was fast turning into thirty. Claudia took her jacket off and roasted on a deck chair while Booey—with her permission—ambled through Henry Becker's garden train display. He had just returned to claim a chair himself when Barbara Becker finally emerged. Both of them stood and waited while she slowly made her way toward them from the house, her cane scraping the terrazzo with every step.

She looked like royalty, with a wide-brimmed hat that veiled the sides of her face and tied beneath her chin with a silk scarf. She wore dark sunglasses and, in what Claudia assumed was a concession to the sun but not the heat, a gauzy, long-sleeved silk blouse with a thousand small buttons that spanned her neck.

Claudia thought sunscreen would have been easier. She also knew why it had taken the old woman so long to get dressed. She greeted the widow and suggested they retreat inside.

"We're here now," Mrs. Becker said icily. She glanced at the pool, then turned to Booey. "Hello, young man. Nice to see you again."

"Thank you, ma'am," he said. "You too. Can I get you a chair?"

"That won't be necessary." She looked pointedly at Claudia. "Presumably this won't take long. Babs said you had something to tell me about Henry?"

"Mrs. Becker, I'm afraid this might be upsetting news. Are you sure you wouldn't rather sit?"

"I'm quite sure, Detective. Now what is it?"

There was no nice way to back into this one, so Claudia told her swiftly and without inflection that, as it turned out, an autopsy had already taken place and the results showed Henry Becker had been murdered. She stood ready to catch Mrs. Becker, but the woman barely moved.

"Mrs. Becker?" she said. "Do you understand what I just said?"

"Of course I understood you. But it's the most ridiculous thing I ever heard. Obviously, there's a mistake somewhere."

"No. There's no mistake."

The woman shook her head, furious. "No mistake? My Henry's burial has been delayed, and now you tell me his body has been . . . mutilated!"

"I regret that, Mrs. Becker, but the larger point is that he didn't drown on his own."

"Oh, come now! They can't even keep track of which bodies are to be autopsied in this foolish town. You expect me to believe the results of an autopsy? They've probably mixed him up with someone else!" She thumped her cane on the terrazzo.

"Mrs. Becker," Claudia said carefully, "your husband was murdered. I'm very sorry. If you'd like, I'll see that you get a copy of the autopsy report. But he was murdered. Believe it, because with or without your cooperation, we're going forward with a full-scale investigation."

"My condolences," Booey said quietly.

The woman shook her head slightly, then shuffled toward the edge of the pool. She gazed at the water for a long time. Claudia counted a minute, two. Then she joined her. "Are you sure you wouldn't rather go inside?" she asked.

"I'm fine," Mrs. Becker said distractedly.

She didn't look fine. Perspiration rolled down her cheek, streaking her makeup and staining the edge of her scarf. Claudia pulled at her own shirt. In Cleveland, it would be in the high seventies. Here, the temperature approached ninety. Already. She felt her face burning.

"An investigation," Mrs. Becker said. She turned and faced Claudia fully. "Who would want Henry dead? Do you think that I did? Do you think I held his head underwater until he stopped breathing?"

"I'm just here to get some additional information right now," she answered. "I'm not pointing fingers at anyone."

"Sure you are." Mrs. Becker sighed. "At Babs too, I suppose."

Claudia didn't answer.

"Everything that Henry endured . . . for it to come to this."

"I'm sorry."

"Yes. You've said that." She tilted her head. "Listen. . . ."

"Excuse me?"

"A mockingbird. Isn't it beautiful? Henry loved them."

Claudia glanced at a gray bird perched high on the screen's scaffolding. She watched its tail flick smartly. This was one bird she knew. Nice, except when it trilled at six in the morning on a weekend.

Booey had come up beside them. "It's the state bird," he said. "Technically, its name is *Mimus polyglottos*. A lot of people confuse mockingbirds with the shrike, but—"

"Later," Claudia said.

"You're a very knowledgeable boy," Mrs. Becker said. She smiled thinly at Claudia. "Well, Detective, what is it you need from me? If you've got questions, please ask them now—and quickly—and then leave."

So much for bird-watching. Claudia clicked a pen open and flipped to a fresh page in her notebook. "Good by me," she said, a little testy herself. "Let's start with Barbara Kensington."

Forty-five minutes later, Claudia fed quarters into a vending machine at a gas station and stabbed at the Orange Crush button. A can clunked to the tray and she handed it to Booey. She primed the machine with another handful of coins and got a Pespi, which she rolled against her forehead before popping the top. She leaned against the gas station wall and drank without pause, hoping it would chase away a headache forming at her temples.

She wasn't sure what to make of Barbara Becker, who eventually conceded that no, she really didn't know much about Kensington's past, but persisted in defending the younger woman, anyway. "Perhaps she *is* a little too spirited at times," Mrs. Becker had said, "but I'm a good judge of character, and believe me, you'll never find anyone more thoughtful or loyal than Babs. Whatever you may think, she's a person of integrity."

Claudia hadn't bothered writing down the woman's words. In fact, she hadn't written down much. Mrs. Becker would not be swayed in her assessment of Kensington, nor could she imagine anyone at all who would kill her husband. She freely admitted that with Henry's passing, she would inherit a fortune; but she stopped short of offering information about the one-hundred thousand dollars Kensington would get when the will was probated. She loved Henry. Babs loved Henry. Henry loved them both. Just one small happy family.

Claudia nicked a limp dollar bill from Booey and finagled it into the machine. She punched out another Pepsi. He was still working on his Orange Crush and had begun to chatter into her headache.

"She could have been on a stage or in the movies," Booey said admiringly. "Mrs. Becker, that is. She's so . . . regal, so . . . centered. Like Katharine Hepburn. Or, uh . . . Olympia Dukakis."

"You *know* their work?"

"Oh, sure. I'm a big movie buff."

Of course.

"Old movies, new movies, comedy, drama. . . ." Booey scratched his left ankle with his right foot. "You wouldn't believe my video collection—and now I'm adding some DVD, too. If you ever want to borrow an old favorite, I probably have it." He drained his soda. "Mrs. Becker could've been big. I mean, look how well she held up while you were grilling her. She *had* to feel your heat, but she didn't let on. That takes a certain kind of talent."

"I wasn't 'grilling' her, Booey." Claudia felt a flicker of annoyance. "If I ever do, you'll see the difference."

"I didn't mean 'grilling' in a bad way," he said quickly. "You weren't nasty or anything. Just . . . straightforward. Bang, bang, bang—question after question."

Yeah. Question after question. And she knew little more than she had before. "So what did you think of Kensington?" she asked, killing time now, not wanting to get back into the hot car.

Booey blushed. "She's good, too. Now her, she reminds me a little of Jamie Lee Curtis, only with longer hair. You ever see her in *A Fish Called Wanda*? Excellent movie! She—"

"No, no, no. That's not what I meant. Forget about who she reminds you of. Just tell me your own impression."

"Oh. Well . . . I was, actually."

Claudia sighed and polished off the second Pepsi.

"No, really. See, I think they're both like actresses, Miss Kensington and Mrs. Becker. I think they're both faking something."

Claudia looked at him, surprised.

"Don't *you*?"

She arched an eyebrow. "Yeah, Booey. I do." Then she grinned. "Come on. Let's get back to the station and try to sort things out." She moved to toss her empty can into a trash bin beside the vending machine.

"Wait. I'll take that," said Booey. "I'm into recycling." She handed it over, and he plucked her first can from the trash as well. He eyed a few other cans buried deeper in the bin.

"Forget it, Booey. You can always come back for them later," she deadpanned.

"Oh, yeah. That's a good idea." He trailed her to the car, clutching their three cans. A moment later they drove off, the AC in the Cavalier gasping warm air while Booey talked earnestly about the earth's ozone layer. He sounded like Robin, but without the edge. Claudia smiled. What a piece of work he was. . . .

CHAPTER 17

SWEAT CASCADED DOWN THE CHIEF'S FACE. It had already stained the rim of his collar. Now it was popping up in patches on his shirt and slicking back the hairs on his arms. Claudia and Booey were sweating, too, but they'd been standing beneath a full sun for more than hour and then navigating through traffic in a hot car. Suggs was at his desk in air-conditioning. He looked up when he heard them outside his door, his face ashen.

"Hey, Uncle Mac, you don't look very good," Booey said, a half-step ahead of Claudia through the doorway. "Are you—"

Before Suggs could respond, she yanked on the back of Booey's shirt and spun him around, giving him a graceless shove back into the multipurpose room. "I'll take it from here," she said. "Go write up some notes from our visit to the Becker place."

"Yeah, but he—"

"I know. Go. I'll take care of it." She launched herself into Suggs's office and slammed the door.

"Hey!" Suggs began to struggle to his feet.

"Forget 'hey,'" she snapped. "Look at you! You're *sick!* You need to get this fixed already!"

"Don't you go tellin' me what I need to do, Hershey. Don't you—"

"I need you tomorrow, so here's the deal. Either you go with me now to the ER and get this . . . *thing* checked, or I'm calling 911." She batted his bottle of Maalox from the desktop. It fell into the trash can with a thunk. "Come on. We don't have time for this."

"Hershey, you are *sooo* fired!"

"Good. That makes this even easier."

"I mean it, by—"

"Me too."

She reached across his desk and snatched at the phone. He was quick, though. He grabbed at her wrist and shook the phone free, his face no longer white but glowing with fury. Claudia swore and fumbled in her purse, then held up her cell phone like an Olympic torch.

"Me or an ambulance?"

He fixed her with a look, part pain, part anger. "Hershey. . . ."

"There's a lot less commotion involved if you go with me. Which way do you want the town to play the story?"

"No wonder you're so lousy with men," he muttered. "That's how the town's playin' *your* story."

It stung a little—but only a little. The context was all wrong, and she didn't respond. She watched him put his hat on, then moved aside when he brushed past her through the door. He glared at her briefly, but the fight was all gone when he reminded her that she was still fired.

She nodded, and they left.

For the second time in one day, Claudia stood at a vending machine, this time grubbing for peanut butter crackers and bad coffee. She knew lots of hospitals that filled their machines with apples, turkey sandwiches, and yogurt. The Indian Run Community Hospital wasn't one of them. She yawned and wrestled a cracker from its cellophane wrapping. Seven-thirty. In another half hour, the hospital would try to give her the boot—give all of them the boot.

Moody, Carella, and Booey were slumped over files in the waiting room. Sally had come and gone. Jeannie, the chief's wife, had left as well, her parting words to Claudia reinforcing what she long suspected—Suggs didn't stray out of character, whether he was home or on the job:

"He's a pigheaded mule; and how you got him to come over here, I'll never know, and he sure won't ever tell me. I don't suppose you will, either, even though it has to be a story worth handing down through the generations. But I'm grateful. And when he starts to feel better, he'll be grateful, too. Eventually."

She was a diminutive woman with vivid blue eyes and thick mocha hair pulled back with a barrette. Claudia had met her on a few occasions and liked her instantly. She imagined that if the chief weren't her boss, the two might be friends.

"Meanwhile," Jeannie had continued, "if he gives you any guff, just tell him you know where his mole is and that if he doesn't ease up, you'll announce it to the world." She laughed, a husky laugh that defied her small stature. "I guarantee *that'll* shut him up fast."

Claudia had no desire to learn about the chief's mole, and she quickly changed the subject. But thinking about the conversation now brought a smile to her face. She ate the last of the crackers and returned to the waiting room just as a nurse called her name. The woman scowled at her, as if Claudia were responsible for the ulcer that tests had revealed.

"You can go in now," the nurse said in a tone that made it clear what she thought of the idea. "Chief Suggs said you first, then the others. But don't plan on staying long. And *don't* upset him. The whole point of keeping him overnight is for him to get some R&R, which obviously he doesn't get at work." She glared once more, then stalked off.

The head of Suggs's hospital bed was cranked up as high as it would go. His arms were crossed over his chest. Claudia supposed he wanted to let her know he was still pissed, and she tried to show a properly subdued expression when she entered. It was tough, though, what with his bare feet sticking out from the bottom of the sheet. He had skinny ankles for a big man.

"You're unfired," he said without preamble. "Embarrass me like this again and you won't be. Might do you well to remember that."

Claudia nodded. "How're you feeling?" she asked.

Suggs grunted. "I been poked and prodded and had somethin' wicked stuck in me all the way to my stomach. I'm surprised it didn't come out my ear." He gazed at the window for a second, then back at her. "Gonna have to change my diet, too," he said glumly. "But the good news is, it ain't stomach cancer. Just an ordinary ulcer that the doc says I let go too long."

"That's what you thought? That you had cancer?"

"Crossed my mind."

"That must've—"

"The guys are all out there?"

"I . . . yes."

"Good. Bring 'em in. I want to know what's happening with the Becker case. And, Hershey?"

"Yes?"

"I coulda made it longer, but the wife is happy that I didn't. So thanks for that, but don't go pushin' any 'favors' on me in the future. Got that?"

"I got it." She turned away so he couldn't see the smile, then went to retrieve the others.

Moody had the best stuff, so after he got his files carefully settled on the window ledge, he went first. "Everybody else already knows most of this, Chief, but here's my personal favorite—and it's one you'll love, too." He paused dramatically, then said, "Barbara 'Babs' Kensington? That's her real name, all right, but here's the one she used as an exotic dancer—'Topaz.'"

Suggs guffawed, his belly sending a ripple of movement under the sheets. "An exotic dancer? Oh, that's good."

"Yeah, she's a beaut, this Babs of ours," Moody said. He checked his notes. "Up until four years ago, she danced all over the place, up and down poles in Dallas, Vegas, and Los Angeles. Looks like L.A. must have been some kind of siren call for her, because she turned her attention to acting and actually landed some movie roles. They were bit parts and, evidently, not enough to keep a roof over her head, because she supplemented them with exercise infomercials and part-time work as an aerobics instructor. Man, the grass never grew under her feet, that's for sure."

Carella looked at Booey. "That true, Boo? You saw her feet. No grass, huh?"

The tips of his ears colored. "I didn't pay any attention to her feet."

The room exploded in laughter.

Claudia smiled, heartened to see Suggs laugh like he meant it. It had been a while.

When they settled down, Moody sobered and said, "That was the easy stuff. What I don't know yet is how she went from dancing and acting to playing nursemaid. But she did. Becker's not the first old man she tended. He's the fourth."

Suggs whistled. "Sugar daddies, huh?"

"Something like that," Moody replied. He flipped through his notes. "The first guy, a Trevor Hallahan, he apparently made her acquaintance on one of those infomercials. He was in his late sixties—a rich widower, lived alone—and Kensington had been all over him like a fly on honey. He liked it. He liked her. Then, one day on the set, he had a stroke. It wasn't all that bad, but two weeks later he had another. She moved in with him. When he died four months later, she got a chunk of his will, some twenty-thousand bucks. He was worth three million, and his two grown children didn't fight it. It probably didn't seem big enough to make a legal fuss over."

"So what're you sayin'?" Suggs asked. "She parlayed the experience into a new career?"

"Yeah, something like that. I think she played for bigger and bigger stakes, learning how to finesse things, learning how to pick her victims."

"They all dead, these old guys?"

"Yep. The second, Arthur MacArthur—and no, I'm not making that up—he was in L.A., too, in his eighties when she met him. He was another widower, a retired biochemist who'd made his money on some patents. But how she met him, that I don't know. He didn't run with the movie people."

"How long was she with him?"

"Seven months. He had a bunch of medical problems, so no one was surprised when he died of a massive coronary. Thing is, he didn't die before he added a provision to his will that left Kensington thirty grand of the four million bucks he had."

"Kids?"

Moody shook his head. "Not this time."

"So who got the rest of his money?"

"It was split between six nieces and nephews, plus a cool million to charities."

"And these nieces and nephews, they didn't fight Kensington's take?"

"No. They squabbled among themselves, and they got downright vicious in trying to get the million designated for charities, but the thirty grand? Not enough to fool with Kensington."

Moody took them through Kensington's third old man, this one a semiretired investment broker who shuttled between L.A. and Chicago. "His name was Roger Engle and he *did* have a wife. She was a patient at the same nursing home where—surprise, surprise—Barbara Becker eventually met Kensington. Anyway, I gather Engle's wife was pretty much out of it. Over a six-month period, old Roger freely began taking Kensington with him when he made duty visits to her."

"Man, that's . . . scummy," said Carella.

"Yeah, but he got his due," said Moody. "He was at his wife's bedside one day when he had a stroke himself. He died before the night was out, at the age of seventy-one."

"How much did Kensington get this time?"

"This time, nothing. I don't think she was done running her game on him when he died. The wife got the whole estate—six million and change—and then she died six weeks later. Everything defaulted to their two adult children. Kensington wasn't even a factor."

"But she had her hooks in Chicago and managed to get her claws into Becker," said the chief.

"That's how it seems to me."

Suggs's nurse froze them into silence when she marched in unannounced and made a show out of taking the chief's pulse and blood pressure. When she finished, she set a Jell-O cup on his tray, looked pointedly at her watch, and departed.

"Nurse Ratched," Carella muttered.

"Here's what I don't get," said the chief. "If she's runnin' a game, then she sure puts a lot of time in it for a rotten return. Not counting Becker, what're we talkin' so far? Three old geezers over some seventeen months for a take of fifty thousand dollars? And spread over a four-year period?" He shook his head. "Even if she gets Becker's hundred grand, that still only brings her to a hundred and fifty, which comes to an annual income of under thirty-eight thousand dollars. That's not exactly somethin' she could retire on, so what're we missin'?"

They all looked toward Claudia.

"I think there might be a couple of possibilities," she said. "For instance, Kensington might be an opportunist, but not a murderer. Presumably, she got gifts from these old guys—jewelry, clothes, electronics, maybe a car or two. It's possible she turned some of those presents into cash. She might also have had other jobs on the side and probably off the books. The bottom line on her income could've been a great deal more than what she turned from wills. Look, even with as much information as Mitch managed to get, we still have gaps."

Voices and the squeal of wheels filtered into the room from the hallway. Someone new was being moved on a gurney to another room. Claudia waited until the commotion died down.

"What's interesting about this is how the stakes for Kensington got bigger each time. Her first take was twenty grand. The second was thirty. The third was a bust, but she stood to get a hundred thousand on Becker. That's a *lot* more. I'm with Mitch. It's almost like she's been refining her technique, figuring out what she could do, learning from her mistakes."

"So how does Barbara Becker fits into this?" Carella asked.

"Good question. She might not fit into it at all. Maybe she genuinely likes Kensington and wanted to share some of the wealth with her. Maybe she thought she deserved it. With her husband dead, she has plenty of money, more than the other old men in Kensington's life. A hundred grand out of Mrs. Becker's eight million would be as inconsequential to her as the twenty grand out of Halloran's three million was. But we need to find out who orchestrated that codicil, and why. It could be—*could* be—that Mrs. Becker didn't want to wait around for Henry to die, either."

"You think they double-teamed the old guy?" Suggs said.

Claudia saw him sneak a yawn and fought back her own. "I don't know. They could've done that, yeah, and for all we know they could've had a third party involved, too." She told them about Aaron at the pool. "We need to get a background on that guy, because something about him doesn't fit. I lifted some empty beer bottles from the pool and got an officer to run them over to Flagg for fingerprints. If this Aaron is on file, maybe we'll get another piece of the puzzle."

Carella stood and stretched. "Here's another tidbit. It's almost anticlimactic, but whichever one did Becker? She did it in the pool." He looked apologetically at Claudia. "I didn't get a chance to tell you this earlier—all right, I forgot—but I fielded a follow-up call from the M.E.'s office while you were out. They picked up on a trace of chlorine in the old man. Actually, they had to send a tissue sample to an outside lab for that, but it reinforces what they already thought, what we already thought."

"Thicker and thicker," said Moody. "It just gets thicker."

Suggs cleared his throat. "Not that anyone's asked, but I haven't been altogether unproductive myself," he said. "First, that Jag in the Beckers' driveway? Registered to Barbara Becker. She's got a BMW too, should anyone care to know. Second, phone calls? If Becker stayed with friends when she went to Chicago, she didn't call them from her house to make the arrangements. What she *did* do on six separate occasions was spend time at the Regency Hotel. Fact is, there's nothin' in phone records that hints at personal calls to Chicago. She's been in touch with lawyers, a realtor, couple of other businesses, but no regular people." He inched up on the bed. "How about *them* apples?"

"Interesting," said Claudia.

Suggs seemed disappointed. "Seems a little more than just 'interesting,' if you ask me."

"Well, let me rephrase then, because actually it's *very* interesting. Aaron drives the Jag like he owns it, so apparently he's even cozier with Mrs. Becker than I thought."

"He's cozy with *both* of those women," Booey said. He looked surprised to hear himself speak. "I. . . . "

"Go ahead, son," said Suggs.

"Well, it's just that at the pool with Miss Kensington, he . . . well, they . . . uh, you know."

A slow grin started on Carella's face.

"Thing is, she said she'd only just met him. It, uh . . . well, it sure didn't look that way." He glanced at Claudia. "Did it?"

"Not to me." She shot a warning look at Carella before the inevitable joke made its way out of his mouth. "Your point is dead on, Booey."

They talked about who would do what next and were rising to leave when the nurse returned. "It's ten after eight," she informed them stiffly. She pointed at the door. "Everybody *out.*"

Carella whispered something to Moody. The nurse glowered at

them, and they laughed, then told the chief good night and followed Booey into the hallway. She watched them, taking a head count, then whirled around to face Claudia. "Everybody means *everybody*," she said.

"Give us a second," said Suggs.

She frowned at him, then retreated, muttering. When Suggs was satisfied she was out of earshot, he beckoned Claudia closer.

"Everything's set for tomorrow," he said. "Just before you blackmailed me into comin' here, I firmed things up with a few more calls. Raynor's on the hook."

"You don't need to be there," Claudia said.

"Oh, I'll be there, all right. I won't be in the office tomorrow, but I'll be ready for the meet. Count on it."

She gestured around the hospital room. "You're . . . up to that, so quick?"

"Hey, Hershey. You got one free pass on tryin' to tell me how to live my life. Don't push it."

"Just asking. I'll see you tomorrow." She gave him a half salute and left, the eyes of the nurse on her the whole way down the hallway.

CHAPTER 18

"YOU WOKE ME UP."

"I'm sorry, honey." But Robin was grousing, really, not quite complaining yet, and Claudia gripped the cell phone harder, as if she could eclipse the distance between them by applying more pressure to the tiny unit that connected their voices. "It's almost nine o'clock," she said. "The sun's out. The birds have been up for hours."

"If I had to grub for worms, I would be too," Robin muttered.

Now she was waking up. Claudia smiled, her eyes on the moving van a half-block down the street. Two men were struggling up a ramp with a hutch.

"How's the kitten, Mom?"

"Good. He's good. He eats like a horse, and he entertains himself by shredding the arm of the couch. I take that as a sign he's happy."

"We should get a scratching post for him. Maybe two. When I get back. . . ." Robin's voice trailed off.

For a minute, Claudia thought she'd lost her. She thumped the phone on the steering wheel, then listened again.

"Mother, what are you *doing?*"

"Ah, there you are. I'm on the cell phone and—"

"Wait. *You* bought a cell phone? *You?*"

"Hey, kiddo, I'm hip."

Robin groaned. "If you were really 'hip,' Mom, you wouldn't use the word *hip*."

Claudia's training never ended. "I know. I was just testing you."

They bantered for a while and swapped a few stories. Already, Brian had taken Robin on tours to the Washington Monument, the White House, the Supreme Court. They'd dined in some of the capital's most fabled restaurants. Today, they had plans for the zoo. No wonder she was tired.

"Where are you, anyway, Mom? You sound like you're sitting in traffic."

"Just killing time," Claudia said lightly. She rolled up her car window to block the sound of passing vehicles. Not that there were many. Before long, neighbors would start cutting lawns and washing cars. But Dennis's street never got unruly, and it was a Saturday. Except for the moving van, not much stirred yet.

"What are you killing time for?"

"I'm working today. Just a couple of things I need to get done."

"Oh."

For once, Claudia was grateful that Robin rarely expressed interest in her work. She didn't care to explain what she was doing later. She certainly didn't care to explain why she was lurking on Dennis's street as if she had him under surveillance, because she hardly knew why she was there herself. What was she doing? She shook her head and focused on Robin's voice.

"Dad's really something on the piano, Mom. And people seem to *know* him here, like he's really a hot ticket. I'm thinking of taking lessons. I bet I'd be good."

Claudia felt the familiar pang of jealousy. Why not the oboe? "That's terrific, honey," she said. "We can talk about it when you get home. There must be someone here who gives lessons."

"Mom?"

Something hesitant in Robin's voice made Claudia sit up straighter in the car. "What's up?" she asked.

"Well, nothing, but . . . you think I could maybe come home sooner than we planned? Like maybe right after the Fourth of July?"

Claudia went on full alert. "What's the matter, baby? I thought you were having a good time. Don't you feel well? Is it because of the kitten?"

"No, no . . . nothing like that. I just miss home."

The catch in Robin's voice told a different story. Claudia made herself take it slowly, trying for a tone that wouldn't signal alarm. "Is it just that you miss home? Or does this maybe have a little to do with . . . your dad?" The silence on the other end lasted so long that she had to resist banging the phone again.

Finally: "Thing is, I *am* having a good time," Robin said. She had lowered her voice, as if worried that she might be overheard. "Dad's great. Everything here is . . . great. But Dad . . . I don't know him that well, you know? I always have to be, I don't know . . . *on,* somehow. It's hard. *Weird.* Know what I mean?"

She knew. Robin hadn't spent enough time with Brian to be herself. Claudia did mental cartwheels, then immediately felt guilty for her reaction. Still. . . .

"Robin, you don't have to stay any longer than you want to, but are you sure about this? Have you talked to your dad about it?"

"I was hoping maybe you could."

Dennis walked out of his house, rolled canvases beneath his arm. Claudia watched. If she was going to say something, if she was going to stop him—*was she?*—now was the time to make her move. She watched him open his car door and ease the canvases onto the backseat.

"He's in the kitchen, probably having coffee," Robin was saying. "So could you, you know, talk to him?"

Claudia watched Dennis talk to one of the movers. They shook hands. The man began shoving the ramp back into the van. *Shit.* She should at least start her car, drive by, see what she would do when she was at his driveway.

"Mom?"

"Yeah, hon."

"So would you? Now?"

She willed Dennis to look up, to look over, to see her. He was watching the mover get into the van. A second later he slapped the side of the truck with his hand, and it slowly began rolling away from the house. Moments now. Just moments.

Look over.

"Are you there?"

"I, uh . . . honey? Right now?"

"Well, he's here now. That's the thing. Please? I want to come home. I don't know how to tell him."

Claudia saw Dennis move toward his car. He paused and stared at the house, his hands in his pockets. *Still time.*

"I'll owe you, Mom. Okay?"

"What? Oh, kiddo, you don't owe me for anything, not ever." She blinked and squeezed her eyes shut, feeling the start of a miserable, undeserving tear. She sighed into the phone. "Put your dad on. I'll take care of it."

"You won't make him hate me?"

"No, no . . . he'd never hate you, no matter what."

"You're sure?"

"I'm sure, baby."

"You're the greatest!"

"Yeah," she said softly. She heard Robin's phone clunk against a hard surface, then heard her daughter's voice faintly in the background: "Dad, Mom wants to talk to you."

Claudia waited for Brian to pick up and watched the man who loved her drive away.

CHAPTER 19

THEY SAW THE HEADLIGHTS THROUGH THEIR FIELD GLASSES before they heard the rumble of the pickups. A few minutes later, the vehicles were clearly visible below the full moon, moving parade-like over a narrow gravel road and then through a gap in dense trees which concealed the old farm property. All that remained was a weathered barn that listed dangerously to one side. Boards had been pried from its entrance door and side windows, which now spilled light like a Halloween pumpkin illuminated by a candle. The pickups bounced toward it across ground studded with weeds and thorny shrubs, stopping finally in haphazard rows a dozen paces from the structure.

Claudia took the binoculars from her face and pushed a finger under her eyeglasses. She rubbed the soft area below her left eye, then tried to shift to a more comfortable position. They'd been here for hours, she and Suggs and twelve others, setting up and then getting in position behind trees, and now, just . . . waiting. Booey and Carella were twenty feet away; Moody and three other patrolmen, ten feet beyond them. She couldn't see them, but she hoped that Booey had remembered to slick himself down with insect repellent.

She groped for the thermos but stopped short of doing anything once her fingers brushed against it. That's all she needed, another cup of coffee. Already her bladder was sending warning signals she couldn't ignore much longer. She groaned, then looked through the binoculars again. She'd lost count, but calculated twenty-five or thirty trucks when the last one was parked. Most carried two people, including a handful of women. Doors were opening and thumping closed again. Laughter rolled from the trucks to the line of trees concealing Indian Run's finest.

Suggs had come through, and she turned to him discreetly, watching him watch people getting out of their pickups. It was hard to see his face in the dark, but earlier, before dusk faded into night, he looked all right—tired, maybe, and of course a little tense, but all right.

"They're a noisy bunch, aren't they," she said to him.

"Who? The cockers or the cocks?" Suggs set aside his own field glasses and squinted at her.

Claudia wasn't up on the lingo. If Cleveland had cockfights, she'd never been plugged into them. "Both, I guess," she answered, presuming he was referring to the men and the frenzied roosters they were unloading. "You'd think they were at a carnival."

Suggs snorted, exasperated. "For them, this *is* a carnival, Hershey. It's why they're so damned excited now. When are you ever gonna get the city mentality out of your head?"

Claudia gave it a rest. She suspected that some of the men down there were Suggs's friends. She knew where he stood on this, he'd made it clear on the ride over. "Next thing you know," he'd growled, "the same bleedin' hearts who put an end to cockfightin' are gonna go after sports fishing. If this thing we're doin' gets out to the press, I'm gonna have to take the bass off my office wall. They're gonna want to know why'd I catch it if I wasn't gonna eat it."

Claudia watched the handlers bring their birds into the barn. The chief didn't like it—she guessed he'd been turning a blind eye to cockfighting for years—but tonight he'd do what the law said he had to do. He'd do it because she'd persuaded him it was one way to get to Raynor.

"Look," said Suggs. He pointed. "Two o'clock, just inside the door."

There he was, the man himself, greeting the cockers with a hearty handshake. Two of the white dogs Claudia had seen at Raynor's trailer stood at his side, tethered to their master by a short leash. Though tension in their bodies signaled keen interest in the gamecocks, which the handlers carried in cages, neither dog moved from its position. And, of course, they didn't bark.

"Well trained," Claudia muttered. "And creepy."

"That's what he counts on. From what I hear tell, they're like a trademark with him, like a family crest or somethin'. He's always got at least two of his dogs with him when he goes out in public. You get one look at them and you know Raynor's not a man to mess with. Nobody does. It's one reason people trust him to organize fights. If nothin' else, him and his dogs keep a lid on trouble." Suggs slapped at a mosquito. "Damned muggy night you picked for this, Hershey."

"So, Raynor doesn't fight his own birds?"

"Uh-uh. *Used* to—used to breed gamecocks, too—but not for years now. He makes his money these days as a freelance organizer; at least that's what we've been hearin'. And it must be true, because the man's here, all right, and he did what we needed him to do by taking care of the arrangements. Of course, *he's* the guy who was hot to put something together. We just made it easier for him, is all."

Claudia heard the irony in Suggs's tone. She bet he never would have mentioned hearing that Raynor was actively looking to arrange a cockfight if he'd known it would open the door for a sting operation.

"Oh, yeah," Suggs said. "We helped him put a bow on this one, all right. We're seein' that he gets a five-hundred-dollar fee on top of his normal cut off the admission price. And I gotta tell you, fifty bucks to get in—even for a private hack fight like this one—well, that's just way off the charts. Most often, in places like Arizona or maybe Oklahoma, you'd pay maybe five or ten bucks to get in."

"I'm surprised the admission price didn't send up a red flag for him."

"Two things, Hershey. First, the risk isn't all that high. Chasin' down fights just isn't a big priority in most places. Raynor knows that. Second, he's a greedy bastard. He sees dollar signs, and so he's plenty happy to believe what we fed him, that the man scouting for a fight is a high-rolling anesthesiologist from out of town. I'm sure he's also thinkin' about laying down a few bets for himself. And anyway, maybe fifty bucks for admission really isn't such a stretch. With cockfightin' being illegal just about everywhere now, getting into a private club or a one-time fight like this is flat-out pricier." Suggs shook his head. "Raynor'll have to peel off a few bills for the pimple-faced kid who helped him get the barn ready, but even so, if this wasn't a sting tonight, he'd strut out of here with a bundle. And those dogs of his would make sure it stayed in his pocket on the way home."

"Nice racket. All he's got to do is stand there and smile and pocket money. He doesn't even have to get his hands dirty by refereeing any of the fights. He's—"

"Hershey, how many times do I have to explain this to you?" Suggs pulled a handkerchief from his pocket and mopped his face. "The referee is paid by the house, which in this case is us, and in this case, of course, the referee is one of our own guys."

"I realize that," Claudia said, annoyed. "I was making a statement, not asking a question." She resisted correcting him about the referee, who was *not* one of "our" guys. He was a Flagg County deputy whom Raynor was unlikely to recognize.

As if Suggs were reading her thoughts, he let loose a profanity about Flagg's involvement in the sting. "Just my kind of luck that Raynor would pick a place both in and out of the town limits," he muttered. The abandoned property, once home to a modest cattle operation, straddled the Indian Run and county lines. "We're no more than a eyelash onto county land, and I had to go hat in hand to Andrews, who's still wet behind the ears but of course wanted to tell me how to run the thing. I'll never understand how that young pup was made sheriff."

"It's just an interim appointment," Claudia reminded him.

Personally, she thought Jared Andrews had more on the ball than his predecessor, a bigot who had keeled over at his desk in the middle of his second term. But now wasn't the time to share her perspective, and she murmured something inane about jurisdictional turf wars. Suggs wasn't listening anyway.

"They got four of their people undercover inside the barn, and none of ours," he said. "We're just decoration. All we're really doin' is babysittin' the outside."

Claudia chose not to point out that Indian Run had no people Raynor wouldn't recognize, or experience with stings, or even enough manpower to pull off a raid on its own. "You put it together, Chief, and it's still our show," she said, then changed the subject before he could respond. "Hey, that Aaron guy from the Becker estate? We got a hit on his prints from the beer bottle. He's every bit the lowlife we thought he was. Maybe worse."

"Yeah? How so?"

"He's been behind the wire twice. Once for breaking and entering. Second time for second-degree murder. That one came out of a home invasion in a ritzy section of L.A. He thumped a guy on the head with a fireplace poker."

"And he only got second degree?"

"Here's the fun part. He bopped one of his *own* guys, claimed he was trying to stop the guy from killing the homeowner. He had a decent lawyer, and the jury bought it."

Suggs swore. "Figures. But L.A.—that's interesting. Kensington spent a lot of quality time there."

"Yeah, and the timing fits." Claudia squirmed, wishing for a bathroom. "Aaron—full name Aaron Rivens—he's plenty well-known to the L.A. police. Before he got into violent crimes, there were a few other charges along the way that never stuck, everything from petty larceny to auto theft to peddling small quantities of dope. Maybe we'll get somewhere now." She held her binoculars to her eyes. "Aah . . . take a look. It looks like everybody's just about inside, even Raynor's demon dogs."

Suggs squinted into his field glasses. "We need to give them a few minutes. They'll be weighin' the cocks and checkin' their gaffs. Someone's probably settin' up sandwiches. The handlers—hang on, hang on; Raynor's little sidekick is closin' the doors. Come on. We need to get in position."

"Wait a minute. How're we going to handle the dogs?"

"We're not. One of the Deputy Fifes inside will. I figured Raynor's dogs would be here, so two of Andrews's people are from canine patrol. They know animals. They'll know what to do."

"I hope so."

Suggs chuckled. "You really are a fish out of water here, Hershey." He spoke quietly into his radio to the others, then nudged her. "Let's go, then. It's showtime."

The plan was simple. Raynor had already been witnessed taking money; and if no one had screwed up, they had it on video. Theoretically, that would be enough. But to avoid giving a defense attorney wiggle room, they'd wait for the first cock to fly before they moved in. Raynor would go down. Spectators and the handlers would get . . . discretion.

Suggs silently motioned for his people to get in place. Booey disappeared with Carella into shadows behind a pickup truck. Moody signaled to a patrolman, and together they crept toward the west side of the barn. Two others took the east side. A show of force, it wasn't. But they had four Flagg deputies squirreled inside, and they had the element of surprise. They'd make do.

Claudia quietly positioned herself two feet from the barn doors and peered through a notch in a board that Moody had widened earlier. Suggs was similarly set up a few feet away. With her nose to the wood and her eyes pressed up against the hole, she felt like a Peeping Tom. An absurd urge to laugh seized her so suddenly that she had to push her face against the board to shake it off. The moment passed, and she concentrated on what she could see inside. The sight sobered her instantly.

Yes, fine—George Washington had been a cocker; Lincoln had been a referee. Cockfighting predated Christianity . . . she knew all that, had actually listened when Suggs lectured her, and she understood— she did—that participants in blood sports were rarely crazed people who hated animals. Hunting was popular. Little old ladies fished in tournaments. Millions watched boxing on HBO. Hadn't she attended a bullfight herself? Blood spilled everywhere, all the time. No one could get enough.

But the hole in the barn revealed a blood lust that she could feel and almost smell, so strong was the anticipation of spectators. They sat on splintered bleachers arranged in a semicircle around a wide dirt pit. Ragged chicken wire enclosed the pit, which was illuminated by bare bulbs powered by a noisy generator. Claudia had seen the arena setup hours earlier, had vaguely admired Raynor's ability to orchestrate everything so quickly and thoroughly. Now, though, with people inside, people catcalling and whooping and shouting their first bets, now that she could see the first of the gamecocks resisting their owners' arms, straining to go after each other, now she felt her stomach sour and wished she could be anywhere else.

Claudia took her eye off the hole for a second and breathed deeply the night air. When she looked inside again, two handlers were moving toward each other, swinging their gamecocks in front of them, waiting for a signal from the referee to release the birds. The spectators roared their approval. Light glanced off something lashed to one of the birds' feet. Claudia could barely see it, but she knew it had to be a gaff. Suggs had described it as a long, needle-like weapon that each cock wore for the duel. They would fight vigorously, and they would fight to the death.

"First up is a Gray Toppie and a blue Kelso," she heard Suggs say. "Good fighters with lots of heart. Good matchup. Watch close now. They're done billing the birds. They're gonna toss 'em, and what happens next, happens fast. Be ready, be ready. . . ."

She didn't see the referee's signal, but suddenly both birds were airborne and flapping furiously at each other. They hovered, as clenched together as lovers, then landed in a cloud of feathers, and instantly clashed, pecking and slashing at each other with their gaffs. The spectators roared excitedly when the Toppie pivoted and sidestepped a few inches away. In the next moment it was back, jabbing at the other rooster's head.

"Now!" Suggs roared.

Claudia saw the Kelso go down in the second she wheeled from the notch and hurried after the chief, drawing her gun. She helped him shove the doors open, but the Flagg deputies inside the barn were already barking orders at the stunned crowd. Raynor had chained the dogs. They weren't going anywhere. She spotted him in a far corner, yelling back at a deputy, and started toward him. Then something caught her eye—a flash in the pit—and she paused, riveted. Like gladiators, the Toppie and Kelso were still going at it, oblivious to the commotion around them, looking for a kill, possessed by their training or an instinct or . . . *something*. Both birds were bloodied. The Toppie was beginning to stagger in circles. Its gaff had loosened and was etching lines in the dirt. The Kelso hopped toward it on one foot, ready to attack again. *Still.*

"If you're not gonna help, then move out of the way," said Suggs.

He pushed past her and scooped up the Toppie and handed it to a bearded man. "Get out of here. Take this foolish bird and go. Hurry up." He looked at Claudia. "Why don't you go have a talk with Mr. Raynor over there. He'd be the one in handcuffs, and I don't believe he even realizes you're here yet."

"Look, I'm sorry—"

Suggs shook his head. "Forget it. Go get Raynor."

Claudia glanced over just as a deputy was pushing him out the door. She turned back to say something to Suggs, but he was already reaching for the Kelso, hollering for the bird's owner to come get it. She looked at the bloodstained dirt and went outside.

The deal was simple. If Raynor went down for Wanda Farr's murder, Indian Run would share credit for the bust with Flagg County. If he didn't, and word of the sting got out to the press, Indian Run was on its own to explain why no one else got arrested. Raynor might have already figured some of it out, but Claudia didn't care. His first priority would be to save his own hide, and she approached him with a smile.

"Well, well, Mr. Raynor. And here I thought you were a homebody," she said. He was sitting on the ground against a tree, his only company a Flagg County deputy, and he hadn't seen her coming. His head snapped up and he glared. Claudia looked at the cuffs on his wrists. "I guess you *do* get out, after all."

"You bitch," he said. "I should've known you'd be behind this."

Claudia laughed. She took the deputy aside for a minute and spoke to him briefly, then told him he could go. She squatted beside Raynor. "The deputy tells me you don't want a lawyer. That true?"

"For what? A cockfight? There's not a judge or a jury in Flagg who's gonna give a damn. I wouldn't spend the price of a phone call to rouse a lawyer out of bed."

"Well, now, if it's money you're concerned about, we'll get you an attorney. It's your constitutional right, you know. Did the deputy—"

"Yeah, yeah, he told me. But I don't need anyone, Hershey, because this is all a load of crap. I know it. You know it. I'll be out before the sun rises."

"That's a pleasant little fantasy. Maybe you don't keep up, but your little party here tonight? Did you know it's a third-degree felony?"

He sighed elaborately.

"Yep. The state frowns on cockfights. It falls under the Animal Fighting Act. Chapter 828 on the Florida books. You can go down for five years. Imagine that—*five years,* just for putting together a friendly little duel between roosters. Doesn't seem fair, does it?"

A slight breeze stirred the air. Claudia hoped it didn't mean rain. She pulled a pack of cigarettes from her pocket and offered one to Raynor. He shook his head. "No?" She lit one for herself. "Suit yourself."

Someone laughed in the distance. A truck started up. Then another. Raynor turned to the sound. "What the hell is this about, Hershey? Where's everyone going?"

Claudia looked over. "Home, I imagine."

"Oh, I see. It's just me who's staying."

She shrugged. "We're allowed some discretion. Most of those folks? They didn't even get a chance to place a bet. I guess we jumped the gun."

"This was a setup."

"Sure you don't want a cigarette, Mr. Raynor?" She held hers up. "I'd offer you some coffee—I know how you like your caffeine—but I'm pretty sure you wouldn't want the swill left in my thermos."

Raynor said nothing. He watched two officers wrestle the barn doors closed, then glanced around. "Where are my dogs, Hershey?"

Claudia blew a plume of smoke skyward. "Oh—well, funny thing about those dogs, Mr. Raynor. We put a call into Animal Control. They're coming, and they're all hot and bothered about them. Apparently they regard your dogs as dangerous. I don't know; maybe it's that no-voice thing." She shifted to the ground. "I'm a cat person myself, but your dogs? In their own way, they're actually kind of handsome. I hope Animal Control doesn't just put them down."

"You're full of crap."

"Oh, it's nothing, really. I can probably straighten it out when I get around to the paperwork." She waved to a passing patrol officer. "Man, I hate paperwork."

"My dogs better not get hurt. For that, I *would* get a lawyer, and I'm not talking about some greenie right out of law school. Believe me."

"Oh, I believe you." She yawned. "Want to borrow my cell phone?" She leaned back, propping herself up with her hands. "It's new. Has pretty good reception."

"Stop yanking my chain, Hershey."

"How about *you* stop yanking mine?"

Raynor spat into the ground. "I told you I didn't kill her."

"I have a good memory. I know what you told me."

"It's the truth."

"I don't know *what* the truth is. But I know when someone's lying, Raynor. And you're lying about something."

"Look, Hershey, you don't have anything on me, or we wouldn't be here now."

Claudia swept her hand in an arc, taking in the barn and the last of the departing vehicles. "I have this, Raynor. From humble beginnings do all—"

"—things start. Yeah, yeah." He scratched his ear. "All right. I tell you a thing or two, and then I walk, right? I get my dogs and I walk."

"You broke the law. I can't make promises."

"But that . . . discretionary thing?"

"Maybe. No way will you walk altogether, but maybe I could make things go . . . easier."

"Not good enough, Hershey."

Claudia sighed and stood. Carella and Suggs were wandering around by the barn. She started to call out to them.

"All right, all right, damn it. Sit back down. Just give me a minute to think."

"You don't need a minute to think. You either have something to tell me or you don't. If you do, let's go down to the station and get it on tape."

He didn't need a minute to think, but he was doing it anyway. Claudia crushed out her cigarette, giving him space. She smiled inwardly. It was all about the dogs. *His dogs!* Hot damn.

"The cuffs come off?" he finally said, looking up, but not quite meeting her eyes.

She had him. "Sure. Once we're there, yeah."

"Coffee?"

"That and toilets."

Raynor grunted while he struggled to his feet. "I'm getting too old for this kind of shit."

"Aren't we all," Claudia replied. She nudged him toward a patrol car. "Let's get out of here."

CHAPTER 20

THE SHOWER HEAD WAS ONE OF THOSE FANCY NUMBERS. It boasted six modes that dispensed water in everything from a steamy tropical mist to a masochistic beat hard enough to leave marks. Claudia chose the latter setting, the one Robin called "the skin scraper," and let hot water pummel her.

Fifteen minutes later, when she finally felt purged of the day's grime and revived enough to listen to the interview tape, she turned it off and groped for a towel. The bathroom was steamed up, but not so much that she couldn't see herself in the mirror when she put on her glasses, and she eyed herself critically.

"You are not my friend," she mumbled at the mirror. She sighed and vowed to get back into her exercise routine soon. When the Farr case was over. When the Becker case was over. When life was discovered on Pluto.

She threw on a robe and headed for the living room, detouring first to the kitchen for something to drink. A glass of wine would be nice. She thought about the mirror and opted for water instead, then made her way to the living room, grabbing her briefcase and a small cassette player on the way.

The kitten was nestled in a corner of the couch, and she eased herself onto the cushion in a way that wouldn't disturb him. He hadn't risen to greet her when she came in at two in the morning, but he lifted his head now, blinked at her once, gave a quick lick to a front paw, stretched halfheartedly, and went back to sleep.

Claudia touched one of his ears with a finger. It flicked twice. Out of nowhere, she felt a powerful urge to call her sister, but she had no idea how to reach her. Anyway, they hadn't been on speaking terms for years. Sydney wouldn't even know her voice. They never. . . .

Don't go there.

She shook it off, opened her briefcase, and pulled out the tape with Raynor's statement. He'd quickly reverted to his usual smug manner once he was seated on a padded chair and in the station's air-conditioned comfort. Claudia had no real desire to hear him again, but the son of a bitch had spun an interesting story. It merited a second listen, and there wouldn't be time tomorrow. She put the tape in the machine and fast-forwarded past the standard introduction that established the date and time and their identities. When Raynor's scratchy voice came on, she stopped the cassette and hit PLAY.

". . . sure this is fresh? It tastes like boot leather."

"If you want better coffee, Raynor, go to Denny's. Tell me about Wanda Farr and your relationship with her."

"Nothing like getting right to the point." Raynor took a swallow of the coffee she'd given him and made a face. "You already know about my relationship with her. We were neighbors, but we weren't friends. She antagonized me every chance she got. And before you ask, I antagonized her too. Nothing you don't already know."

"When's the last time you saw her?"

"I need to take a leak."

"Come on, Raynor. Let's get this done."

He cackled, then turned serious. "I saw her on a Thursday, early afternoon."

"What Thursday?"

"I don't know, a couple weeks ago?"

"Like maybe June 22nd?"

"Could be. Probably."

"All right. Where did you see her?"

"This isn't gonna sound good. You're likely to jump to conclusions."

"I'm not jumping anywhere. Just tell me where. And tell me why."

"Well, shit." Raynor fidgeted and scratched at his beard. "All right. I went to her trailer. She'd been to mine earlier, hollering and making a big to-do about one of my dogs, threatening to call Animal Control on me. Again. That bitch, she—"

"She *came* onto your property? Wasn't she worried the dogs would go after her?"

"Hell, no. You can believe this or not, but my dogs are trained to respond only to my commands. They're made to look meaner than they are. Works, too, nine times out of ten."

Claudia wanted to ask why they made no noise, but it wasn't relevant and Raynor was on a roll. She nodded, encouraging him to continue.

"The dogs'll go after strangers, they'll chase them some, they'll corner them, but they are *not* trained to kill. Farr learned that much by living so close to me. She knew them. They knew her."

"So why'd she come over?"

"Aw, because one of my dogs killed one of her cats. Well, that's what she *said*. She said one of my dogs went over to her place and mauled a cat. But that's what she was always saying. The woman was wicked crazy."

"You're saying that your dogs left people alone *and* her cats?"

"No, I'm not saying that. A dog's a dog. It can be trained in some ways, but not others. Mine would take off after birds, squirrels, raccoons, and anything else on four legs. If one of her cats happened to stray too close to one of my dogs, well, it's possible he'd go after it."

Claudia stopped the tape for a minute and sipped her water. She gazed at the kitten, shook her head, and hit PLAY again.

"So the day she came over, this Thursday, what happened?"

"Nothing. She screeched at me, I yelled back, and then, like always, she went away."

"So what was it that brought you to her trailer later?"

"I got a call from Animal Control. That witch must've actually gone out and found a pay phone and called them."

"And?"

"And I told Animal Control it was just Wanda Farr making a lot of noise about nothing, as usual. Sometimes they'd come out anyway. Sometimes they wouldn't. This time they didn't. They gave me the usual spiel on the phone, told me to be nice, or whatever, and that was that." Raynor paused to drain the rest of his coffee. "I'll take one of those cigarettes now."

"This is a nonsmoking building," Claudia said. But she lit one for both of them anyway. "So what happened next?"

"I watched TV. Did some stuff. Had a couple drinks. Got pissed all over again. I mean, who the *hell* was this woman to call about my *dogs*, when her stinkin' cats roamed all over the place, wailing whenever they were in heat, fighting and screeching amongst themselves? I like things quiet. My dogs are quiet. They know how to behave. Her cats were a blight on the neighborhood. They'd—"

"So on this particular occasion you built up a real steam about them, is that it?"

"Yeah."

"And you went over there . . . to do what?"

"I don't know."

"You don't know?"

"I don't know!" Raynor flicked ash on the floor before Claudia could stop him. "I didn't have a plan. I don't know, I guess I was going to yell back, scare her a little. I was working on my fourth drink, maybe my fifth. I wasn't thinking as clearly as I usually do."

"So you went over."

"Yeah. I leashed a couple of my dogs and I went over. I took my dogs and my drink, and I sought her out."

"When?"

"Probably about dusk. She was just outside her trailer, doing whatever, and the minute she spotted me she started right back up. I wasn't there long."

"So what happened?"

Raynor examined his cigarette, avoiding Claudia's eyes. His voice dropped an octave. "The truth? I lost my cool, totally. We were about four, five feet apart." He grew silent for a moment and ran a grimy fingernail around the rim of his coffee cup. Then he blew a pocket of air from his mouth. "What I did was, I threw my glass at her, not thinking about it, just reacting, and it . . . well, it sort of thudded off her head. For a split second nothing happened. She just looked at me. Then she stumbled back, like she was dazed or something. She put her hand on her head where the glass hit her, and then she started to go down a little. She didn't fall, though. She walked in a little crookedy line, a few steps forward, then a few steps back, but she didn't go down."

"And what were you doing?"

"Me? I . . . nothing. You got to understand, this thing happened so fast, I . . . all I did was watch her. And then, then I just . . . left. It made me nervous, the fact that she was doing these screwy little circle-like walks, and now she wasn't saying anything either."

"You went back to your trailer?"

"Yeah. I was a little panicked, maybe."

"What about the glass?"

"You already know the answer to that, is my guess."

"Tell me anyway."

"I left it there. It's got a heavy bottom, and it fell on some weeds, so it didn't break. Amazing, isn't it? The thing hit her head. It hit the ground. It didn't break. But I wasn't thinking about any of that at the time. I just wanted to leave." He fidgeted. "Look, can I hit the can now? Seriously, I really do have to go."

Claudia had paused the tape recorder at that point, giving each of them a break. She stopped it now, as well, and quietly rose from the couch to stretch. Raynor was like any other bully she'd ever known, and just as cowardly. Anger drove him to Farr's trailer. Fear drove him away from it. She thought about him while she did some sloppy knee bends and then, annoyed with herself for the half-assed effort, punished herself with a dozen serious crunches and an equal number of side leg lifts.

To her surprise, she felt herself getting into it. She rolled toward the coffee table and hit the PLAY button again, listening while she worked at working out. The sound of Raynor's hearty voice made her skin crawl.

"Whew! I feel like a new man," he said. "I'll tell you what, when you hit a certain age you got to take the horse out of the barn a lot more than you do when you're young."

Claudia had rolled her eyes then, and she rolled them now. "Let's pick up where we left off," she said. "You left Wanda Farr walking in circles, and you went home. What next?"

"Nothing next, leastwise not then."

She waited.

"Okay. Come morning, I half expected the old lady to storm my property again or set the cops on me. I was surprised she hadn't already called them the night before, but I figured that what with it being dark and all, she just didn't want to go hunt down a phone. So in the morning I waited, thinking about what I'd say, did a couple chores, worked my dogs some—like that."

Raynor's face had taken on a troubled expression then, and he'd wet his lips, apparently thinking how best to phrase what came next.

Claudia shifted to her back and put her legs into the air, her knees at ninety degrees. She bicycled past a lengthy pause on the tape, marveling at the self-restraint she'd shown in not rushing him through his narration.

Finally, he continued: "Well, she didn't come and she didn't come, and neither did anyone else. It began to gnaw on me some."

"Why?"

"Why? What a stupid question." Raynor shook his head disgustedly. "Obviously, I was starting to worry whether the glass had maybe knocked the old fool senseless."

The glass. Not him, of course. The glass.

"You went back?"

"Yeah. It was midafternoon or so, and I headed on back, this time without my dogs. She wasn't outside, so I knocked on her door. I had twenty bucks in my pocket. I figured on giving that to her, sort of to make amends, you know?"

Big whoop. "Uh-huh."

"Anyways, she didn't answer the door. I must've stood there like a jackass for five minutes, knocking and knocking, but nothing."

"Did it ever occur to you to maybe call 911 or something?"

"No, I can't say that it did." Raynor leaned forward, bristling. "Let's not forget that I didn't start this thing, she did." He grunted, apparently satisfied with the moral choices he'd made. "Besides, the glass was gone, so I figured that she must've been okay, because she obviously picked it up off the ground and brought it into her trailer. Probably didn't have anything but dirty paper cups inside. This was a good glass. It would've been like a prize to her, well worth the headache it might've caused her."

"Okay. Let's see if I have this straight, Mr. Raynor. You hurled a glass at Wanda Farr and hit her in the head. She staggered, but didn't actually fall. You went back to your trailer, fretted over the prospect of the cops coming out, and when they didn't, you fretted even more that maybe they hadn't come because she was too dead to call them. Is that about right?"

"Close enough."

"All right, good. You went back with twenty bucks to make things up to her, but she didn't answer the door. You were all right with that, because the glass was gone, which you interpreted to mean that she'd taken it inside. It was an unfortunate misunderstanding between neighbors, but in the end, everything worked out because Wanda Farr got to keep a good glass. How am I doing?"

"You can see where it was all logical."

"Uh-huh. So then what happened?"

"Again—nothing. I didn't see her. She didn't see me. I put the whole thing out of my mind until I heard that she was found dead in her trailer."

"You kind of thought she died after the fact? That maybe you really did kill her after all?"

"Want to know the truth? I didn't think that at all, not in the beginning. Fact is, I laughed my ass off. Here I am, worrying about a little bump on the head, and as it turns out, the old gal drowned herself. What I felt was mighty relieved."

"So you didn't make a connection between hitting her in the head and her drowning in the tub?"

"Not until you showed up with that little monkey sidekick of yours."

"His name is Booey."

Raynor waved a hand. "Whatever. Point is, everybody was talking about how Farr drowned in the tub. Everybody said it was an accident. Then you were in my face with questions. I started to wonder about the bump all over again, like if maybe she had a delayed reaction and drowned accidentally because of it. It *still* would've been an accident, but I could see how you might could take it in another direction, make it into a 'contributing circumstance' or whatever you call it. So I began to ponder on that glass again."

"You wanted it back."

"Tried to get it, too, which you already know, because you called me up trying to spook me, asking if I found what I was looking for." He shrugged. "So you got the glass and you got my prints on it. That's why we're here. Only thing is, I didn't kill Farr and you know it."

"Persuade me. Tell me something I don't know, Mr. Raynor."

Claudia sat up, a little out of breath. She looked at the tape player and listened intently to what she already had heard.

"Here's something you don't know, De*tect*ive." Raynor grinned hugely. "Here's *two* somethings. First off, I know that you and Booey were out by my trailer, stirring up my dogs. You think I don't know what goes on there? But second, I wasn't the only one out at Farr's trailer that night. And I got proof. It's a prize, all right. You want it, it's yours. Just drop the nickel-dime cockfighting charges, bring me my dogs, take me home, and I'll give it to you."

Even though the hour approached four in the morning, she thought it would take her a long time to fall asleep. She'd crawled under the covers feeling overstimulated by the exercise and churning with the possibilities that Raynor's "prize" suggested. She scowled into her pillow. It wasn't proof, of course. Nothing could be that easy. But what he'd given her . . . perhaps later it might just develop into evidence.

Five minutes later, with the kitten at her feet, she slept.

CHAPTER 21

"LIEUTENANT?"

Claudia jumped, startled from a concentration so fierce that she'd locked out everything around her but the notes she was writing. Her last stroke ran in a flat line off the edge of the paper.

"What are you doing here, Booey? It's Sunday." She checked her watch. "And it's early."

"Not for me. I usually get up at five. I hit the shower first thing. By five-thirty I'm already having cereal with skim milk. Then I—"

"Admirable, Booey. Very healthy. How's your uncle doing, anyway?"

"You wouldn't believe it! He's like a new man, laughing a lot, full of energy. It's like a miracle—that's what Aunt Jeannie says. She dragged him to church this morning. Told him he had a lot to be grateful for and he should let God know he is."

Claudia smiled. She wondered how long it would take Suggs to sneak a chili dog. "You know when they'll be back? I need to fill him in on some things."

"Probably by eleven o'clock."

She saw his eyes dart to her desk. They narrowed with the strain of trying to read her notes upside down. She almost laughed out loud. "Don't hurt yourself there, Booey."

He looked away guiltily.

"I'm just having some fun with you. Go on, have a seat. I'll bring you up to speed."

The chief should hear about the developments first, but Booey was here now, and he'd been in on everything else so far. Besides, he had a squirrelly way of thinking that every now and then produced surprising insights.

The whole time she talked, his feet thrummed against the floor as fast as a hummingbird's wings, which she knew by now meant his brain was turning. When she finally finished, though, he shook his head apologetically. No neurons firing today. They both looked at the evidence bag on her desk.

"So what *did* bring you in here today, Booey? You never actually said."

He slid three pages across her desk. "I found this on-line, from the archives of *Rail and Whistle Journal*. It's a magazine similar to *Model Railroader* or *Finescale Railroader*."

She nodded as if she were familiar with them.

"This particular article is a profile on Henry Becker from two and a half years ago. It's mostly about how he got started in model railroading, plus details on some of his models, but the writer also talked to Barbara Becker a little."

Claudia glanced at the pages. The magazine had published a spread on Becker, plus a brief sidebar on his wife. The main article included a tightly cropped picture of the man, holding up a model locomotive, plus a wider photo showing one of his layouts. Claudia realized this was the first time she'd seen a picture of him alive. If Mrs. Becker kept photographs of her husband in their house, she hadn't put them on public display.

"He looked like a kind man, didn't he?" said Booey.

Even in health, Becker was thin, with fine features in a narrow face that combined to give him something of a patrician appearance. But it was his eyes that drew Claudia in, for they radiated lively intelligence and an undeniable enthusiasm. Without a hint of the Alzheimer's that would doom him, he looked like he could've lived to be one hundred. She agreed that he looked kind—a person she might have enjoyed knowing.

But it was Barbara Becker who surprised her. For the picture that accompanied the sidebar, the photographer had captured her beside a window in an unguarded moment, her mouth open and her head thrown back in laughter. Her expression reflected a warmth and lack of self-consciousness that made Claudia want to laugh along with her. But she wondered if the woman had been horrified by the picture when the article came out. Her hair showed serious gray, and the window light was unflattering, revealing her age in a wrinkled neck and a network of feathery lines on her face—everything she worked so diligently to conceal with heavy makeup.

"What's interesting," said Booey, "is that in the sidebar, Mrs. Becker says she loves model railroading almost as much as her husband does. And in the main article? One of their friends is quoted as saying the same thing. But Mrs. Becker told *us* she didn't like his trains—or didn't share his passion for the hobby—something like that. Here, look."

Booey popped from his chair and moved around the desk to stand beside Claudia. He jabbed a finger on a paragraph. Claudia read: "Sharon Drake, a longtime friend of the couple, described the Beckers as 'proverbial lovebirds' who can't take their eyes off each other unless it's to look at a new model train."

Claudia skipped a paragraph in which the writer described one of Becker's newest acquisitions, then read Drake's concluding comment: "Whenever I call Barbara, I have to let the phone ring a dozen times because it takes so long for her to pry herself away from Henry, or his trains, or both." The author of the article had asked her whether that might be an exaggeration, and Drake had laughed and replied, "If it is, then it's only a small one."

While she read the rest of the story, Booey fidgeted at her side. There wasn't a lot else to learn. The author had effectively captured a man and his hobby, making more of technical details than Claudia cared to know. The sidebar on Barbara Becker was a respectful nod to the wife, a device she knew was intended to flesh out Henry's character more than anything else.

"Why would she not be honest about her interest in Mr. Becker's trains?" Booey asked.

Claudia wondered the same thing. She looked at Booey. "Do some of your magic for me," she told him. "Get me a phone number for this Drake woman. Let's see if we can put this into some kind of context."

He was halfway out the door when she stopped him. "Hey, Booey? Nice job."

"It was nothing, really. I was just trolling on-line. You would've—"

"Look, this is as good as it gets from me, so stop fishing." She smiled. "You found something good. We don't know why it's good yet, but we will."

He beamed, then pivoted into the multipurpose room, in pursuit of an unoccupied computer. Claudia went back to her notes.

After she talked to Suggs, Claudia drove into Flagg and dropped off the evidence bag at the crime lab, with little optimism that what it contained would produce anything worthwhile. The evidence clerk who logged it in chided her for not bringing it in earlier, but Claudia barely listened. She was thinking about Sharon Drake. Booey had come through with a phone number for the woman in record time, but Claudia elected not to leave a message on the answering machine when it picked up. She wanted to catch Drake cold, though she wondered now if fatigue was beginning to interfere with her judgment. She was going nowhere fast with the Becker case, and she worried that waiting for the right moment to catch Drake might be less a tactical move than an indication of inertia, which she knew could strike any investigator when a case got bogged down.

Claudia yawned and aimed her car toward the gourmet grocery store in Feather Ridge. After she picked up a sandwich for herself and Booey, she'd call again. If Drake didn't answer, she'd leave a message. End of story.

Milo Aggastino spotted her before she saw him, and he interrupted a conversation with a stock boy to boom out a greeting. "Detective Hershey! Looks like I'm not alone in working a Sunday." He said something else to the stock boy, clapped him on the back, and strode to meet her. "What can I get you? And please don't tell me a bagel and cream cheese. That's all anybody seems to want on a Sunday, and it's no substitute for real food."

Claudia smiled. "I need two sandwiches to go. Something mildly sinful. Surprise me."

"Done and done," said Aggastino. "Give me one second."

True to his word, the grocer was back shortly and handed her two fat packages. "You'll like these," he said. "I can't take credit for them—they're the work of a new deli guy I hired—but I watched what he did, and if you're disappointed, then I'm in the wrong line of work. How about coffee to go with them?"

"No thanks. I'm pretty much tanked out on caffeine for now."

Aggastino patted his vast belly. "You ought to put some weight on. You'd be surprised how much you could absorb of anything." He followed her toward the checkout lanes. "I should apologize for not calling you after your last visit here. I *did* ask around about the cat lady—casually, of course—but none of the employees had more than a vague recollection of seeing her here and there. She seemed to have about as much staying power with them as last night's dream."

"Wanda Farr was invisible to most people."

"Maybe that's just the way things are these days." Aggastino waited for Claudia to pay, then he walked her toward the door. "The old people, they're dropping like flies lately."

She looked at him curiously.

"Okay, not dropping like flies, exactly, but—do you read the obituaries? No? Well, I do." He laughed at her expression. "It sounds more gruesome than it is. I keep up so that if one of my customers dies, I can send the family a small fruit basket. It's part of a cradle-to-grave philosophy my father handed down to me. 'Milo,' he'd say, 'shake hands when new customers come into your store. Send fruit when old ones die.' I've always done that."

"Sounds like your father had good business sense."

"He did. But just lately, I wish he'd been less insistent I follow the obits. In the last ten days I've lost five customers. I didn't hear about the cat lady from the obituaries, of course, but she was the first. Mrs. Lakely and Mrs. Sapperstein—both went from sudden heart attacks. Then there was Mr. Becker and, just this Friday, Mr. Torres. He had—"

"You knew Henry Becker?"

Aggastino shrugged and held open the door. "I knew him like I know most of my customers, which is to say not much. And with Mr. Becker, it was even harder to know him because he had some kind of dementia, or at least that's what I heard. He— I'm sorry, was he a friend of yours?"

"No, but I knew of him," Claudia said quickly, surprised and grateful that for once the town's rumor mill was running on empty.

"I guess everybody did. With those long walks of his, he was becoming something of a fixture in the neighborhood. Anyway, he didn't have a lot to say, and he always looked a little lost to me. But he was nice enough, and I was sorry to hear he'd died."

"So he was one of your regulars?"

"Oh, he didn't always buy anything, but he wandered in here most days, usually by himself. Now and then he was with some woman, a flashy young thing who I took to be his nurse. That's not unusual here. Most of the Feather Ridge people can afford private nurses when they need them. Anyway, she'd sashay in like she owned the place and ignore Mr. Becker while she played to the crowd—or at least that's how it looked to me. She'd buy groceries and a fistful of lottery tickets, and she'd flirt with the stock boys. Poor Mr. Becker, he'd just sort of stand around and go 'Barbara? Barbara? Where's Barbara?' This woman would roll her eyes and say 'I'm right here, sugar plum.' But it was like she was annoyed with him."

"That's our Babs," Claudia murmured.

"Excuse me?"

"Nothing. I take it you didn't think much of her."

"Let's just say she could've been a little more respectful."

"What about Mrs. Becker?"

"Her, I never met."

They'd reached Claudia's car. Huge clouds shaped like mushrooms scuttled east across a sky so blue it almost looked fake. She watched a plane shoot through one of them.

"They're beautiful, aren't they?" said Aggastino. He smiled. "My theory is that when God decided to create the heavens and the earth, he started right here. There isn't another state in the union that displays it all so perfectly."

"You might be onto something there," Claudia replied. She unlocked her car door and threw the sandwiches on the passenger's seat, then slid behind the wheel. "Thanks for the personal treatment."

"Anytime."

She started up the car. "One last thing? If anything else occurs to you about Mr. Becker—if you remember anything more, anything at all—would you get in touch?"

Aggastino's jaw dropped. "I . . . a second ago we were talking about clouds. Now we're back on Mr. Becker? I can't believe that's not by design. Are you saying that his death wasn't an accident?"

"You've still got my business card, right?"

"My afternoon just went down the toilet." The grocer leaned toward Claudia's window. "I suppose your whole day has been there. If . . . sure. I'll call."

"And—"

"Yes, that too. I'll be discreet."

Claudia thanked him and waved as she pulled away. He didn't wave back. She understood. The grocer liked her just a little less. She could hear it in his voice, see it in his expression—all familiar territory. Some people sprinkled fairy dust wherever they went. Not her. She powdered the world with toxic information, and they would look at her, and they would wonder . . . *Does she* like *this?* They would wonder, *Doesn't she see the beauty all around her?*

A pickup burdened with a frayed couch and love seat belched gray exhaust in front of her. Nothing was tied down. The taillights didn't work. Someone ought to pull that guy over. But not her, not today. She *did* have a life, and she didn't live it all in the dark.

When the road widened into four lanes, Claudia sped around the vehicle. It was Sunday. She would check messages, eat at her desk, and go home, maybe spruce the place up. If she couldn't reach Drake from the station, then she would do that from the house, but that was it. She did so know the clouds were beautiful. Did so, did so, did so.

CHAPTER 22

SHARON DRAKE DIDN'T GET IT. She thought Claudia was making a courtesy call to inform her that her friend's husband had died. She didn't get that Claudia was talking about murder, and she didn't get it because she was too drunk to get anything except a fresh twist of lime for her gin and tonic. She told Claudia that much without prompting, and she told her a whole lot more in a phone call that should've topped out at fifteen minutes but ballooned into thirty.

Claudia threw a load of whites into the washer while she considered their conversation. Her left ear was still numb from the press of the phone. She imagined Drake was merely numb all over. If it was five o'clock in Florida, then it was four o'clock in Chicago, which meant Drake must've started drinking seriously by two o'clock or earlier. But her "newly acquired fondness for liquor," as she'd put it to Claudia, played no role in the disintegration of her friendship with Barbara Becker.

"Honey," she'd said in a Texas drawl she hadn't quite erased, "after Barbara moved south, she turned into a hermit or she turned into a bitch. Or she turned into both. She never called me or even returned my messages. She didn't come to visit, and she sure as hell didn't invite me down. I don't know what happened, and frankly, I stopped caring after she couldn't be bothered to send so much as a sympathy card when my Bobby died six months ago."

Claudia set the washer dial to PERMANENT PRESS and turned it on. So there it was, Barbara Becker caught up in another lie. Her R&R trips to Chicago had nothing to do with former acquaintances. She understood why Drake would feel hurt.

The two women had been good friends for seven years, almost from the day Drake and her husband had moved to Chicago from Houston. They met at a country club where they played lousy tennis, enjoyed reasonably skilled bridge, and ate leisurely lunches twice a week.

"Why Barbara and I hit it off is a mystery," said Drake, "because our personalities were like night and day. In fact, if anyone would've been likely to move to Florida, you'd think it would be me. I've detested Chicago since we moved here. Too damned windy. Too damned cold. But Barbara—she loved it. She'd begun to put in a beautiful garden out back, she had season tickets to the theater, she was talking about remodeling the house. Why on earth she up and left, I'll never understand."

She hadn't said *understand*. She'd said *unnershtan*, but it was close enough. Claudia had learned how to distill language from drunks long ago. She had also learned how to put aside impatience and let them ramble, which Drake seemed perfectly content to do.

"Look, I get that once Henry went and contracted that head disease, that, that. . . ."

"Alzheimer's?" Claudia supplied helpfully.

"Yeah, that. Once he got that, life as they knew it was on its way to being over. I am one hell of a lot more sensitive than Barbara, if you care to know the truth, and so I recognized that things were going to change. But from what I could see, the man was a long way from being brain dead. He was a little forgetful, and he got moody, and now and then he'd do mildly peculiar things—but he could still carry on a conversation. There was no reason to move him, and there was certainly no reason to bring in that trollop Barbara found in a nursing home."

"I thought Henry liked her," said Claudia.

"Well, honey, of *course* he liked her! Just because his brain wasn't firing on all cylinders didn't mean the rest of him wasn't. She's the kind of woman who can turn men into mush just by batting her eyelashes, which she loved to do. My Bobby was ten years older than Henry, and I was afraid he'd have a stroke just by being in the same room with her."

Claudia heard ice cubes rattle. "But Henry was devoted to Barbara, no?" she asked. "And she was devoted to him?"

"Oh, you are naïve." Drake huffed impatiently. "Being devoted to each other and having a healthy respect for firmer, younger flesh are not mutually exclusive concepts."

Of course, she'd asked Drake about the Beckers' interest in model trains, and Drake repeated what she'd said in the magazine article. Henry and Barbara both enjoyed the hobby, though Drake insisted that Barbara's interest was dependent on Henry's.

"If one day he decided he liked bungee jumping, then she'd probably get involved with it, too," Drake said. "Don't get me wrong; she genuinely admired the trains, and she could practically write a book on what was what with them—that's how much she knew. But there was an equation there. And if you subtracted out Henry, the trains would be less than knickknacks to her. That's what happened when he got diagnosed with that disease. Her interest in trains plain out flatlined. She'd keep him company while he tinkered with them, but she couldn't have cared less."

Then Drake began to cry. Not counting her Bobby, she'd been through three husbands, bypass surgery, an addiction to painkillers, and two terrifying years of actually being broke. She had three grown children. All of them avoided her. So did Bobby's dog, a Chihuahua that trembled constantly and peed on the carpets during thunderstorms.

Claudia thought she might lose her patience after all, but Drake made her point just in time. "I know what pain is all about, but Barbara didn't. She'd never been crapped on in her life. She had a storybook romance and a storybook marriage. Up until the day some doctor trashed it all with a single word, the only bothersome thing in her life was a touch of arthritis—and that hardly even slowed her down. But after the Alzheimer's thing, she turned numb, and then I suppose she got panicked, and I should've stayed with her, but I didn't. I let that floozy waltz in, and I know, I *know* that she wound up in Florida because of her."

The washing machine chugged monotonously. Claudia realized with a start that it had already completed its fill cycle and she hadn't moved. She grabbed a rag and plucked a can of Pledge from a wire shelf above the dryer, then headed for the living room, her mind still hostage to the woman's boozy voice.

According to Drake, the move had been sudden. Barbara Becker casually talked about the possibility of leaving, and then one day the Beckers were simply gone. She continued:

"You know what I got? I got a call from the damned airport! Can you believe it? She made all these apologetic noises, said something about it being too hard to say good-bye face to face, and told me she'd call as soon as they were settled and we could talk, really talk. Like that ever happened. Fact is, the only thing she apparently cared about after she left was the half-assed garden she started, which she must've hired someone to keep up, because it's gorgeous now. But the rest of her house, she let it all go to hell, just like her friends."

"I'm sorry," Claudia said.

"Yeah, well, when you talk to her next, you just tell her that she's got dandelions in her grass and the paint is peeling around the window frames. *That* oughta get her attention."

Claudia had offered something sympathetic, then managed to extract the names and numbers of a few more of Mrs. Becker's

Chicago friends before they hung up, at which point she would have been happy for a drink herself. But that could come later. She had calls to make, furniture to polish, a carpet to vacuum, and two more loads of laundry to do. Plenty enough to keep herself occupied in the space that Robin and Dennis would have shared on any other Sunday night.

She was dreaming, something convoluted about the dentist, when the phone flogged her from sleep. At first she mistook it for the alarm and batted at it with a hand still caught beneath the sheet. The kitten hit the floor at the same time the clock did, and Claudia throttled to a sitting position. Her mind spun on possibilities, none of them good, as she grabbed the phone and creaked a hello.

"Babs is missing."

Claudia tried to clear the cobwebs. "Mrs. Becker?" She groped on the floor for the alarm clock and squinted at the red numbers. Five in the morning.

"She's missing, and so is my jewelry and car."

There was an edge of hysteria in the woman's voice. Claudia snapped on the light. "Slow down, Mrs. Becker, slow down." She cleared her voice. "Now what do you mean, 'she's missing'?"

"I mean she's missing, Detective! How hard is that to understand?"

Claudia automatically reached for her cigarettes, remembering in the next second that they were on the kitchen counter and she was on a phone with an actual cord. "Tell me more," she said, rising. "How do you know she's missing?"

"We were supposed to have dinner at eight. She had plans to go out—I'm not sure where—but we'd agreed to eat together later. I let her use the Jag, which I often did, and I really didn't think much of it when she was late. She's young, after all. But by nine o'clock I was getting irritated, so I went to watch some TV while I waited for her to come in. I guess I drifted off."

The kitten leaped back onto the bed and found the warm spot that Claudia had vacated. He began to groom himself. She watched him distractedly, listening to Mrs. Becker carry on. Her ten-thousand-dollar Rolex was missing. So was a diamond necklace, her pearls, and two rings. There might be more; she hadn't looked thoroughly yet.

Claudia rubbed sleep from her eyes. "You're sure she took them?"

"Well, who else?" she snapped. "She's gone, along with my Jaguar. My jewelry is gone, too. Now are you coming over or not?" Her tone held no forgiveness. She had refused to see Kensington as a murderer but apparently had no trouble imagining her as a thief.

Claudia looked at the clock again. "How is it you discovered your jewelry missing at this hour?" she asked.

The woman sounded exasperated. "Oh, for heaven's sake. I don't know why . . . all right, never mind." She sighed dramatically. "This may sound foolish, but I keep my watch on the bathroom counter. When I got up to go to bed, I remembered I hadn't taken my arthritis medication, so I went into the bathroom to get it out of the medicine cabinet. That's when I noticed the watch was gone. Of course, I was only half awake, and at first I thought that perhaps I'd put it in my jewelry box. That would've been unusual for me, but . . . well, old people sometimes do unusual things when they're distracted."

"I understand."

"That's when I realized that other pieces of my jewelry were missing as well."

"I'm surprised they weren't locked in a safe."

"Locked in a— Detective, this is my *home*! It never occurred to me that I needed to think like a thief myself in order to protect my property! Now, are you coming over?"

Claudia looked at the kitten and the warm bed. A fragment of the dream flickered in and out of her consciousness. "Give me twenty minutes," she said. "I'm on my way."

To her astonishment, the crime-scene techs got to the Becker estate ten minutes after Claudia called them en route from her house. She filled them in, then escorted them to the bedroom and adjoining bathroom. She told them what she was looking for and where to dust for prints, but the exercise was more for Mrs. Becker's benefit than anything else. Kensington had lived in the house, was staying there still. Finding evidence of her in any of the rooms would prove nothing, unless luck blew their way and she'd been foolish enough to leave prints right in the jewelry box itself.

Mrs. Becker appeared rumpled, but she presented a calmer demeanor than she had shown on the phone. She rested her cane against the kitchen counter and busied herself making coffee while Claudia called in an APB on the Jaguar. No Jag. No jewelry. No Babs. Probably no Aaron Rivens either.

Surprise, surprise.

"Detective Hershey," Mrs. Becker said tentatively, turning from the sink, "I don't want to think what I believe you're thinking right now." She hobbled to the table and set down a cup of coffee for Claudia, then clutched her robe tighter around her, as if a sudden chill had pierced the air. "Stealing is one thing, but . . . I can't even say it."

Claudia blew into the cup. "Go ahead, Mrs. Becker. You think that Miss Kensington might've been involved in your husband's murder. You think that maybe she isn't quite the woman she presented herself to be."

Mrs. Becker nodded. She poured herself some coffee, then joined Claudia at the table, groaning slightly as she sat. "Please forgive me for waking you. I suppose I should've just called 911, but you'd written your home number on your business card and—"

Claudia waved away her concern. "Doesn't matter. Dispatch only would've called me anyway." She didn't give voice to her real thought, which was that it would be a cold day in hell before she passed out her home number again. To anyone. "I don't suppose you have any idea where Miss Kensington might've gone?"

Mrs. Becker shook her head. "No. I tried not to interfere with her privacy." Her voice quavered. "Obviously, that was a mistake. Maybe everything I did with her was a mistake."

"There's more, isn't there."

"Well . . . yes." She took a sip of coffee. "I didn't tell you this earlier because I was afraid of how it would sound, but now, it may be more important than I thought."

"Go on."

"About a month after Babs moved in with Henry and me, she asked for more money. Frankly, I thought she was being paid quite handsomely already, but she was looking into the future in a way that I wasn't. She told me that perhaps she'd been rash in making such a dramatic move, especially to a small town, and said she was worried about how she'd be left once Henry died. She'd forfeited a steady job, she'd given up her friends, she'd moved from a lively city to a place that held no prospects."

Claudia knew what was coming. She nodded for Mrs. Becker to continue.

"I think I've told you how much Henry adored her. I did, too. Well, Babs had a way of being persuasive, and because I felt panicky at the thought of being without her help all over again, I said that perhaps we could work something out. She suggested that she be included in his will."

"That didn't seem calculated to you?"

"Not at the time, no. In fact, I thought her proposal reflected a shrewd business sense that these days seems very uncommon in a young person. Part of me admired her, not only for that, but ironically because she wasn't insisting on money up front. I saw this as an investment in each other's future. When Henry passed on, she would have enough money to comfortably go her own way. Meanwhile, I wouldn't have to worry about her abandoning us midstream."

"How much money?"

"One hundred thousand dollars."

"That was the figure you gave her?"

"Actually, no. I suggested sixty thousand, imagining that to be adequate for a new start. She said that one hundred thousand would be more appropriate. I didn't argue very strenuously. Truthfully, one hundred thousand dollars to me or Henry wasn't much."

"And your husband was okay with this?"

"Of course. I mean, I'm not sure he entirely grasped what our agreement was all about—it wasn't always easy to know what he really understood or didn't by then—but he went along. He and I stopped at a lawyer's office just outside of town and had a codicil drawn up. It took no time at all. I never gave it another thought, not even when you told me Henry had been murdered."

"Now you do."

Mrs. Becker's shoulders slumped. "My jewelry and car are missing, and so is Babs. I trusted her with everything, and I'd told her all that you'd told me. She had to know she would have come under scrutiny. She would know she had to leave, and apparently she wasn't going to leave entirely empty-handed." Mrs. Becker shuddered. "What happens now?"

Claudia swallowed the rest of her coffee and stood. "We find Miss Kensington. That's what we do."

CHAPTER 23

IF RON PETERS WERE CLAUDIA'S TYPE, which he was not, and if he weren't married, which he was, she would have leaped from her chair and knocked him over in an embrace certain to leave him with carpet burn. As is, she stood so quickly she had to steady the table before her platter of French toast slid to the floor.

"Sarge! You're back early, and thank goodness, because you have no idea how— What's with the cast?" A sling supported his left arm at a ninety-degree angle. "Vacations are supposed to be good for you."

Peters flexed the hand protruding from his cast. "And mine was, up until the time we stopped the van for a surprise visit with my wife's brother. He was painting his house. I made the mistake of offering to help on the second story. The sun was out. The beer was cold. Unfortunately, the ladder had a bad rung—which I suspected on my way up and knew for sure in the split second it took me to go down."

Claudia winced.

"Yeah, but it could've been worse. It might've been my leg." Peters pulled out a chair when Claudia moved to reclaim her seat. "The chief told me where to find you." He looked around. "I've never understood how you can see in here. It's dark as a cave."

The bowling alley didn't open to customers for another hour, but the owner welcomed cops and firefighters in early while he prepped the lanes. Claudia had anchored herself to a cocktail table in the bar, a dimly lit room with two pool tables and a dartboard. She could think without distraction here; and if she was lucky, as she was this morning, the short-order cook had already fired up the grill.

"I can't believe you cut your vacation short," Claudia said. "I'm thrilled that you did—for one thing, I'm lousy at doing roll call—but still. . . ."

"Well, the thing is, we got back late last night, and I couldn't see wasting my leftover days hanging out at home. So I came in. When the chief saw me, he went nuts. He smiled so wide you'd think he had a dinner plate jammed in his jaw. If my arm wasn't in a cast, I swear he would've pulled me into a bear hug. I *never* saw him like that."

Claudia told him about Suggs's ulcer. "Getting it under control seems to have made a huge difference in his outlook."

"Oh. So you mean he's becoming a human being?"

They both smiled.

"You know, I wondered about an ulcer." he said. He looked at her plate. "Go ahead and eat."

He cracked his knuckles lightly, a pure Peters reflex that drove Claudia wild. But having him back—early no less—she could live with it. She pushed some French toast onto her fork.

"Yeah, he was colorful, all right," he continued. "When I asked him what I'd missed, he grabbed his neck and played like he was choking, then told me you'd give me chapter and verse."

"So you don't know anything?"

"I heard that Mitch shaved his mustache off last week, and I saw that we got new computers. I also met Booey, and I just now learned that the chief has an ulcer. That's what I know."

Claudia paused with her fork at her lips. Mitch had shaved off his mustache? A *week* and she hadn't noticed?

"So is this going to be a long story?" he asked.

"Long enough for you to have some coffee. I recommend a large."

He groaned good-naturedly. Everything about him was good-natured. Claudia watched him head for the snack counter, then polished off her breakfast while she waited for his return. *Mitch had shaved off his mustache?*

They got down to business a few minutes later. Peters sipped steadily at his coffee while Claudia laid out the Farr and Becker cases in chronological order. Now and then he popped his knuckles but, otherwise, did not interrupt. By the time she finished, bowlers had begun to cluster around a rack of house balls. Claudia ignored them. The overhead lights in the bar would remain off until it opened at eleven for the early beer crowd.

"I can't say I'm sorry I missed the action," Peters finally said. He lifted his cup, then set it down, seemingly surprised to discover it empty. "Two old people dead, both drowned, both murdered. One, a man, on the right side of the tracks. The other, a woman—definitely on the wrong side." He worried at a cuticle on his good hand. "No wonder the chief's ulcer picked now to blow up on him. I'm surprised *you* don't have one."

"I'm probably working on it," said Claudia. She looked at her own cup, annoyed to find it empty, grateful that it was. "When it was just Wanda Farr, and Raynor looked good for it, things made sense. With

— 159 —

him out of the picture, I don't know."

"But he could be lying about the pocket, couldn't he? He could've made the whole thing up, just to take the heat off himself."

"I wish," said Claudia. "It would be convenient as hell." She thought about the piece of denim material Raynor had triumphantly handed her the night of the cockfight. She thought about his expression when he told her where he got it—how he got it. "I wished he was lying so bad that I talked myself into believing it, then I talked myself right out of it. What he said, in his own way, it had the feel of truth."

He'd claimed that when he went back to Farr's trailer for the second time, someone was already there, someone low to the ground and deep in the shadows beside the trailer door. He didn't see the person at first, but his dog did, and it alerted him with the same gurgling sound that Claudia herself had heard and would never forget. Raynor looked into the shadows at the same time the person looked back. A man, he thought. A man with what looked like a gun pointed at him. Hard to know in the dark, but foolish to risk being wrong.

"If I hadn't've been so distracted, I would've known something was up," Raynor said. "Usually there's a bunch of those diseased cats hanging around the outside of Farr's trailer. They would've skittered under the trailer once they spotted me and the dog, of course, but it was night and I should've still seen a flash of those glow-in-the-dark eyes they have. They're not as damned clever as everybody seems to think they are."

For Raynor, it was obviously familiar territory. Claudia wondered how many times he'd taunted his old neighbor at night.

"Anyway," Raynor continued, "when I saw that gun aimed at my head, I dropped flat as a manhole cover and told the dog to go get him. He tried, too."

That's when Raynor had dangled the pocket. "The guy was quick, but not so fast that my dog didn't get his teeth sunk into his ass end. I just wish he'd of taken a chunk of flesh too."

If Raynor's story could be believed—and Claudia reluctantly leaned in that direction—then she wished the dog had drawn blood as well. There was just the pocket, though, nipped cleanly from the intruder's faded blue jeans as if by a seam ripper.

"His car must've been on just the other side of the trailer, because I didn't see it. But I sure as hell heard it when he took off. I don't know what it was. I can only tell you it didn't sound like a truck, because trucks I know—almost like I know dogs."

He refused to concede that the shadowy figure might have been a woman, because the person was tall and, he insisted, "No way would a woman get away from one of my dogs." Claudia had refrained from commenting.

She pushed the episode from her mind and looked at Peters. He was toying with a coffee cup, waiting out her silence.

"You know how they do that? he said. "How they make dogs go silent?"

Claudia shook her head.

"There's surgery that a handful of veterinarians do for situations like when someone's maybe threatened with eviction if they can't get their dog to shut up. Obviously Raynor's got a different motive."

"Yeah. Like intimidation."

"But there's a bright spot in all this, right? The lab ought to be able to give us a fix on the pocket."

"I don't know, Ron. It's off to the FBI and, theoretically, yeah, they'll be able to match the pocket to the manufacturer and maybe even give us a brand name. But that could take up to ten days, and without fibers to match, I'm not sure what good any of it will do, at least in the short term. If Raynor's dog had taken some blood with the pocket, we'd get some DNA, but even with that, it'd only support a conviction, which—"

"—we'll never get if we don't get a fix on a suspect first."

"You got it."

"So all we know so far is that someone besides Raynor had a reason to want Wanda Farr dead."

Nothing in Peters's tone hinted at an accusation, but the reality of his words overwhelmed Claudia with defeat. If Suggs had been there and offered her half a week's severance pay to slink back to Cleveland, she would probably take it.

"The Becker case," he said, "at least that sounds promising."

"I'm sorry, what?"

"Becker? It's got to be Kensington and maybe her Aaron Rivens. *Probably* Rivens. Like you said, they knew each other before, and you saw firsthand that they're lovers now. That can't be a coincidence."

He was right. Their history didn't lie.

Peters shrugged. "The way I see it is, they played a major head game on Mrs. Becker. The woman's distressed over her husband's diagnosis, she's fearful of the future, she's not sure how she's going to keep her own sanity together while she watches him lose his. Kensington—and then Rivens a little later—they buddy up to her, get her confidence. They're like these scam artists who prey on old people's fears and persuade them to pay for new roofs or buy a whole new air conditioner, only Kensington and Rivens were a lot more sophisticated and they had higher stakes."

Sophisticated wasn't the word that sprang to Claudia's mind, but he had a point.

"All they had to do was wait for an opportunity," Peters continued. "When it came, they drowned the old guy in the pool, then chucked his body into the No-Name. He had Alzheimer's and a pattern of wandering, so what they put together was a convenient tragedy. And Kensington, what with her history of targeting old guys, she had to be the brains behind this. She— Wow, someone just rolled a strike."

An exultant whoop from the lanes sailed into the bar. Claudia pictured an old man with a slow ball high-fiving his teammates. Good for him. She turned her attention back to Peters.

". . . where she screwed up was in assuming everyone would buy into the idea that Becker's drowning was an accident." Peters held up a finger. "One, she took us for backwater stooges who'd fall all over ourselves to help Mrs. Becker get her husband buried proper. You know how I know that?" He held up another finger. "Because two, she sure didn't count on an autopsy."

And she was almost right, thought Claudia. She twisted her napkin into a spiral and nodded for Peters to continue.

"When things didn't go the way they planned, when everything backfired instead, Kensington and Rivens cut their losses. They took what they could and vanished. And this *Babs*—the arrogance! She didn't even care anymore what we knew or suspected."

Claudia followed his thinking. As expected, the crime lab had quickly put a match to Kensington's prints on file and those they'd found liberally distributed in Mrs. Becker's bathroom and bedroom. The younger woman hadn't even made an effort to conceal them in the jewelry case itself.

Peters knocked lightly on the table to get her attention. Claudia looked up from her napkin.

"How long have I known you, Lieutenant?"

"Long enough to call me Claudia when we're drinking coffee in a bowling alley."

It was old territory for both of them, and Peters grinned. "I still call my daddy 'sir.' You really think I can bring myself to call *you* by your given name?"

She flicked her napkin at him. He flicked it back. "I can never read anything much by your face, Lieutenant Claudia."

She smiled.

"What I *have* learned by now is that your silence has a language. And since you haven't said anything to my masterful summary, I have to think that what seems so obvious to me doesn't sit the same way with you. Am I right?"

Suggs would've been out of his chair, ready to throttle her for not spitting out an answer. If he still had a mustache, Moody would finger it, and Carella would be talking into the silence in a bid to hurry her along. Peters sat unblinking, with the same Zen patience he showed when he filled out inventory forms and scheduling sheets.

"The problem I have with all of this," she finally said, "is not with what's obvious. It's with what isn't. All of Kensington's moves have been obvious, almost predictable, at least in retrospect. But Barbara Becker . . . now there's some kind of queen bee who looks to me less and less the way she appears."

"You lost me."

"Well, Mrs. Becker's smart. I have trouble seeing her getting as addled as she would have to be to go along with Kensington as much as she did. Kensington suggested a move to Florida? Mrs. Becker went along. Kensington insisted on a codicil? She went along. Kensington left Henry alone? No problem. And anyway, the idea that she'd just pluck Kensington out of a nursing home where she was working as an aide . . . I don't know. It doesn't play—and what else doesn't play is the Houdini act she pulled on her friends."

The bar's fluorescent lights flickered twice, then flashed on. They hissed steadily. Claudia nodded to a young man who positioned himself behind the bar. It wouldn't be long now before they'd have company.

"Where my money is, Ron? She's sandbagging us on something."

"Are you thinking that Mrs. Becker is working *with* Kensington and Rivens? If she is, then why didn't *she* bolt too?"

"Good question, Ron. It could be that—"

Claudia's cell phone rang. She picked up and listened, mouthing "Sally" to Peters. She muttered "uh-huh, uh-huh" a few times, shook her head, and disconnected.

"Sally's in love with my cell phone," she told him. "She doesn't have to fret over codes. Anyway, I guess we should get back. She says Booey's practically wetting his pants, he's so excited about something he wants to show me. He won't tell her what."

Peters laughed. "I only met him briefly, but I bet he even sleeps with enthusiasm."

"Wouldn't doubt it."

On their way out, they waved to the bartender, then paused at the snack counter to put in a takeout order. Sally wanted a burger and fries. Claudia watched the bowlers while they waited. It occurred to her that the dispatcher might be covering for the chief. She hoped not.

CHAPTER 24

NO MATTER WHAT HE SAID, Booey clearly believed he had something. It showed in his voice. It showed in his posture. Claudia thought it even showed in his hair, which stood in sparks off his head from his anxious poking at it. He'd brought in his own computer, a high-end laptop that he described in tones so reverential she wondered if he lit incense in front of it at night. He ushered her to a chair in front of the computer before she had her purse off her shoulder.

Booey had chosen a desk in the multipurpose room as far from the distraction of the dispatch console as possible. "This is probably nothing," he told her sheepishly, "but it won't take long."

Claudia slid her purse to the floor. "Go for broke, Booey."

He cleared a screen saver from the computer, revealing an image of a train. The perspective showed a locomotive looming in the foreground. The screen rendered the image sharply, impressively.

"That's a freight train," he said. "It's not real, though. It's one of Mr. Becker's models."

"Okaaay," she said slowly. "And I'm looking at it because. . .?"

"Well, it's just an introductory shot—sort of an opener to get us started. See, I went through the digital pictures I'd taken at the Becker place, and I put them in a certain kind of order, and then finally I burned them onto a CD-ROM so that everything I show you will make perfect sense."

She hoped they would get to that soon.

"Pretty good image, isn't it?"

"It's terrific, Booey."

"Thank you."

He stood behind her so that his voice floated over her head. With every word he spoke, she felt his breath move her hair. She would never make it through his entire presentation that way, so she asked him to pull up a chair alongside her. After he complied, she looked back at the train on the screen and told him to continue.

He put his hand on the mouse but stopped short of clicking to the next frame. "This is a little awkward," he said uncomfortably. "The pictures, well, they're all from that day when I, you know, went unauthorized into the Beckers' garden, where Mr. Becker had his G-scale train display. Those are the large models. You probably remember. . . ."

Sure she did. She'd wanted to kill him. "That was then. This is now. I presume you have a reason for bringing it up again, so let's just move on."

He clicked the mouse. The first image vanished, replaced by a panoramic scene that captured a horizontal slice of the garden. Booey must have crouched to get the shot, because except for a hint of the patio's screening in the background, the image showed a scaled landscape that appeared real. A tall tree and a scattering of scrawny trees and shrubs that Claudia couldn't name partially concealed a train track that ran parallel to a canal. The canal appeared to widen in the middle, but it was further obscured by yellowed grass. She remembered Becker's impressive displays inside the house—villages, city streets with skyscrapers, beaches, farm communities—each of them elaborately detailed and fixed on camouflaged scaffolding. The image on Booey's computer, though realistic, lacked the excitement and mastery of his other work.

"I'm pretty sure he wasn't finished with this," said Booey. "I was standing at a distance and so you can't tell it on this picture, but some of the details are a little rough, and part of the painting he did is spotty. But watch when I zoom in closer to this." He pointed at some of the yellow grass in the image, then clicked the mouse. "Now look."

Claudia leaned forward and studied the new picture. It took her eyes a second to adjust, and at first she didn't see anything but the grass, a tree, and a shadowy cluster of shrubs. Then she realized that Becker had included a figure by the shrubs.

"That's clever," she said. "What is that? A person?"

"Watch." The image disappeared and a new one took its place. "This zooms in even more."

Now it showed more clearly. Claudia could make out the figure well enough to understand that Becker had crafted a person who appeared to be kneeling or sitting, and reaching toward some . . . rocks? She sat back in her chair and removed her glasses to rub her eyes.

"It's not a great angle," said Booey, "and it's not up to Mr. Becker's standards. I think he probably just found a doll of some sort and then dressed it up."

Claudia yawned. "It's no Barbie doll, that's for sure." She put her glasses back on and looked at the screen again. "Do you have any more shots, or is this it? I'm not sure I get what you're driving at."

"Watch the next one. This one brings you in even closer."

She was about to tell him to just explain the point of his demonstration when the new image flashed onto the screen. She sighed and looked, then stiffened. They weren't rocks. They were cats, a dozen or more of them, each poorly constructed and, even to her untrained eyes, out of scale. But they were cats. More significantly, in this shot, the figure was that of a woman.

"I'm looking at Wanda Farr and her cats, aren't I," Claudia said quietly. "This is the No-Name Pond."

"You think so?" Booey's voice hitched an octave. "Because that's what I thought, but then I decided, no, my imagination was probably running away with me. Sometimes it does that, and so I almost didn't show you. I thought that maybe Mr. Becker was only—"

"Oh, no. It's Wanda Farr. It's her. It's her, and those are some of her strays, and Becker knew her. Damn it!" Claudia exploded off the chair. "Carella, Moody, Peters—anybody who's in, get over here, now!" She pivoted to Booey and pointed at him. "You—you're promoted. I don't know to what, but you're promoted. Now go find your uncle."

"Promoted! Wow, I— But wait, I have other pictures. Some of the angles—"

"And we're going to look at them all. I need to make a quick phone call, and then we're going to look at them again and again and again. Now go. Get the chief and then back this up." She gestured at the computer screen. "I want the whole show all over, from the beginning. You just gave us something huge."

The fingerprint examiner at Flagg County's crime lab balked—not at her request, but at the urgency. "Listen, this is nothing against Indian Run—I know you think you have something with the Farr case—but besides Flagg's own cases, we serve a lot of small departments. We have a backlog that could stretch from here to Tallahassee."

Claudia wished she'd taken the time to personally meet more of the crime lab's people. She didn't know the examiner—a Liz Hurd—and though the woman sounded sympathetic, she wasn't likely to be persuaded.

"Look," said Claudia, "all I'm asking is that you pull the glass out of evidence again and take another look at it. You can do that, can't you?"

"We can dust it with fluorescent powder and check it under high-intensity light," Hurd replied, exasperation evident in her tone. "But it'll take a day or two. I can't get to it any faster."

The smudged fingerprint on the glass at Farr's trailer showed only four points of identification, not enough for a match. But a fluorescent examination—potential gold. It might reveal more, maybe even ten or twelve points. The lab could shoot a photo and work off that for a match. It could work, and if it did, the match might give them Farr's killer.

"Please," said Claudia. "I need this."

Hurd let a moment pass. "You should've asked for this sooner, you know. Like when you found the victim."

Nothing would be gained by getting into a pissing match with the woman. If Hurd had been around the block even once, then she already understood that precious few fingerprints ever went beyond routine analysis. Of course, it didn't help to know that Hurd was right, or close enough to being right for Claudia to chafe. She did sit on the prints too long. She'd waffled with indecision. Plain and simple. A beginner's mistake, and a big one.

"I'd consider it a personal favor if you'd try to rush things, Ms. Hurd. I'll owe you."

"That's what everybody says," she muttered, but Claudia sensed some give in her tone. A second later, when Hurd said she'd try, Claudia thanked her with uncharacteristic enthusiasm. As soon as she hung up, she asked Sally to fax a formal request to Hurd's attention, then returned to the multipurpose room where the others were waiting.

"About time, Hershey," said Suggs. He stood in front of the laptop with his arms crossed. "Booey's gone about as numb in the mouth as you are and won't tell me what's going on. I'm about out of patience."

"Sorry for the delay," Claudia said, ignoring his sarcasm. She took a place beside Peters. "Where's Mitch and Emory?"

"While you were sucking up breakfast at the bowling alley, I sent them out to a traffic accident that was turning unfriendly fast," said Suggs. "Two pickups and a car. No injuries, but seven people involved."

"You sent them *now*? Now's when we need them most."

Suggs held up a hand. "I know that, Hershey, but here's a little reality check for you. Much as I might want to throw everyone I got onto these cases, and as much as I know you want me to, I can't put the whole town on hold while we figure things out. All of patrol had somethin' going and I needed a man out there, so I sent Moody. He radioed in for backup because some joker was startin' to take swings at the driver who rammed him. I had no choice but to put Carella on it. They'll be back before long, all right?"

"I'm sorry. You're right."

Suggs nodded. "Damned right I'm right. So what is it that's got you all worked up?"

Claudia turned to Booey. "It's your show, Boo." Had she just called him Boo? She shook her head. "Show them what you just showed me."

This time, she narrated, at least up until the point when Booey put some additional pictures on the screen. They all captured parts of the same scene, and though one included what must have been the footbridge, none showed the doll-like figure or cats as clearly. Still, together, they made a powerful statement for a link between the two victims.

"Wanda Farr and Henry Becker both wandered," said Claudia. "They lived on opposite sides of the train track, but both were in walking distance of it. Farr included the No-Name in her walks because there were strays there. Becker included it because he loved trains. Even though trains don't run by the No-Name anymore, it still had a track. That was attraction enough for him. It's no coincidence that he put Farr in his model display."

"Wow," Peters said softly. "I can't figure out if this is a lucky break or rotten luck."

"Maybe neither," said Suggs. "Look, this thing makes me uneasy—I'll grant you that—but I don't see how you can make a case that the murders are related. Farr and Becker were as different as you and me, Hershey. Why would the same person want them both dead?"

"Because maybe Wanda Farr saw the killer dump Becker's body in the No-Name."

"And the killer saw her witness it?" said Peters.

The chief made a face. "Sounds pretty speculative to me."

Claudia reminded him that the medical examiner's reports indicated both had died around the same time.

"Yeah, so? If the killer saw Farr when he dumped the body in the pond, don't you think he would've panicked? Don't you think he'd just bang her on the head or shoot her? Why go through all the trouble of finding her at home, pouring liquor down her throat, and drowning her in the tub?"

"Because he needed it to look like an accident as much as he needed the Becker drowning to look like an accident."

From the corner of her eye, Claudia saw Booey's hand waving tentatively. He'd been plowing the air that way through her entire exchange with Suggs. "Yeah, what, Booey?"

"Sorry. I don't mean to interrupt."

"Go ahead, go ahead."

"Okay. I . . . well, would it mean much if the display in Becker's garden was different now?" He jangled coins in his pocket when they looked at him. "I mean, different from what's in my pictures?"

"Different how?" said Claudia.

"Different like if things were missing? If—"

"Criminy, son!" Suggs put his hands on his hips. "What the hell are you trying to say, and can you just please get it out already?"

Booey straightened like an army grunt at attention. "Sorry." He cleared his throat. "What I'm saying is that when Lieutenant Hershey and I went back to the Becker place, that time we saw Miss Kensington and the ponytail guy at the pool, I had a chance to look in the garden again." He glanced at Claudia. "You remember? This was when Miss Kensington had gone inside to get Mrs. Becker for us?"

She nodded.

"I didn't have my camera with me, and I didn't make any kind of connection to the first time I saw the garden display. But later, after I fooled with these pictures, I realized that on the second trip, the doll and the cats were gone. Everything else was there. But not those. Someone must've been in the garden. Someone must've taken them out. Does that mean anything?"

"You're sure about what you saw?"

"I'm sure."

Claudia grinned. "Then off the top? I'd say it means a whole lot, Booey. You've just been promoted again."

"What's this about a promotion?" said Suggs.

"I want another look at the pond."

"The— Hershey, what are you imaginin' you'll find out there, all this time after Becker's been dead?"

"The last time we were out there, we thought Becker was an accidental drowning. This gives us a new perspective. A new perspective means a new look."

"And I suppose this 'new look' has to be now?"

"No point in waiting."

Suggs sighed. "You think you can handle that on your own, or do you need a whole army? 'Cause I need Sergeant Peters here, and your two sidekicks aren't back yet." He gave Peters a meaningful look.

"Lieutenant?" Peters said. "I think I'll just excuse myself, if that's all right. I need to see what came in on the overnight reports."

"That's fine, Ron. Booey and I can handle the pond. Chief, you want to come?"

"Nooo, I do not want to come, Hershey. Number one, it's busy here. Number two, I'm still pluckin' spurs out of my socks from the last time I was out there. Number three, the first press call on Becker's murder came in just before Booey's picture show here. From a radio guy, no less. He told me they aired a little news brief late last night. It didn't have any details. That's what he wants now—and you know this means the other press people will be callin' next."

"Rotten luck. I thought maybe we'd catch a break and they wouldn't pick up on this for a while."

"Wishful thinking." Suggs tapped the laptop with a finger. "I put the reporter off for this, but I told him I'd call back. If I don't, he'll make things up and put that on the air next. Probably already has. You know how they do."

"Okay. I'll talk to you as soon as we get back."

"You do that." Suggs turned toward his office, then paused. "And hey, Hershey, when you're done foolin' around out there? I'm gonna want to know what this business is about a promotion, too. I'm the chief. I make the promotions around here."

Claudia smiled. "Yes, sir," she said to his receding back. She wasn't sure, but she thought she heard him chuckle. "Booey, close up your machine, and let's go 'fool around' at the No-Name. And bring your camera, just in case."

"I'll bring both, the digital and my 35mm. I also have a—"

"Take whatever you want."

She didn't care if he brought a desk with him. Her mind was already at the pond. She headed to her office for her jacket and purse. Five minutes later they were out the door.

CHAPTER 25

PHOTOSYNTHESIS. She couldn't shake the word from her head. It played over and over like a bad song that cements its impression in your brain the minute you turn off the radio. It was Booey, of course, who'd put the word out there, running it into a commentary about the dense growth around the No-Name Pond. But she didn't need a science lesson to recognize that the sun had done its part in boosting the foliage into an ever higher, ever thicker jungle. What she needed was a machete—*anything* that would spare her hands from parting the thorny weeds in search of . . . what?

They'd been at it for almost two hours, plumbing the thickest of the scrub some six feet from the south side of the canal bank, where Becker's train display suggested that Wanda Farr visited. Perhaps the cat lady had carved a path. If she had, it was gone now, grown over with persistent vines and razor-sharp grasses. Of course, Becker's display likely didn't conform to any kind of scale, which meant they could be searching in the wrong area entirely. And that only brought up another point: The doll and the cats might have been a figment of the old man's imagination altogether, having nothing whatsoever to do with Farr.

Claudia straightened for a minute to stretch her back. She wiped her forehead, wincing when sweat leached into a cut above an eyebrow. In some places, the grass rose nearly to her waist. What was she doing out here? She hadn't even noticed that Moody's mustache was gone. Now she was going to make a case linking two murders because of some toys that an old guy with Alzheimer's included in his train display? She bent to the task again. Someone had removed the toys.

"Hey, look!"

She stood again and peered past the grass toward Booey, some seven feet away. He was holding something aloft. She cursed silently. She'd told him not to touch anything that looked promising.

"I think I found an arrowhead!" he said. "You want to look? I found it by some—"

"This isn't a treasure hunt, Booey," she snapped.

His shoulders slumped. "I know. I'm sorry. And anyway, this is probably just a stone. But . . . well, there's some scat here too. At least I think it's scat."

"Some what?"

"Scat. You know, animal . . . poop? It could be from cats." He looked at her hopefully. "Couldn't it?"

Or raccoons. Or opossums. Or squirrels. But Claudia fought past the weeds to take a look. She hooted at the image she must be presenting. Tough city cop, moving crab-like on all fours to examine scat, when the only experience she had with animal dung was the cat shit she religiously sifted from the kitten's litter box.

When she finally reached him, Booey pushed aside yellowing weeds that tapered into spidery tendrils. "It's hard to spot because this weedy stuff is all knotted together with the grass, but the growth here is actually thinner at the bottom. See the tops, though? They're locked together, like they reached over the ground to shake hands or something—kind of like what confederate jasmine does." He sat back on his haunch to give her room, then pointed. "Look low," he said. "See it?"

She saw it. Just behind the curtain of growth was a pocket of space showing faint new life. Dried clumps that looked like feces lay partially concealed near a small mound of dirt. From cats? She thought they fastidiously buried their waste, though it occurred to her that Robin's kitten wasn't always zealous about it. So . . . what? She was looking at an abandoned cat bathroom?

The grass rustled as Booey nestled beside her. "If Wanda Farr wasn't coming here to feed them anymore, then maybe they stopped coming here, too," he said. "Don't you think it kind of looks that way?"

"You're reading my mind," she said, straining to see farther into the narrow opening, if that's what it was. It *could've* been a path recently, a strip of ground not quite filled in with new growth but blocked from sight by the scrub all around it. Claudia backed out of the hole, feeling her revolver press against her ribs from one side, her portable radio from the other. She slapped at something on her elbow, then moved to the canal bank and sat, looking north across it to the Feather Ridge side. Booey settled beside her.

They were west of the sprawling camphor tree—too distant from it to enjoy the shade it cast. Claudia wished she had thought to bring her cigarettes, but they were locked in the trunk with her jacket and purse. A hot breeze raised her hair briefly, then pushed it back against her neck. It was hot and buggy, but they couldn't leave yet. She had to go deeper into the hole. Just in case.

"It's peaceful here, isn't it," Booey said quietly.

"I guess." Claudia watched a pair of dragonflies flirt above the canal. "On the right kind of day, it would be."

They lapsed into silence, Claudia's mind turning over the possibility of snakes out here, wondering whether she'd find any slithering in the grass. "Look, Booey," she said, "I'm going to take another look in those weeds. Think you can find your way back to the car?" She struggled to get her keys out of her pants pocket. "I have a small evidence kit in the trunk. Can you—"

"Sure." He was scrambling to his feet. "Shouldn't take more than a few minutes. Are you going to bag the cat stuff?"

Was he nuts? "Not if I can help it," she said. "Wait here for me when you get back."

She watched him bound away on his mission, then stood stiffly and returned to hers, back on all fours, "photosynthesis" still fooling with her head.

Sometimes, you'll find what you're looking for only when you stop looking. Fourteen feet into the depression, Claudia had just about given up, her hands raw and her knees aching from scrabbling over the ground. Once, she'd tried making her way on her feet, but then the brush blocked her view and horseflies dove at her unprotected face, forcing her low again. She crawled another couple of feet, then simply stopped and sat—not winded, but thirsty, disgusted, and discouraged. An insect the size of toenail clippers skittered past her. Warily, she watched until it disappeared beneath something shiny. She shuddered. No telling what was living in her hair by now. She pushed blades of grass from her face and struggled to turn around in the cramped space. It was definitely time to go.

Should she bag the cat shit, if that's even what it was? It proved nothing. She *had* nothing. The only light at the end of this particular tunnel had already been claimed by a bug that probably *ate* cats for dessert. It was certainly big enough to—

She stopped abruptly. *Cat food can.* The shiny something—that's what it was; that's what the bug took cover under. She laughed. Photosynthesis—yes! Warped, but there. The light had reached her brain.

Claudia clumsily twisted around, then crawled back a few more paces, her eyes locked onto the can. As she drew closer, she saw more of them, maybe even a dozen. Friskies this, Friskies that . . . a smorgasbord of flavors. Tentatively, she pushed aside some whiskery weeds. Her mouth opened. More of them, maybe forty. She grinned. Wanda Farr was a litterbug. Better yet, she was either forgetful or purposeful. Claudia didn't know which, but a cheap can opener lay next to the discarded cat food cans. It was one of those hand-crank devices and still new enough not to show rust.

Her knees screamed, but she crawled past the cans and farther into the tunnel. It widened slightly and finally opened on the other side, not far from the train tracks. She'd found Wanda Farr's path, the one she took to feed wild strays, the one that intersected with the path of an old man who might have been her only friend and tried to tell their story with his garden display.

Claudia had a beginning. She had an end. All she had to do was fill in the middle, and she had an idea for that.

By the time she bagged the can opener and as many cans as she could fit in the evidence kit, put markers on the ground, and scribbled some notes, another hour had passed. They ate up thirty minutes more while Booey shot some photos, first digital and then with a 35mm camera. Dark clouds were rolling in. Claudia almost wished it *would* rain. Maybe it would wash the grit from her face and arms, and ease her prickly sensation caused from rubbing up against unmerciful foliage.

Four hours without anything to drink, without a cigarette, without a toilet. She yawned while she watched Booey tuck his camera gear into his backpack. He bent to tie a shoe, then hitched the pack to his shoulder and joined her. They looked like beggars as they fell into step together.

"That was productive, wasn't it?" he asked.

"We'll know for sure once I get this stuff over to the lab. But off the top, yeah, I'd say it was productive." She glanced at him. "Maybe you ought to shift that pack to your other shoulder. You've got all your weight on the canal side. One little stumble and you'll be swimming."

"Good idea." He paused to make the change. "I'm not the best swimmer in the world." He told her a convoluted story about an Olympic swimmer who'd been booted from competition when a drug test revealed he was on steroids.

Claudia half listened while she made a mental list of what she still needed to do when they got back to the station, which thankfully wouldn't be long now. They were almost to the camphor tree. Ten minutes more and they'd be in the car. Of course, it would be hours before—

A sudden boom sounded from their right. A chip of the camphor flew past Claudia's face.

"Fireworks already!" Booey said. "You'd think—"

She launched herself at him, knocking them both over the bank. The camphor's mighty roots jutted erratically from the slope. By an accident of her shoe, she stopped them on one, less than a foot from the water. A second boom rang out.

"That's not fireworks," she hissed, her body pressed against his. "Someone's shooting at us. Stay down. Don't move."

Her body muffled his response, but she felt the terror in his thin frame. "Shhh. I'm going to get us out of this."

They clung to the camphor's roots, clipped to the bank like earrings. She freed one hand and reached for her radio, choosing her moment at the same time Booey shifted his weight. The portable slipped from her grasp. It thudded against a tree root and splashed into the water. There would be no help.

Claudia felt her pulse roar in her ears. She inhaled once, twice, a third time. Then she processed their position. On the negative side, the bank pitched more steeply below the camphor than elsewhere along the canal, as if the weight of the tree were a burden too great for the bank to bear. They leaned into the pitch at an unsettling seventy-degree angle. If they let go of the tree roots, they would tumble into the water. On the plus side, the roots provided an uneven latticework that extended in both directions a good fifteen feet. Claudia looked up into a fringe of grass hanging over the bank. They were less than two feet from the top—another plus, except for the not knowing. Not knowing who was out there. Not knowing how close that someone was. Not knowing whether that someone was approaching them even now.

"Listen, Booey, I need to move to the other side of you. If I go east along the bank, I think I can come up behind the shooter." The shooter. What he had was a rifle or a shotgun. She knew the sound, and knew that her .38 revolver was no match for it, but she didn't tell him that. "Can you hang on here?"

"I think so," he said in a voice so faint she hardly heard.

"All right, good." She let go of a root long enough to give his shoulder a reassuring squeeze. "Now look, this is going to be a little tricky when I climb over you. Just stay as still as you can."

"Okay."

Her left leg was already partially clamped over him. She lifted it slightly, groped for purchase on the other side, and shifted her weight until she was on him and then over, grappling for a new root. Sweat poured into her collar, and she felt a sliver from the root in her left hand. She glanced to her right. Booey looked like he was nailed to a cross, but he stayed still.

"I won't be gone long," she said. "You might hear splashing—my left foot's going to slide in and out of the water while I'm moving—and later you might hear shooting. *Do not move unless I scream at you to move.* Understand?"

In a voice that trembled on the point of hysteria, he asked about alligators. Would he know if the splashing was her, or a gator?

"It'll be me," she said firmly. She craned her neck uneasily, looking into the water. Once before, she'd been close to an alligator. It was— She shook her head. She couldn't think about that now. Gators were a possibility. The shooter was a definite. "This'll all be over in a few minutes."

She began to move off, shuffling along the roots as quickly as she could, unable to stop her left foot from plunging into the pond now and then, feeling the water ride up her slacks, surprised at how warm it was. But she remembered that it was deep by the camphor, that the pond dropped off quickly. It was not her friend, not now.

She strained to keep a grip on the roots, cursing once when one of them snagged at her pants pocket. Then they began to run out. The roots were spaced farther apart and seemed smaller. Claudia struggled to stretch from one to the other, wishing they extended farther, but grateful, too, that the bank itself pitched less harshly here. She turned her head to the right. Booey hadn't moved. Good. She glanced downward. The water shimmered, catching a burst of sun breaking through the clouds.

For a second, she paused, talking her heart rate down again. She knew what was below her. It was time to see what lurked above. With a strength powered by an adrenaline rush she knew would leave her weakened later, Claudia pushed herself up and cautiously peered past the grass and over the bank. Nothing. She scanned left and right. Whoever was out there—and she had no doubt someone still was—wasn't showing himself.

Eight feet from the bank, a pair of stubby trees poked through a generous carpet of tall weed. They offered cover, if she could get to them, if she could haul herself up without getting shot, if she could rely on legs that burned from her gymnastics on the roots. She ached to pull her gun, but getting over the bank required both hands. The next eight or ten seconds would take more than skill or strength. Claudia sent up a fast prayer and pushed off while, at the same time, clawing at a snatch of grass and pulling. She threw herself flat on top, then shoved off with a knee and ran in a ragged crouch to the safety of the trees, not daring to look around.

To her ears, she sounded like an elephant thrashing through a jungle, but no shots sounded. A second later, she knew why. The shooter, likewise moving in a crouch but with conviction in his posture, moved steadily from behind his own tree some forty yards to her right and farther from the bank than she was. His concentration never strayed from the slope where she and Booey had taken cover. He counted on them to be cowering where he'd watched them go down.

Claudia freed her weapon from her trouser holster. She had one chance at this. One. She readied the gun and silently crept at an angle through the weeds, taking refuge behind trees when she could. Her eyes stayed on him. His eyes stayed on the bank, his shotgun leading him toward the edge like a divining rod.

The sun flickered again, then retreated once more behind clouds. She saw him in the flicker, though—saw him clearly.

Rivens.

Why here? Why now? Why wasn't he halfway across the country? She shook the thoughts from her mind. Later. She would find out later. For a few more long seconds, she watched him, giving him time to get in front of her. He passed an oak tree, which incongruously looked dead on one side but alive on the other, probably from a lightning strike. If she could get there without drawing his attention, she would have cover and an advantageous point from which to confront him. It had to happen fast. It had to happen now.

Claudia sprinted, weeds whipping against her slacks as she ran. Rivens paused once and looked to the side, but he was lazy—too confident—and he didn't turn enough to see her. She dove behind the tree, then inched up into a crouch, peeking past its trunk and breathing hard. She was two dozen paces from him. He was half a dozen from the bank. She shifted beside a low-hanging branch, kneeled, steadied her arms against it, and aimed the revolver.

"Rivens! Police! Freeze!"

He dropped low while he pivoted, and fired. The shot went wild.

"Drop it, Rivens! Do it now!"

Her voice, the second time, gave him a fixed location. His next shot exploded into the ground two feet in front of the tree, sending up an angry cloud of debris. Claudia felt a pebble cut into her cheek. She fired back two rounds, both going high.

"That's your only warning, Rivens! Now drop it!"

He flattened against the ground, partially obscured by weeds, but she saw him roll to the right. His shotgun came up again.

"Don't do it!" she screamed, pulling back into the tree just as he fired again. The end of the branch flew off. He brayed and began edging toward her, his head low, firing one shot after another. Claudia sucked in her breath, sank as low as she could, and slithered to the other side of the tree. She didn't care if she killed him now. She anchored her heels, then leaned out as much as she dared and fired back three fast rounds.

He roared and whirled, his shotgun flying to his left. Smoke from their exchange clung to the air. Claudia squinted through it. She'd only winged him, and already he was on the run, clutching his shoulder and bulling his way east through scrub brush, taking the route she had used to reach him. She took off after him on shaky legs, begging her lungs to cooperate.

The dogs came out of nowhere, or at least it seemed that way. At first, she didn't recognize them as dogs at all. She heard nothing and saw just a blur of white, speeding from behind some wild oleander and streaking toward Rivens. By the time she understood what she was watching, they were on him, three of them, aiming to do what she had only thought. He screeched and tried to protect his head. Claudia moved uncertainly forward. She had one round left—not enough for anything.

They stopped abruptly on a single word, not hers: "Hold."

Claudia whirled. Raynor stood behind her, an amused expression on his face. "I heard the shots from across the tracks. I saw what's what and thought you could use some help. Figured it'd buy me a 'get out of jail free' card for now or later." He looked at Rivens. "The fella down there looks a little winded, don't you think?"

Rivens wasn't moving. Claudia couldn't tell if he was dead or unconscious. Blood seeped from his shoulder, but that was the least of it. She glanced at the red-stained muzzles of the dogs, then looked away quickly. Nausea knotted her belly.

"I told you they listen to me," Raynor said.

Claudia holstered her revolver and forced herself to kneel beside Rivens. His face had gone gray, and he wheezed shallowly. She thought he would survive, but not if she didn't get help for him quickly. She stood, swallowed, then turned to the No-Name and hollered out Booey's name.

"I'm still here," he called back, his voice hopeful.

"All right. I'm on my way." She looked at Raynor. "Give me a hand."

"How about that," he said. "You've got that cute-as-a-button boy with you!"

"Shut up and help me."

"Well, golly. Here all this time I thought that's what I just did." He walked beside her as casually as if they were taking a stroll through a park. The dogs trotted after them, wagging their tails. "Looks a little like rain, don't you think?" He clucked. "Too bad, really. The day started out so nice."

"Shut up, Raynor," she repeated. "I don't want to hear you talk."

The words were barely out of her mouth when the first ping of rain hit her. Raynor laughed merrily, then fell back a few steps to croon "attaboys" to his dogs. He was having the time of his life.

CHAPTER 26

SUGGS PROMISED SHE WOULD HAVE HER WEAPON BACK THE NEXT DAY, and Claudia believed him. Indian Run had no internal affairs department. It had no police shooting review board. What it did have was the police chief and the mayor, and unless the media got riled, taking Aaron Rivens down would show in the books as a justified use of deadly force. Suggs didn't see it as a tough call. Preliminary ballistics tests, courtesy of the Flagg County Sheriff's Office, already supported the scenario Claudia described and Booey heard.

She frowned into her glass, rattled the ice cubes, and polished off the rest of her iced tea. That made four glasses in the hour and a half since her return home, but she still felt thirsty—that and edgy, dispirited and achy . . . more than an iced tea could handle. Then again, it could be worse. She'd chosen the good-guy team and the right side of the tree. Rivens took the wrong side of both, and thirst had to be the least of his problems right about now.

She poured another glass and took it into the living room. She slumped onto the couch and put her feet on the coffee table, sloshing tea onto the gray sweats she'd changed into. Didn't matter. No one was around to see. Not Robin, not Dennis, not even the kitten.

Of course, Rivens would probably pull through—doctors gave him good odds—but even if he did, his life would be a shadow of what it had been. It wasn't because of the bullet from her gun. Minor surgery had already repaired that. The dogs, though . . . Claudia shuddered. Rivens would be in the hospital for a good chunk of time, and at whatever point he came down from his morphine high there, he would be shuttled to jail.

She closed her eyes and sank lower into the couch. The idiot had tried to kill her. He was looking at a life term, which could be sharply abbreviated if they got him on Becker's and Farr's murders and a jury recommended the death penalty. Lots of *ifs*, Claudia thought. Too many. She didn't have a case for murder yet. Rivens didn't want her to have one. It's why he came at her, but she imagined a shrewd defense lawyer arguing that he was merely out hunting and mistook her for a rabbit. Tall grass, lots of trees. . . .

"I can't believe *I'm* the one with the glass that's half full," Suggs had said in high spirits after the mess at the No-Name was cleared. She was writing her report, the chief perched on the edge of her desk. "Sure, you got knocked around pretty good. And Boo! His hands are still locked in the death grip he had on those tree roots. But while you were foolin' around at the pond"—he winked—"we were takin' calls for you here, and guess what? We *are* makin' a case for Rivens, oh, yeah. Whatever you said to that fingerprint whiz at Flagg, she hustled those latents on the glass from Farr's trailer. He might as well've signed his name 'cause his big paw stood out all over it this time."

So Liz Hurd had delivered. Surprised, Claudia jotted a note to call and personally thank the woman. Rivens's fingerprints at Farr's home still didn't give them everything they needed, but it *did* bring them closer. He'd been on both sides of the tracks—Farr's trailer and the Becker estate. They knew that with certainty now. They held proof of that much. What they didn't have was the Jag or Kensington. They could only guess at how Rivens had made his way to the No-Name; no trace of a vehicle had been found.

Suggs had yammered on for a while, then sobered. "You almost got yourself killed out there," he said. "Rivens was packing a shotgun as mean as they get. You see it?"

Claudia nodded. The bastard had armed himself with a pump-action shotgun modified by a five-shot magazine. No wonder he came at her so leisurely.

"You saved Boo," Suggs said gruffly. "Don't think I didn't notice." Then, before she could respond, he banished her. "Go home. It's already seven o'clock. You need to get some rest." He grinned. "Besides which, if the press asks, I can truthfully say we took your weapon and you're off the case while we take a hard look-see into the circumstances of the shooting. I don't have to mention you're only off overnight."

He was still such an innocent when it came to the media. If he hadn't been, he might not have "mentioned" to the radio reporter that they had a suspect. He might not have teased the reporter by "mentioning" that his lead investigator was in the field now, "probably slappin' at bugs and gettin' a sunburn" while she followed a "hot lead." None of it would have meant much to a casual listener. It would've meant a great deal to Rivens, who'd had plenty of time to look for her, a good idea of where to look, and obviously, plenty of reason to want to.

Claudia didn't tell him that, however. Not now. She *wanted* to be home, where she could suck down something cold and think or not think or do whatever the hell she wanted to do without an audience.

She glared at the fruit basket on the kitchen counter. If nothing else, Barbara Becker was efficient, at least when it suited her. The basket arrived at the station within two hours of the first broadcast about the shooting. Claudia didn't bother to remove the cellophane wrapping. Even now, she wasn't sure why she'd brought it home. She read the card again: "Thank you, Detective Hershey. I'm grateful you weren't seriously injured, and I'm very, very sorry that I ever doubted you. —Barbara Becker."

Chief Suggs didn't get a basket, but he got a call. Mrs. Becker wanted protection. She wanted someone at the house, guarding the front door. Babs didn't frighten her; goodness, no. She was probably long gone, comfortably tooling along in the Jag. But Rivens—did the chief not understand how cunning the man was? How powerful? He could escape, and if he did, what was to stop him from coming after her? She could implicate him in her husband's murder. He'd want her dead. So please, would the chief send someone over? Now?

Suggs talked her down from her panic, lying a little, telling her Rivens probably wouldn't survive anyway, assuring her that even if he came to, he couldn't even hobble to the bathroom on his own.

But the chief brooded. "We gotta be real careful with this thing, Hershey," he'd said. "If she comes back at me again on this and we don't belly up, she'll be callin' the governor next. I don't have to tell you what kind of new ulcer that'd give me and maybe everyone else, too."

Claudia untangled a ribbon from the fruit basket and searched out the kitten. He was asleep on a chair under the dining room table, but he woke instantly for the colorful dangly. She got stiffly to her knees and pulled the ribbon across the carpet.

She yearned for Robin to get home, although she felt a rush of gratitude that her daughter wouldn't fly in until the day after tomorrow. She didn't want to alarm her with the angry bruises and scrapes on her face, her arms, her hands, her legs—everywhere, really. Last year Robin had seen worse; she'd *lived* through worse. They both had, and no one needed the reminder.

The kitten waggled its rear end, then pounced at the string. Claudia raced it over the carpet, again and again, until he inexplicably paused to lick his shoulder. She laughed. No getting around it now; the foolish thing was getting to her. She thought she might be leaving her mark on him, too. Well, Robin could still name him, but now she was just going to have to share, damn it.

By morning, her body screamed. Claudia would have preferred to make that discovery slowly, but someone was at the door, pounding on it, and she lurched from the couch before she remembered why it was important to ease into the day. She sidestepped the coffee table and pushed a hand through her hair on the way to the door. It better not be some high school kid selling overpriced candy bars to win a Disney trip.

She squinted through the peephole. Carella. Carella holding a tiny American flag. She unlocked the door.

"Good morning, Lieutenant, and happy Fourth of July!" He gave the flag a wave. "Like it? The bowling alley was handing them out this morning. Boy, you look like you got run over by a truck."

Claudia didn't need a mirror to know what he was seeing: stained baggy sweats, circles under her eyes, cuts on her face, hair sticking out. She stood back a little. No doubt she had morning breath too.

"I've felt better," she said. "What time is it, anyway?"

"Almost eleven."

"What!"

He laughed. "The chief said to let you sleep in. That was at eight o'clock. He said it again at nine and then at ten. At quarter to eleven, he said, 'Where the hell is Hershey already,' and sent me over to roust you."

"You could've called."

"The chief said no. Said he didn't want any 'damned phones' jarring you awake."

"Like banging on the door wouldn't?"

"Hey. I'm not the chief. I don't think like the chief."

"No one does. Come on in." She stepped aside, then closed the door.

Carella whistled. "Big night, huh? You didn't even make it to bed."

Claudia saw him looking at the couch. An ashtray heaped with dead cigarettes sat on the coffee table beside her iced tea glass. Her oboe lay on the floor. The living room lights were still on.

"Shut up, Emory. You want coffee?"

"Nah. Had a few cups already."

"Fine. Then go away. I'm up."

He trailed her to the kitchen, picking up the ashtray and glass behind her. She ran hot water and reached for a jar of instant coffee.

"You're *not* going to make tap water bilge, are you?"

"It's fast. It's efficient. I need to haul myself into the shower and get going, Emory. Farr's dead. Becker's dead. For all I know, we have the wrong person in jail or, at least, not enough of the *right* people there."

Carella snatched the jar from her hand and turned off the faucet. "I can't let you do it. This stuff isn't coffee. Go shower. I'll make real."

"Emory—"

"Go on. This is just as efficient."

Claudia went. By the time she returned, Carella had put a steaming cup of coffee on the counter along with a plate of fried eggs and toast. The flag was propped against the coffee cup. He'd already washed up the pan.

She stared at the plate. "Anyone ever tell you you're nuts?"

"My wife. Every day."

"She's right." Claudia thanked him and sat down to eat. "You're in an awfully good mood."

"Yep, and I'm trying to get you to the same place. If breakfast doesn't do it, then maybe my news will."

"I'm listening."

"Eat first."

Claudia set down her fork. "Come on. Delayed gratification isn't high on my list."

"All right, all right." Carella poured himself some coffee. "Two things. First, Farr's prints were everywhere on the cat food cans. Better yet, Henry Becker's prints showed up on some of them too. So there's your link."

Claudia nodded. She expected that, but the confirmation hitched her spirits a notch.

"You got any cream?" said Carella.

"No. Sorry. What else?"

"Well, I called that grocery store guy over at Feather Ridge."

"Milo Aggastino?"

"Yeah. He seemed surprised that I wanted to know what Becker bought when he came into the store, but he checked around and called me back."

"Cat food, right?"

"You got it. The cat food was a consistent purchase, but occasionally he bought other things too—weird things, random things—stuff like toothpicks, string, shoe polish." He shrugged. "Just . . . stuff."

Probably items the old man used to work on his train displays, Claudia thought. "What about the can opener?"

"They sell can openers identical to the one you found, but the lab didn't pick up his prints on it."

"Well, it would be nice to have Becker's prints on that too, but we can probably get by without them. We still have the cans."

"And I haven't even told you the best part yet."

"But you're going to, right? And in my lifetime?"

"Remember the stolen Eldorado that wound up in Daytona Beach? Two dimwits ran it into a stop sign, got busted, then whined they bought it from another guy and thought it was legit?"

"Vaguely."

"Turns out these guys were telling the truth, at least a little. When Daytona processed the car, they picked up some interesting prints, which—"

"Let me guess. Rivens?"

Carella gave the flag a little wave. "Hey, they don't call you 'detective' for nothing."

"Not a hard call. We already knew that Rivens cashed in on stolen vehicles before he decided to dabble in murder. And it's Rivens we're talking about. But I'm guessing there's more to the story, yes?"

"See? You elevate the concept of 'detective' to a whole new level."

Claudia feigned a punch at him, then refilled their cups while Carella told her the rest. The Eldorado thieves had done business with Rivens before. He'd bring them cars. They'd turn them over to a seedy chop shop, which had aspirations for a bigger market until the Daytona police shut them down with their newly acquired information.

"Daytona had been looking at the shop for a while but couldn't quite get a handle on it, at least not one good enough to move in," said Carella. "The Eldorado thieves, they figured they could shop a deal with the police, though. Once they started talking, they didn't care who they gave up. Daytona found all sorts of vehicles there—some just brought in, some already dismantled. It was a regular potpourri of parts."

Carella told her how Daytona inventoried whatever they could, how they matched parts to cars, and cars to particular thieves. Rivens's name had meant nothing to them until news stories began to leak out of Indian Run.

"Guess what one of the parts with Rivens's name on it turned out to be?" said Carella. He didn't wait for her to answer. "A BMW, or at least the skeleton of a BMW. Still had the VIN on it."

"I think I know what's coming. The vehicle identification number is a match for Barbara Becker's BMW."

Carella nodded, revved. "And it *still* gets better. Daytona called this morning, just in case it might mean anything to us. The interesting thing? The BMW apparently wound up in the shop almost a month ago. But it was never reported missing. This from a woman who just about had a stroke when her Jag took a hike yesterday. I mean, come on! No way could she not know her other car was gone. *No way.*"

He slammed a palm on the counter for emphasis, accidentally flicking the flag like a tiddlywink. It danced off Claudia's coffee cup and sailed toward the floor. Carella cursed and snatched at it, missing.

"You move like an old lady," Claudia said. She watched him slide off the counter stool to retrieve the flag.

"I feel like one some days," he said. He grinned sheepishly and set the flag back on the counter. "Think I ought to shop for a cane now? Something turbocharged and color-coordinated to match my uniform?"

She began to chuckle, then sobered in the next instant, her eyes fixed on Carella's face, a thought dancing at the back of her mind.

"What?" Carella finally said. "I got something unsightly stuck in my nose?"

"Shhh. Wait."

"Wait for what? If—"

"Shhhhhh!"

She stared through him, the thought nagging at her, dragging Barbara Becker's manicured face before her eyes, almost as if the woman herself had taken his seat. She thought about her for a long moment, then about Babs Kensington, and finally, the sullen-faced Rivens. It hit her, what she'd missed, how perfectly constructed everything had been, how wonderfully elaborate the simple ploy. Of course. There all along, in plain view.

She burst out laughing. She laughed until tears ran down her cheeks. Carella laughed uncertainly, then got caught up in it, too. They couldn't stop, not either of them. He didn't know why and she wouldn't tell him—not quite yet—but it was good. It was the best.

CHAPTER 27

LOTS OF CALLS TO MAKE. Lots of favors to call in, and some to ask. Claudia steeled herself for all of that and for a backward look through a case file that told more than she had thought, but not enough, still not enough. She put everyone on it—Carella and Moody on calls, Booey on the computer. They were good sports, asking what she asked them to ask and nothing more, ferreting out scraps of information that seemed out of context. But they were shooting in the dark because she didn't tell them what she was thinking, didn't want them asking extraneous questions or arousing suspicions. She would explain it all later, when she felt certainty overpower speculation—strong speculation, but speculation nevertheless.

Except for the murmur of their voices on phones and the occasional chatter of dispatch, the station barely stirred. For most people, it was a day off. They were hanging last-minute flags and already staking claims at the park in anticipation of the town's fireworks display later. Claudia didn't blame them. For a town so small, Indian Run always got it right, putting up a spectacular and loud show that lasted a full thirty minutes. The uniformed officers would get busy soon, though, directing traffic, settling territorial disputes over barbecue grills at the pavilion, and chasing off purveyors of illegal firecrackers. She hoped Suggs wouldn't need to send anyone else out. She needed them here.

While they worked in the multipurpose room, she labored over notes and constructed a new timeline, throwing out the old one altogether because she didn't want it to distract her with doubts. That could happen, it *did* happen. You'd get stuck in a way of seeing things, fixed on a point you thought you were moving, when all you were really doing was rearranging the pieces around it. Claudia didn't want a better mousetrap. She wanted a new one.

Once, she put in a call to Barbara Becker to let her know that Aaron Rivens had died. He hadn't, and she didn't exactly say that he did—not in so many words—but she dangled the suggestion, and the woman made the leap, gushing relief, coming to life, her voice shifting from frightened to confident.

Claudia listened intently and she listened differently, not to her words but to her tone. It told her nothing that would go in her notes, but it helped to move the point a little more.

Then she explained to Mrs. Becker that the information about Rivens would not be shared with the public, not yet. Protocol demanded that his next of kin be notified first. They were working on that now. Becker understood, of course she did, and then she shared news of her own. She had put up a fifty-thousand-dollar reward for information leading to the arrest of Babs Kensington.

Claudia already knew. It had been on the air since one, ushering in an avalanche of bogus calls that taxed even the patience of the unflappable Sergeant Peters. But she pretended otherwise because it really didn't matter and because she knew something else, too. She knew that Barbara Becker would never pay out, no matter what.

From time to time, Suggs paced outside her office. He poked his head in around three o'clock and growled something about "this latest business being worse than the cockfight sting." Him, she'd told—all of it. But even then, he left her alone. They all did, and by seven-thirty she had enough to put it all together and tell them, finally, why they would miss the Fourth of July fireworks.

CHAPTER 28

CARELLA AND MOODY FLIPPED A COIN to see who would catch the disturbance call that came in just as they were leaving. Moody lost on tails. He scowled and brushed his phantom mustache with an index finger, then hurried off to a patrol car. Peters took a pass, too. The station couldn't be left with only the night dispatcher on duty.

"You guys have all the fun," he groused.

"Yeah, but you're a sergeant. You get the big bucks," said Carella.

"Big job, little town, small bucks. In Miami I'd be making real money."

"Hah! In Miami you'd. . . ."

Claudia tuned out their banter while she checked her revolver and slid it into the holster. She clipped on her portable and slipped into her jacket. Robin was right, she thought idly. The sleeves *were* too short.

". . . besides, Sarge, if it gets slow tonight you can always doodle on your cast to pass the time," said Carella, rubbing it in just a little. "You could draw some—"

Suggs gave him a shove toward the door. "Someone oughta doodle on your head," he said. "Now come on, already. Let's go pick up the lovely Babs and be done with it. Booey! Hershey! Let's go, let's go, let's go. Maybe we can still catch the tail end of the fireworks."

"She'll *be* the fireworks!" said Booey. He high-fived Carella and dodged a cuff from his uncle, all of them hooting like fans psyched for a Super Bowl game.

Claudia watched grimly, recognizing the tension beneath their horseplay. She felt the same band of steel just under her skin. They were one bluff away from closing two cases.

They took two vehicles and headed out.

Because the woman would not be alarmed to see her at a late hour, Claudia went alone to the front door. Carella crouched to the side five feet away, obscured by shadow. Suggs and Booey stayed out of sight behind a trio of dwarf palms tastefully set near the walkway. Claudia heard Booey tell his uncle to be careful, the palms' feathery fronds concealed three-inch thorns sharp as daggers. She shushed him, then glanced around. They had coasted in on idle and without headlights. She'd pulled the Cavalier around the circular driveway, parking a short distance from the entranceway. The chief stowed his pickup on the other side of the fountain, all according to plan.

"The house sure is dark," Booey had whispered when they got out of their vehicles. "If I were as scared as she says she is, I would have every light in the place on."

"She's not scared," Claudia said flatly.

"Oh, right." He wiped his palms on his pant legs. "What if she doesn't answer the door?"

"She will. But she'll make me wait."

"You're sure?"

"I'm very sure."

The chief ended their conversation with a sharp tug on Booey's arm, pulling him away to get in position. Now they were ready. As ready as they would ever be.

Claudia took one last look behind her. She couldn't see Booey or Suggs behind the palms. Good. She looked toward Carella and gave him a thumbs-up. He gave her one back and set his weight slightly. She heard his knee joint pop.

Surprise, not alarm. That was the ticket.

She inhaled deeply, exhaled slowly, and leaned on the doorbell.

Five minutes, then eight. Almost ten when the light above the entranceway finally came on. Claudia felt eyes on her through the peephole. Another thirty seconds passed before the door itself opened. She braced herself with a smile.

"Detective Hershey! If you're here, it can only be with good news."

"Good evening," Claudia said pleasantly. "I apologize for the late hour, but it couldn't be helped."

"It's perfectly all right. I'm sorry it took me so long to get to the door." She tapped her cane against the foyer floor. "This foolish hip slows me considerably, I'm afraid."

"I'm sure it does."

Claudia kept her smile but said nothing, her eyes unwavering, checking. No doubt. Not now.

"I . . . Detective, I don't understand. Is there something you need from me? Something I can help you with?"

"Oh, yes. I'm sure you can. I'm here for Babs."

"You're . . . here?"

Claudia's smile widened. She watched the woman hug her robe tighter against her. She watched her glance anxiously backward, into the gloom of the foyer.

"You think she's . . . *here? Now?*"

"Oh, I *know* she is."

"That's not possible! How could she have slipped past me? I've been— Oh, no. The key. The key! I'd given her one, of course." She shuddered. "Should I . . . do you want to search the house?"

"I don't think that'll be necessary." Claudia inclined her head. "Do you? *Babs.*"

"Pardon me?"

"You're good. You had me fooled to the end, and I don't have Alzheimer's."

"I don't know what you're talking about."

"Sure you do, Miss Kensington."

"I don't know what kind of stupid-a . . . game you're playing, but I'm going to call your superiors!"

"Stupid-ass game? Is that what you were going to say? Because that's exactly the sort of thing Babs would say." Claudia shook her head. "I know you've had some training, but still, it must've been tough, going in and out of character like that."

"This is nonsense! And it's outrageous!"

"Show me your neck."

"Excuse me?"

"Your neck? It's the one thing that's really hard to camouflage, isn't it?"

She clutched the robe tighter.

"See?" said Claudia. "There you go again. You can make your face look older with a ton of makeup. You can put on an expensive wig. You can walk stooped, like a little old lady. And by the way—the cane? Nice prop. Convincing. But your neck? It's young and it's uncooperative as hell. Bad for you. Good for Henry Becker and Wanda Farr, and probably Barbara Becker, as soon as you tell us where her body is. And, *Babs*, that would be a really, *really* good idea, to tell us. This is a death-penalty state. If there's any way at all you can cop a life sentence, it would only be if you cooperated, because see, you're under arr—"

The cane whistled toward Claudia's face, but she was ready. She caught it with her left hand and shoved the door all the way open with her foot, pushing Kensington against the foyer wall with her right hand. The woman's robe fell loose, showing off a lovely neck free of wrinkles. Claudia dropped the cane and kicked it aside. Her left hand hurt like hell.

Carella was instantly beside her, wheeling Kensington around, putting the cuffs on. "You all right, Lieutenant?" he asked.

She heard Suggs and Booey coming up behind them. "Yeah," she said. "That's a wicked stick she carries, but yeah."

"Turbocharged," said Carella. "Gonna get me one of those babies some day."

Claudia laughed and turned to Suggs. "Looks like we'll need a patrol car for transport now. Think you can tear anyone off the road yet?"

"Already radioed for Moody," he said. "He's on his way over. Nice job, Hershey."

Booey glared at Kensington. "You think you're smart, but you're not. All you are is evil, and you—"

"All right, Booey," Claudia said gently.

"There's a word for her," he said.

"I know."

Kensington strained toward Booey. "There's a word for you too, you stupid little boy." She snorted. "There's a word for all of you. It's called *multimillion-dollar lawsuit*."

"That's more than one word," Booey shot back.

"I want a lawyer."

"Of course you do," said Claudia. "There's that nice fella over in Flagg. What's his name? Frederick Montgomery? Oh, you know . . . the one who prepared the codicil for you? But don't you—"

Kensington kicked at her, clipping the top of her shoe. Carella pushed her back against the wall.

"Now that wasn't nice," Claudia said smoothly. She glanced at her shoe. "Look, you've left a scuff mark, and I was only trying to be helpful."

"Bitch."

"Again, not nice."

"I want a lawyer *NOW*."

"And you shall have one." She pulled her cell phone from a jacket pocket. "Got the number off the top? No? Well, don't worry. We've got a phone book at the station. Meanwhile, don't you want to know what-all we're arresting you for? We've got a list as long as my arm, beginning with murder."

"I'm not saying a word."

Claudia shrugged. "At this point, you don't have to. I get to do all the talking." She winked and then recited the formal charges, recited

Miranda, and would've recited the Gettysburg Address if she knew it, just to unhinge this very dangerous woman for a blissful moment or two.

"You'll never make all of that stick," said Kensington.

"Sure I will, or enough of it. Want to know why? Because I don't have to pretend. That was your job and you blew it. Oh, and by the way? Aaron Rivens is undead. Amazing. He'll probably have a lot to tell us."

Kensington opened her mouth, then shut it. Her makeup had smudged, leaving a beige streak against the collar of her robe. Claudia pointed it out to her as Carella and the chief began to walk her away. Then she bent to retrieve the cane and followed, just in time to catch a spectacular burst of color light the distant sky.

CHAPTER 29

GINA ROHR LEANED ON THE BALCONY RAIL and gazed at the night sky. Another hour and a half and dawn would break, and they were still at it. "I know what you're thinking," she said to Claudia. "You've been thinking it all night, wondering how an assistant state attorney can afford a place like this."

Claudia didn't bother to deny it. She yawned as she pushed out of a wrought-iron chair and went to stand beside the young woman. "So how can you?"

She laughed. "I inherited a filthy fortune. It's legitimately mine and I didn't kill anyone to get it."

Rohr was the sharpest prosecutor in the Flagg County State's Attorney's Office. She was also the youngest and unabashedly outspoken, attributes that defense attorneys occasionally tried to leverage against her to no avail. She battled fiercely and fearlessly in court, stalking the floor in short skirts and stiletto heels that riveted judges and jurors alike. Now, though, she wore faded jeans and an oversized man's shirt that fluttered at her thighs with a light wind.

"Nice breeze," said Claudia.

"It's an advantage of being six floors up. Besides, I didn't think you'd mind enduring an inquisition here as much as you would in my cramped office. Want a refill on your drink?"

"No. Yes. I don't know. I'm bushed."

Rohr smiled and retrieved both their glasses from the table. "We'll be finished pretty soon. Back in a minute."

Claudia looked over the railing again. Stars twinkled faintly, a reminder that they'd all missed the town's fireworks while they got Kensington processed and transported to a holding cell. No way would a judge let her out on bond, but Rohr wanted as many details nailed down as she could. Her questions were efficient but endless, and they always came back to the same thing: *How does a thirty-three-year-old woman masquerade as a woman more than twice her age with no one noticing?*

Because her target victim had Alzheimer's and no one heeded much of what he had to say. Because the Beckers were newcomers to the community, presenting only the history she chose to present. Because she counted on a small town to favor her with sympathy, not scrutiny. Because she had professional training as an actress. Because she was willing to set the stage and play out every act. Because she *did* have the advantage of an uncanny resemblance to Barbara Becker. Because a lot of money was at stake. Mostly, because *no one was looking.*

But Wanda Farr looked one day. She saw Henry Becker pitched into the No-Name. Kensington sent her errand boy after her, an errand boy smitten enough to do her bidding and stupid enough to imagine she would ever let him share the reward. Claudia bet that if Kensington hadn't believed Rivens was dead, she even would've figured out a way to excise him before he left the hospital. What she would *not* do was walk away from a fortune, not when she believed she had already convinced the police to look elsewhere.

"It was an incredible scheme, wasn't it."

Claudia whirled around.

"Sorry. Didn't mean to startle you." Rohr handed her a glass. "Pinot Grigio. I'm out of Chardonnay."

"Thanks." She took a sip. "I can't decide if I'm drinking too late or drinking too early."

"Doesn't matter. You can crash in the guest bedroom."

"That's not necessary."

"Yeah, it is."

They settled into the chairs. Claudia leaned back and stretched her legs as far as possible. The chair cut into her spine, but she ignored it.

"You know, Detective, you left me a lot of legwork on some things."

Claudia translated silently: *You made mistakes.* She nodded, thinking about the things she should've done but didn't, errors that would not have prevented Farr's murder but that, combined, would make Rohr's job more tedious now. She waited too long to request a fuller analysis of the prints on the glass. Later, she didn't ask for comparison prints on Barbara Becker when the crime-scene techs dusted for Kensington's prints in the bedroom. If she had, she would've known there weren't any. Barbara Becker never made it as far as Indian Run. If her assumptions were right, she never even made it out of Chicago. Kensington stepped into Indian Run already in costume. She wore it as sparingly as possible, but enough to establish a presence as the concerned wife of Henry Becker.

"Kensington led me by the nose for a long time," Claudia said. "She set everything up so beautifully, so persuasively, right from the beginning."

"She manipulated everyone, not just you. Right away she made sure to establish a record of Becker's wandering. When he showed up in the No-Name, no one gave it a thought. Deflect, deflect, deflect. Look, this chick constructed a scheme around her own persona—police record and all—so that you'd have an obvious suspect."

"Who we'd never catch, of course."

"You have to admit it was a work of art, or almost—and ballsy, too, even to the end. I mean, come on. How many people would report a car stolen and keep it hidden in their own garage?"

"I could've lived without that reminder," Claudia said glumly, thinking of the Jag they'd recovered in the Becker garage, pristine beneath a tarp all the while. "Everything was right under my nose."

Rohr shook her head admiringly. "My guess? After a respectable period of time, the 'grieving widow' would quietly move, then vanish—and probably in the damned Jag. You'd still be looking for the phantom caregiver. Kensington would've settled somewhere on a beach with an expensive umbrella drink, and she'd be laughing her ass off."

"I should've caught on sooner, though. She was always covered up to the neck. She kept her hands in her lap as much as possible. Barbara Becker and Babs Kensington were never seen together. She did most of her business outside of Indian Run, and almost entirely in cash. She kept her old friends at arm's distance and didn't establish any new ones here. I assumed her remote behavior was because she felt overwhelmed by her husband's condition—"

"—which is what she counted on you thinking—"

"—until Aaron Rivens left a track at Farr's trailer."

"Farr was an annoying problem for her. Becker's autopsy was an unexpected challenge. But Rivens, he was a disaster. He left his prints on the glass and his pocket in a dog's mouth. He—"

"We don't have a match on the pocket yet."

Rohr waved a hand. "We will." She took a sip of her wine. "He made Kensington start to punt on a lot of things, and then it only got worse. The way I see it, he got impatient for things to happen, so he reverted to form and sold hot cars for ready cash. I doubt Kensington knew about any of them except for the BMW. And then the jackass tried to shoot you! Mistakes were happening everywhere, and they were getting a lot harder to deflect. Kensington had to—"

The phone rang from inside. "No rest for the weary," Rohr said, sprinting from her chair. "Don't fall asleep on me while I'm gone."

Claudia took a swallow of her wine, then set it down distastefully. She didn't want any more. She closed her eyes and began to doze, her head inching toward her chest. It couldn't have been more than a minute when she felt Rohr shaking her shoulder.

"Hey! Dream on your own time."

Claudia struggled to a more upright position. "Sorry." She squinted, bringing her vision back into focus. "News?"

"Score one for the good guys. Chicago just dug her out."

She pictured the Chicago police, their high-intensity lamps flooding the garden while their shovels churned up lilacs and roses behind the Beckers' northern home. She saw them hoping to connect with something solid, hoping that they wouldn't.

"Kensington didn't let anything get in her way," Rohr said somberly. She downed the rest of her wine, then looked at Claudia's glass. "You're not keeping up with me."

"Can't." She tried to stifle a yawn. "I'm so past tired I'm not even sure I'm alive."

"You are, but it's marginal. Look, just one more question. I'm curious. How'd you finally figure Kensington for the imposter she was?"

"You don't want to hear this. It's boring."

"I can go with boring."

Claudia picked up her glass, then set it back down. "It was the cane. I was at the estate having an initial interview with Barbara Becker—*Kensington*, I mean—and the cane was leaning against the kitchen table. I accidentally knocked it off and she swiveled to catch it before it ever hit the floor. It was an instinctive catch, and at the time, it blew right by me that it was way out of whack for an old woman with an arthritic hip. In fact, my brain didn't catch up to me until yesterday, when Emory Carella bumped something off my own kitchen counter and he made the same kind of grab. It was like watching the remake of a movie. I started to see everything about her in a different way."

"In other words, you had an epiphany? One of those 'Aha!' moments?"

"That's a stretch. This was more like a brain bump."

"Well, you're right about one thing." Rohr smiled. "It makes for a pretty dull story, Detective."

Claudia took her glasses off and scrubbed her eyes, not even trying to hide the yawn this time. "It is what it is. Now give me a pillow, or I'm out of here."

CHAPTER 30

BEING TALL HAD ADVANTAGES. Claudia could see over the jostling crowd when the passengers finally started streaming out of the gate. She tracked Robin from the moment she emerged and waved her over, shedding fatigue with each step that brought her daughter closer. When she was finally within reach, Claudia swooped, pulling her into an embrace that pinned Robin's carry-on bag between them.

"You're crushing me," Robin protested, her words muffled against Claudia's jacket.

"I know. I don't care. I missed you."

Robin let her cling for a few more seconds, then struggled free. "Jeez. It's not like I was gone a thousand years."

Sure. Now she'd be brave.

Robin shifted her carry-on to her other hand. "How's the kitten?"

"Fine. How are *you*, baby?"

"The fireworks were great. The food on the plane sucked. You didn't name him, did you?"

Claudia laughed. "No. Here . . . let me take your bag." She caught Robin examining her as they walked toward the terminal. "We can grab something to eat on the way home, if you'd like."

"How come your eyes are all bloodshot?" she demanded. "You worked all the time, didn't you?"

"Not *all* the time, but it did get a little busy."

Robin shook her head. "Boy, I bet Dennis gave you some grief over that. Is he coming over tonight? I picked up some charcoal pencils for him. They have 'Washington, D.C.' printed on them. I got you a souvenir, too. Plus I got something for the kitten."

Claudia guided them around a group of tourists. *No, honey, Dennis won't be coming over tonight, or any night. Your mother is lousy with men.* But later. She would explain it all later. Sort of.

"Actually, kiddo, I'm kind of in a selfish mood," she said evenly. "I figured it would be just you and me tonight. Well, us and the kitten, of course. You really do need to come up with a name."

Robin groaned and began reeling off prospective names, discarding each the moment she presented it, moving on to another. Claudia half-listened. What was it Rohr had said? *Deflect, deflect, deflect.* Yeah. It wasn't that hard.

By the time they'd paid the extortion fee to get out of airport parking, Robin had temporarily exhausted her interest in names for the kitten. On the drive home she chattered about Washington instead, telling Claudia about where Brian had taken her, what they'd done, the people he'd introduced her to. Then she asked whether she knew that Brian had a girlfriend.

Claudia said she didn't.

"Well, I don't know if she's a girlfriend, exactly, or just *trying* to be a girlfriend. But she's about a hundred years younger than he is and . . . giggly. I don't know what Dad sees in her."

Oh, Brian. . . .

"You know what he told me, though?"

"What?"

"He told me the one woman who matters most to him is you."

"Me? He said—"

"Well, you know, because if not for you, he wouldn't have me."

"Oh." Claudia concentrated on traffic while Robin fussed with the radio. She finally found something she thought tolerable, and they finished the drive home as if neither of their lives had changed.

There were two messages on the answering machine. Claudia set her purse on the coffee table. She looked toward Robin and smiled. Two seconds in the door and her daughter was already on her hands and knees, urging the kitten to come out from under the couch, trying to renew their acquaintance. She hit the machine's PLAY button. One call was a hang-up. The other was from Booey:

Lieutenant? Sorry I missed you. You had to pick up your daughter, right? I hope I can meet her sometime. She's probably as, well, as . . . amazing as you are.

Robin stopped cooing at the kitten and turned around. "Who's that? Someone have a crush on you?"

"Shhh."

. . . two-week internship is just about up. Uncle Mac says I did a good job for a rookie, but that the only promotion I could look for is a letter of recommendation from you, if you think I deserve one. This isn't any kind of pressure, though, okay? I mean, if you think I deserve one, fine. If you don't, well, the dog-by-the-tree thing . . . I would understand.

"What's he talking about?" Robin said.

"Shhh."

Filmmaking. That's how I'm going to go. I think. I have a terrific idea for a documentary about police work. Maybe you would star in it?

Robin scurried over, the kitten momentarily abandoned. "Hollywood! Is this guy legit? Who is he?"

Claudia held up a finger.

. . . know you'll want details, so I already have an outline. Uncle Mac says you're taking the rest of the week off. Could I fax this over? Or I could maybe stop by sometime?

"Like we have a fax machine," Robin muttered. "I told you we're way out of the loop with technology, Mom." The kitten darted at her shoelace, then retreated behind a coffee table leg, warming to her now.

I'll call later. Or tomorrow. Or you could call me back, if you aren't too busy. You're probably worn out, of course. You have my number, right? Oh. By the way, this is Booey. Sorry. Uh, bye-bye.

"His name is *Booey*?? He can't be from Hollywood." Robin sighed and crouched by the kitten. "Boy, Mom. You really know how to pick them."

Claudia smiled. She didn't pick him, but so what? It worked out. "Here's an idea," she said. "If you shorten 'Booey' to 'Boo,' you've got a pretty good name for a kitten."

"*Boo?*" Robin flipped to her back, teasing the kitten with a finger.

"Oh, come on. Think about it. He scared me when I found him—a kitty 'boo' if I ever saw one." She thought about tripping over him, scaring the crap out of both of them, but that wasn't a story she planned to share. "Anyway, it fits his personality."

"Boo." Robin pursed her lips. "Boo, Boo, Boo . . . not bad. A little lame, but not *bad* bad. I'll have to think about it."

"Don't give yourself a headache."

"Funny. Har har har."

Robin was home. Life was good.

ALSO BY LAURA BELGRAVE

IN THE SPIRIT OF MURDER

When a medium turns up dead in a backwoods Florida town, police Detective Claudia Hershey is thrust into a nightmarish case that reaches from the secretive heart of a psychic community to the powerful corridors of the state Legislature. Unraveling the truth could end her career—maybe even her life.

"*In the Spirit of Murder* is a promising debut, and Claudia Hershey an engaging heroine."
—About.com

"I couldn't put it down until I was sure Claudia had won. Overall, an enjoyable book and one that could promise a series."
—*Mystery News*

"*In the Spirit of Murder* is a fascinating read with a colorful locale. Claudia Hershey is an interesting character, tough and intelligent, and an excellent crime solver."
—*Romantic Times Magazine*

" A very well told mystery."
—femaledetective.com

"Readers who enjoy a police procedural cozy will find *In the Spirit of Murder* to be a delightful read that is filled with action under every bush, but almost totally void of gore."
—Bookbrowser

"A beguiling mystery from the dark side of the Deep South."
—Patrick Lynch, bestselling author of *Carriers* and *Omega*

Trade Paper 1-57072-124-6 $15.00
Hardcover 1-57072-108-4 $24.50

CHECK OUT OUR WEB SITE AT
www.silverdaggermysteries.com

ALL SILVER DAGGER MYSTERIES ARE AVAILABLE AT YOUR LOCAL
BOOKSTORE OR DIRECTLY FROM THE PUBLISHER
P.O. Box 1261 • Johnson City, TN 37605
1-800-992-2691

CATCH THESE OTHER GREAT TITLES
FROM SILVER DAGGER MYSTERIES IN 2001

May
Closer Than the Bones — Dean James
Three Dirty Women and the Bitter Brew — Julie Wray Herman

June
The Ambush of My Name — Jeffrey Marks

July
The Valley of Jewels — Mary Saums

August
Crimson Creek — Dean Feldmeyer
To Kill the Truth — Kayla McGrady

September
Whose Death Is It, Anyway? — Elizabeth Daniels Squire
A Sonnet for Shasta — David Hunter

October
Dying to Meet You — Amy Talford
Murder at Markham — Patricia Sprinkle

November
A Dead Man's Honor — Frankie Y. Bailey
Aliens of Transylvania County — Patrick Bone

ALL SILVER DAGGER MYSTERIES ARE AVAILABLE IN BOTH
TRADE PAPER AND HARDCOVER